Praise Routine Number 4 is the manuscript with which the author obtained his Masters Degree in Creative Writing (UCT) under Prof Etienne van Heerden

Human & Rousseau
a division of NB Publishers
40 Heerengracht, Cape Town, 8000
www.humanrousseau.com

Cover and title design: Michiel Botha
Editor: Cecily van Gend
Set in 11.5 on 16 pt New Baskerville
Printed and bound by Paarl Print, Oosterland Street, Paarl, South Africa

First edition 2008

ISBN 10: 0-7981-5003-3
ISBN 13: 978-0-7981-5003-3

PRAISE ROUTINE NUMBER 4

A NOVEL

MICHAEL RANDS

I t was the end of another long evening and I was on my final cigarette. The smell of ass sweat that hangs about the change room was making me feel ill, so I took a stroll outside along the wooden boardwalk that surrounds the sandy area in the centre of the restaurant. The last fires had been extinguished and there was a smell of wet ash and disinfectant.

I happened to pass the entrance to Vusi's office, just as Charlie was saying 'For the second time.' I stood dead still, afraid even of exhaling the smoke in my lungs.

'In as many weeks,' I heard Vusi say.

'Ai, Byron,' said Charlie. 'I like him. But eish, sometimes.'

Of course I knew what they were referring to. I'd forgotten praise routine number four.

I waited for Charlie in the staff parking lot. Like the change room it's rundown and stinks of garbage. I sat waiting for so long that the motion detector light had gone off when Charlie finally emerged. He was visibly shocked to see me sitting there on the sand still dressed in my skins.

'What was that about?' I asked him.

'You have to stop smoking that shit,' he said to me. 'When you don't smoke, you clever. But when you smoke it, wena Byron. You become stupid!'

'I need it to get into character. I've told you before.'

'We give you the skins, Byron. Wena. Come on now! Pull yourself together. Vusi will fire you.'

I wanted to make a good impression. And so the following week I smoked my last joint four hours before work started. I went through early to impress the management, but got there before anyone else arrived. I spent the first half-hour walking up and down the parking lot, kicking around a flat Coke can and smoking cigarettes. Then I remembered that in my cubbyhole I had half a bankie of weed and a box of Rizzla. I tried not to smoke it. But I was starting to sober up and the boredom was intense. So an hour later me and the head chef's fourteen-year-old son, Faizel, were stoned and playing a game of soccer in the dusty parking lot, using the flat can as a ball and our shoes as goalposts. Young Faizel made no mention of the fact that my shoes were different sizes, and so I relaxed and enjoyed the game. But when Vusi arrived he asked me why my eyes were red.

'It's from the dust,' I said. 'Very dusty.'

He shook his head and started laughing. Not knowing how to respond, I too burst into laughter. He raised his large hand and stuck his index finger into my chest. He was wearing a black suit and a pink shirt, I could smell his aftershave.

'It's not funny,' he said, and walked away.

And so, there I was, sitting on the bench in the staff change room half an hour before the first guests arrived. There was a constant drip noise coming from the shower and the room smelt like fish. I'd tied the skins around my ankles and finished tightening the leather skirt around my waist. I stood up and clicked my back, then stuck my hand into my underwear and shifted my balls to the spot that Charlie and I have jokingly named the praise poet's position, or the triple P. We have to wear tight briefs and pull the entire package right to the front to ensure that our balls don't get squashed during the more athletic manoeuvres. I stood up and started stretching my legs and arms, then washed my hands to remove the musty smell of balls.

'You ready, my friend?' Charlie came into the change room. He's always better dressed than I am. His entire outfit is genuine, made by a brother of his who lives in the Eastern Cape. Mine on the other hand was bought from Xhosa World, a wholly-owned subsidiary of Bhakhuba, the restaurant at which I work. Apparently it was set up for tax purposes, and supplies the restaurant with everything it has, from the artwork in the chief's hut, to the skins worn by the guests.

'Nearly ready. Just stretching,' I said to him.

He has a perfectly cut body, an eight-pack, perhaps a ten-pack; wiry, but well-defined arms. He's the real thing. He comes from a long line of praise poets. When I first took the job he explained to me that praise poets have a similar licence to that held by jesters in times gone by. They can say what others cannot. But Charlie overstepped the mark and offended a corrupt local leader in the rural Eastern Cape. It was during the early nineties, and fearing for his life, he fled to Cape Town and changed his name.

I've learnt a lot from Charlie but the privileged position held by praise poets was not handed down to me. I only have good things to say about our guests.

'Come now my friend!' He was getting agitated. 'The people they will be here now.'

'Who's coming?'

'The German people. One full bus. Maybe two bus. From the Waterfront. They want to wear the skin.'

'Lots of them?'

'Sure. We won't use routine four tonight.'

'Charlie. You sure?'

'Sure, Byron.'

'Thanks man. Thanks a lot.'

'Just one two three five.'

'OK.'

We waited for the guests to hand in their day-to-day clothes at the exchange counter and get changed into the skins. Unfortunately the female clientele get to wear leather straps around their breasts. The dresses of both sexes come down to the knees, and for the most part the guests look more like pale Polynesian islanders than Xhosas.

I stood close behind Charlie; I could feel my heart beating in my neck. I still get terrible nerves. And although they'll never accept it, the weed helps me transform.

'OK, they ready. Come!'

Charlie had been keeping watch, and the first guests had come out of the change room. I stepped outside, keeping myself close to Charlie. The air was warm and the fires freshly lit. As always we moved slowly at first, past the rural Xhosa scenes painted along the walls, keeping our heads down and our footsteps light. I imagined myself to be in a far-off land, my name is Byronkhulu and my people respect me. So long as I keep this image in my head, and my right foot slightly back when standing still, I will be safe. No one will know my real name.

Charlie held two fingers in the air, raised his knees and started sprinting along the boardwalk. I stayed just behind him. Although it's not in his job description, I suspect he enjoys frightening the shit out of Europeans. He'd chosen his man: the shorter of the two, a balding fellow with thin-rimmed glasses perched on his Germanic nose, tufts of hair sprouting out of his deep navel. The man was waiting for his wife, silently admiring a mural of a topless black woman when Charlie started screaming.

'Amandla akho agqithisile! Akekho umntu onokugqitha! Bazakubuya gxengxeze kuwe!'

The German stepped sideways, then backwards, tried to gain his composure but was clearly rattled. This was my cue. I took a deep breath and jumped out from behind Charlie, my right leg raised high in the air. In the triple P I place my faith.

'Your strength is legendary!' I shouted as I came crashing to the floor, the skins slapping against my legs. 'No man should ever wish to cross your path!' I raised my hands in the air. 'For they will surely come to know of your might!'

Charlie held up one finger, and moved in on the other man: a tall fellow with a fat nose and an aura of ignorance.

'Uyindoda esisityebi ehlabathini lonke wonke umntu uyakwazi ubutyebi bakho bobanaphakade'

'And you!' I screamed. 'You are the richest man around. All the people know you, for your wealth is legendary!'

The men gave us silly bows as they backed off and made their way across the soft sand in the inkundla. They took their seats on the raised platform, at tables that are really glorified bar benches covered by decorative cloths. Besides the outside seating, there's a large indoor area, and several private rooms fashioned on African huts. At capacity the place holds three hundred. It wasn't going to be full tonight, but there'd be plenty of work.

Other guests were handing in their clothes to Lindi who works behind the exchange counter. The dancers had just arrived. They greeted Charlie in Xhosa and gave me a nod, then made their way into the change room. The two of us stood underneath the palm tree overhangs that decorate the bar. They'd been hung with colourful lights in late October the previous year. Now it was May and they showed no sign of leaving. I sometimes wondered what the European guests would tell their children about Xhosas. Anyway, I wasn't a cultural educator. I'd taken the job out of desperation. Ironically, it was the one place where my skin colour had counted in my favour. I was an amusing little add-on to a themed restaurant. Their reasoning, I guess, was simple. If tourists arrived and saw only black faces they might think they were walking into an ambush and leave. My pink skin softened the blow.

'Not bad, Byron,' Charlie said to me.

'Thanks,' I said.

Then we stood in silence and waited for the next customers to emerge from the guest change room, which, unlike ours, is a five-star joint. If I know Charlie, we'd be moving on to routine three, maybe followed up by a five. I poured myself a glass of water. My throat was sore from the screaming.

* * *

It was on a night like this that Victoria found me; she was doing freelance photography for a magazine at the time. Or at least, this is what she was paid to do. As far as I could tell, she spent the best part of the evening spying on me, following me around, peering around corners, trying to catch me with her lens. She had an intensely nervous energy about her. Her camera swayed around her neck, bouncing off her chest. A lock of curly brown hair kept popping out from behind her right ear; she'd tuck it back, only to have it pop out a second later. She'd scratch her forearms, the back of her neck; clumsily make some adjustment to her camera. On her hands she wore purple gloves.

As she followed me around, I felt like an endangered animal trying to hide from a tracker. Something about her scared me and I really wasn't in the mood for talking to a stranger. I'd take all my smoke breaks down the dark alleyway that runs behind the toilets; drop my butts in the drain. During the praise routines I'd try not to make eye contact, and when the end of the evening came, I changed fast, snuck out the back past the garbage in the chained-up courtyard and into the parking lot. Assuming that she'd gone home, and feeling overwhelmed with relief, I rolled myself a fat joint in my car. I shared it with one of the chefs, behind a metal dumpster out of eyeshot.

'I'm going to lock up,' he said to me after squashing the roach.

'OK.'

'I'm going back in though. So you off into the parking lot?'

'Ja.'

I stepped into the dusty lot, alone. I was so stoned that my head was vibrating and my eyes stung. I really wanted to go home.

But then there she was, standing alone in the centre of the lot, lit up by the motion detector light. She had her hands behind her back, her hair tucked behind her ears. She looked like a big child.

'Hey,' she said.

She raised one of her hands and stepped toward me, then interlaced her fingers and took a step back. Then she held her hands against her chest. Her movements were graceful, I was fascinated by her, but for some reason still wanted to escape. I raised my hand, then looked down at my feet.

'I'm sorry,' she said, and started coming closer. She paused five metres away. I looked behind me. The back entrance was locked and there was nowhere for me to go. I was so stoned.

'I just wanted to. You know. I'm sorry. I just – '

'What?' I said.

'Can I speak to you for a moment?'

'OK.'

She walked right up to me and stopped an inch short of my private space. The parking lot was empty, the sky was dark and there was no moon. I looked back down at her and decided that I'd just walk away, but then froze and looked up again. She held her hips to the side, her right foot twirled in the sand. Her body had some strange tension in it, like an elastic twirled around itself. A green blouse, which exposed her upper chest and shoulders, clung sensuously and obediently to her body, revealing an inch of transparent bra strap on her left shoulder. She was fiddling with her fingers again. Her nerves were making me nervous. Or maybe I was making her nervous. All I knew was that the sooner the whole thing ended, the better. Just as I was about to burst past her, she stuck out her hand, and took the final step that closed the gap between us. I looked down at her takkies: black with white toes. Then she stuck out her purple gloved hand, and the material felt smooth on my fingertips and I calmed down for a moment as I held it.

'Victoria,' she said.

'Byron.'

'Nice to meet you, Byron.'

'Ja.'

As she started speaking I became transfixed by her wide mouth, home to her wide teeth. Her teeth looked unnaturally white, and her lips unnaturally thin. All her features were angular and chiselled.

'Are you all right?' she asked me.

'Yeah, yeah,' I said.

I realised I was zoning out.

'I wanted to ask you something,' she said.

'What?'

'Umm. Well, I'm a photographer, as you can see. But I also am doing art photography. I'm working on a project at the moment. And you would be perfect.'

'For what?'

'It's all about people out of. Well. I can explain another time. Would you mind me photographing you wearing the skins?'

'When?'

'You can come to my house. I have a room there. I'll call you. Can I have your number?'

I couldn't think of anything to say, and so I gave it to her. Sure enough, the next morning I was awoken by the sound of my phone vibrating on the floor. At first I didn't know what it was and lay staring at the ceiling for several seconds. I've never stuck anything on my walls and so the whiteness of the room shocks me each morning as I wake up, especially if I forget to close the curtains. I leant over and watched my phone move across the chipped floor as it vibrated. I was still hung over and hazy and she wanted me there later that afternoon. More from an inability to think of an excuse than through genuine desire, I agreed to go.

She lived on High Level Road in Sea Point in an old double-storey building. The property was surrounded by a green security fence and I couldn't remember what number she'd told me to buzz. But someone had left the security gate ajar and so I walked straight up the short path to the lower balcony. She lived on the lower level, I remembered her telling me that. The floor beneath my feet was painted red and was stained dark from all the feet that had passed over it. A thick fern in a pot was thriving like a pubic bush in frigid panties. I got the feeling the sun seldom shone where I stood.

I tried to peer through the stained glass panes in the centre of the first door. But they were grooved and dented and I could see nothing. So I plucked up some courage and rang the bell, hoping it would be her who answered. It was. Her eyes were big, her hair was tied back. I felt like a child who'd stumbled across a strange house in the middle of the woods.

'Come in,' she said, and opened the door.

There was a brief one-two, should we, shouldn't we, a step forward, a step back. She broke the situation by kissing me on the cheek. The entrance way was painted yellow and there was hardly enough space for us both to stand comfortably. Above my head was a stained glass light, and the whole house smelt of clean linen.

'We'll be using that one.' She pointed at a closed door to my immediate left. 'Just go change quick.'

'OK.'

I walked through her yellow, shoebox-shaped lounge and into her bathroom. I shut the door behind me and sat down on the toilet. I got undressed and changed into the skins. I'd decided to wear the tight briefs and pulled my balls into the triple P. When I was changed I stuck my legs out in front of me and stared at my stupid feet. The big right and the baby left. I suddenly thought of a way to hide them from her.

Her bathtub was an antique, separate from the wall. It was raised a few inches off the ground by golden eagles' feet, and the taps were antiqued brass. I turned the hot tap on and the whole house began to shake and scream as the water made its way through the piping. I waited for steam to rise from the bath then quickly held my left foot under the hot water hoping it would cause it to swell a little. But I just burnt it.

'Are you all right in there?' she called from outside the bath-room door.

'Yes!' I said.

I went to the room near the entrance and closed the door behind me. Through the large windows I could see my car parked on the street. There was a blue-grey backdrop stuck on the wall behind me, a stool in the centre of the room. Her floors, like mine, were made of wood, but they were much wider, yellow and recently polished. I sat down on the stool and watched my feet hanging there stupidly at the bottom of my legs. Now, thanks to my ingenious plan, the left foot was not only visibly smaller, but also red instead of white.

Suddenly the door burst open and she came walking in, a gust of wind following her.

'Sorry,' she said. 'I forgot to close the front door properly. It's windy today, hey?'

'Yeah.'

She fiddled with her camera. Her fingers were fidgety, but she didn't seem nervous. She looked like a possessed person, totally focused on what she was doing.

'OK, Byron, I want you to just push that aside. The stool. And then stand. OK?'

I tried to hide my left foot behind my right, then swapped it around and tried to hide the right behind the left. Then I tried to stand on the floor, and nearly tripped over myself.

'Oopsy,' I said, and tried to laugh.

'What are you doing?'

'Nothing.'

I stood up straight and moved my right heel backwards so that the toes of my right foot were level with those of the left. She had the camera to her eye and was focusing it on me. My fingers nervously picked at the leather skins. Moving my right foot back causes my body to go slightly out of line, and my right knee to look unnaturally straight.

'No,' she said. 'You really don't need to do that.'

She dropped the camera from her face and looked at me with her eyes. She smiled, and shook her head.

'You really don't need to do that.'

And so I didn't.

I smiled at her, and suddenly felt completely relaxed. It was as if we had discussed the issue at length. As if lawyers representing both parties had met and drawn up a prenuptial understanding, that the feet were fucked up, but that it was fine.

She laughed some more, and shrugged her shoulders.

Then she raised the camera to her eyes again and focused it, while directing my body into the right position. Then she paused for a moment and again dropped the camera from her eyes.

'There's something,' she said. 'It's not uniform thinking. Well what is, I suppose? But I think it's important. Things must be accurate. Even where the lens can't see.'

'All right,' I said. I didn't have a clue what she was talking about.

'It's just that well. Here's the thing. Real tribesmen. And Scots too. You know. With their kilts. They don't. Ug. OK. Please would you take your underwear off?'

Now that we were past the feet, the request felt suspiciously normal.

She raised her shoulders and laughed some more. But now her laugh was more like a little girl's giggle. She held her purple-gloved hand over her right eye, and said 'Am I being rude? I don't know. I'm sorry.'

'No.' I shook my head.

'It's weird I know. But, it's important.'

'OK.'

'I'll cover my eyes if you want.' She raised both hands over her eyes, and made an obvious show of peeping through them.

'No peeking,' she said, and started laughing again.

'OK,' I said.

She dropped her hands from her face. I leant against the blue grey backdrop and pulled up the back of my skirt. I felt like one of the dirtier hobos I've seen in my neighbourhood, pooing against the wall of a house. I blocked the thought out of my mind, and slipped my fingers around the elastic and pulled the underwear down my legs, making sure never to lift the front of the dress up too high. Victoria kept covering her eyes with the front of her hands, then dropping them again.

'Sorry,' she said, and started laughing. 'It's just a bit funny.' Then she raised her hands to her face, covered her eyes again and said, 'No it's not. I'm only joking. I feel so awkward now. Should I feel awkward?'

'No.'

When I'd taken them right off, I sent them skidding across the floor towards where she was standing.

'Those look quite um, sorry. But they look quite uncomfortable.'

'We need them to protect ourselves.'

'I see. OK. I've just had an idea. I'll be back. Wait. Just wait.'

She ran out of the room and returned a moment later with an extension chord and a fan. She left again and came back with a collection of boxes under her arm. There were clearly more than she could manage and so she had to stand at an awkward angle, and keep shifting them about to stop them from falling. I made no attempt to help her, I felt like my feet had sunk into concrete.

She made a little pile out of the boxes, constantly shifting them and rearranging the order in which they were placed. She was muttering under her breath, and seemed oblivious of my existence. When the boxes were ordered she placed the fan on top of them .

'Come stand above it,' she said.

'What?'

'Yes, above it. And hold your dress down. Like Marilyn Monroe.'

'OK,' I said, and did as she asked.

She leant down and turned the fan on, adjusting it to its strongest output. It blew straight up my skirt and the cold air caused the sensitive skin on my balls to harden and the penis to curl up a little.

'Yes, yes!' she kept saying as she moved around the room. As I got used to it, I started enjoying the freedom of wearing no underwear, I even began to fancy the tickle of air against my scrotum. All the little hairs on my balls stood up and an involuntary smile made its way across my face. Yes, I do believe I was the happiest I'd been in ages.

But after we'd finished taking the pictures and I had changed back into my clothes I started getting nervous again.

'I have dinner,' I said.

'Oh. I was going to. But you must come again. To see the pictures. Alright.'

'Sure. Yeah. I'll come.'

* * *

There was something about the way I'd felt standing above the fan, my feet had melted away, my balls felt free and I couldn't help associating this freedom with her. I wanted more. And so, when she called me again and invited me back, I agreed, honestly.

Her property was quite high up the mountain, and because her flat was on the corner of the block from where I parked, I was able to see right down the steep road to the ocean. It was early evening, a Friday, and the sounds of the bustling Sea Point centre below came drifting up the valley. The sky was almost black but still had traces of blue and I was feeling a little cold, but in high spirits. On the inside of her security gate someone had stuck a note written in large black permanent letters: MAKE SURE GATE IS PROPERLY CLOSED. And below that: FOR YOUR OWN PROTECTION.

Below the notice a newspaper article had been fastened to the fence. The caption read: SEAPOINT WOMAN MURDERED IN FLAT. I skimmed the article, but didn't pay much attention to the details. Such sensationalist bullshit had long since lost its effect on me.

I walked up the steps and rang Victoria's doorbell.

She opened and hugged me. I put my arms around her body and could feel her ribs through the thin T-shirt, her thin flesh. I could smell the soapy clean deodorant scent. She seemed to favour subtle perfumes to scent her body. As she stepped away from me, she kept her hands extended: they were still wrapped in the purple gloves and felt smooth between my fingers. She smiled.

'Why is that article on the gate?' I asked her.

'It's just so – well you should be anyway, all the time – but it's just so that people are careful, and lock, and that sort of thing,' she said while closing the door and pulling the security latch into place.

'Would you like?' She pointed toward the green leather couch in the corner of her shoebox-shaped yellow lounge. I was feeling much more relaxed than on my first visit. The first time I'd been so preoccupied with hiding my feet that I'd barely taken in the surroundings. I noticed now that there were a number of large, framed pictures hanging on her walls. One of a naked black man, solid build, leaning against a stripper's pole, another of a young girl in a business suit, holding a cellphone in her hand.

I sat down.

There was incense burning in the room, I saw the packet resting on the windowsill, it was opium-scented, and so I guessed – although I did not know for certain – the room now smelt like an opium den. I stood up and looked out the window, and was able to see the narrow side road where I'd parked my car. Some workers were making their way down the street, dressed in blue overalls and shouting loudly in a language I didn't understand.

I sat down again, and she came in with a large brown envelope in her hands and a bottle of wine tucked under her armpit.

'I'll just quickly get the glasses,' she said, then scampered out the room after dumping the contents of her hands next to a fruit bowl in the centre of the glass table in the centre of her lounge.

'Would you like to see them – the photos, that is?' she asked as she came back in with a glass in either hand.

'Yes,' I said.

She poured us each a glass of red wine, then sat down next

to me on the couch, not close though, perhaps half a metre. I couldn't smell her.

She took them out of the envelope and handed them to me.

'They are small, well smaller than they will be when I blow the nice ones up. We can decide together.'

I flipped through them. There was Byron, holding his leather skins down against his legs as the wind blew up his skirt, and there was Byron running his fingers through his hair. But of course what I looked for was not Byron's skins or his hair or his hands. Of course what I looked for was his feet. They were there, of course. I could not say that the size difference wasn't notice-able, it was. But it was pleasing to the eye. The right was larger, the left smaller, but it looked somehow as if the feet belonged to two separate stages of development, as if the right belonged to the present, and the left to the past: to Byron the child. It looked as if the size difference was a deliberate artistic decision, instead of a subject deformity. She hadn't violated the sacred, prenuptial understanding: the foot was there, and fine, and normal.

So we spoke, and she told me about the project, and how her father owned an art gallery, and how she was going to have her own exhibition with a collection of photographs, some of me, and some of the subjects on the wall – she pointed with her hand – and some that she had yet to take.

'Do you like them?' she asked.

'Yes,' I said.

She shifted her weight slightly on the couch, and for the first time, I could see, beneath the thin material of her white T-shirt, that she wasn't wearing a bra. To be sure, her breasts were not large, but now from the angle at which she was sitting, and some-thing that the light was doing, I was able to see her pink nipples against the pale top. I felt as if I were being rude to watch, to stare, when I had not been invited; but then I noticed that she was turning herself toward me, inflating her chest slightly, directing my attention to the exact spot that I wished my attention to be directed toward. She was wriggling her butt cheeks slowly on the couch as she spoke, and she laughed a little, and one of the strands of brown hair fell forward, and she tucked it back with her purple-gloved hands.

'I need the bathroom,' she said, and left the room. It was obvious where this rendezvous of ours was headed. I wondered at which point she'd decided that I was to be her lover. Or perhaps she hadn't decided this yet. Perhaps she never would. Maybe I'd gotten the wrong end of the stick. I considered leaving to save myself any embarrassment. But when she returned she sat an inch closer to me, and as her body sank into the couch I could smell the soap and water rising off her skin. And my heart sped up as her knees clapped together and she rested her hands on the end of her legs.

'What is it that you do, at your work, that is?'

'I translate Charlie's poetry. From Xhosa to English. The guests are all foreigners. Ninety per cent.'

'So they want to know what's being said?'

'Charlie is a praise poet. And I tell them, yes. What's being said about them.'

'Are they English people?'

'Some. Germans. Lots of Germans. Also some French. Even Japanese sometimes. All sorts.'

'Oh, that's nice,' she said, the way someone says, that's nice if you tell them you're a nursery school teacher. And as she spoke she pointed her right leg slightly toward me, causing the gap between her legs to widen ever so slightly. I imagined what I would be able to see if she weren't wearing anything over her legs, if

I were lying on my back, on the floor, and she made the same movement. I imagined what I would be able to see, and then I said, 'I will be getting a promotion though. Sometime.'

'Oh really?' she said, with a hint of enthusiasm.

'Deputy Manager, perhaps,' I said, and went on to list the perks I'd receive. I'd be able to change out of the skins and into a suit, maybe get my own office, a phone contract paid for by Bhakhuba, a company car was in the pipelines, medical aid, insurance, retirement funds, UIF, bursaries to study further.

She shifted her buttocks a little closer now as I spoke, and kept the angle of her legs open to the same degree; there was a long and deliberate tear from the top of her jeans down to the knees, and the first part of it had been covered by a patch, and she wasn't wearing any shoes, and her toenails weren't painted, and she smiled now, and her teeth were slightly stained from the red wine, and there were traces of spittle on the corner of her lips, and these too were stained red, or mauve, or perhaps purple like her gloves, and then she opened her leg a little more, and moved her bare foot across the wooden floor toward the rug, and held my hand in hers and raised it to her face.

'I like hands,' she said 'Hands are interesting'

All the while I had not moved. But now it was my turn, and I placed my hand on the sewn-on patch on her jeans. It was perfectly positioned, as if placed as a guidance tool for first-time hands: any lower could have been platonic, any higher, overly familiar. So I placed my hand on the patch, and moved my head toward hers, and closed my eyes as my tongue slipped into her mouth and I tasted the red wine on her breath. Then she stood up, and stumbled slightly, and offered me her hand, and led me toward her bedroom, and with her free hand gave me a 'come here' wag with her purple finger, then smiled and giggled, and when in the room pulled herself toward me, held her breasts against my chest for a second, and said 'Whisper Xhosa in my ear.'

My mind ran over routines, trying to remember what I said when the guests came and Charlie rattled off the poetry. The smell of fresh sheets and incense was strong in her room, and I placed my hand on her hip and tried to think of something to say, but in the end all I got was some guttural groans and hopelessly inaccurate clicks. I kept on going as she guided me toward her small bed in the corner of the room, where she pushed some pillows aside and drew me toward her as we both fell down. I ran my hand up the inside of her top and took her small breasts in my hands, and ran the fingers along the flesh from top to bottom, touching the nipples, then retracting. But she was wasting no time trying to get my jeans undone, and I didn't want to stop her, and kept mumbling half-baked Xhosa into her ear, then shifting my own hand down toward her jeans, and struggling with the buttons, and then a zip, and then a clip, and I found the underwear, and tried to pull the jeans down, but for some reason couldn't get them past her buttocks, and now she'd managed to get her hand into my pants and taken hold of my penis, but kept grabbing my pubic hairs, it was too sore for me to relax and enjoy it. My hand kept going, I felt pubes, then went further down, and fingered her pubic bone, and managed to get my fingers, finally, to the entrance of her private hole, and played with the flesh as romantically as I could, while still trying to remember some Xhosa phrases. Her pants were stuck and she was unable to open her legs any further, unable to do what I'd imagined her doing, unable; and she kept tugging at me, hurting me, and in the end we both sort of gave up, and sat up, and I carried on telling her about the potential benefits of my fabricated promotion.

* * *

'Why don't we get you some nice shoes, Byron?' Victoria asked me one evening.

We were sitting in front of her television watching a documentary about spiders, and eating popcorn. She'd oversalted the popcorn, and my mouth was already dry from getting stoned. A strong breeze blew almost every evening, and so I was able to smoke out of her bathroom window. I'd wash my mouth out and splash water in my eyes.

'Why shoes?' I asked.

'Because. Well, because we've bought you all sorts of other nice things in the last while. So let's get some shoes too.'

I'd decided to lie to her, and tell her that I'd received the promotion at work. And so, in order to look like a manager, I'd had to start spending like one. The little savings my father had left me when he emigrated had transformed into expensive cocktails – I avoided two-for-one specials, just to enhance the image – and fancy clothes.

'I don't know about that,' I said, and left the room.

I went back to her bathroom. The underside of her freestanding bathtub was overrun with cobwebs. It was the only place in her house that had been neglected, and so I assumed she never looked underneath it. I hid my bankie of weed and Rizzla there and pretended to have diarrhoea as an excuse for constantly returning to the bathroom. I sat on the toilet and rolled myself another joint. I was still stoned from the last one.

The little bathroom window was covered by a lacy curtain with a strange elastic lining which made it difficult to hold open. But I forced the windowpane outwards, and stuck my head outside. The wind was still blowing hard. The building directly behind hers was a single storey, and so from her window I was able to see the flickering lights surrounding the black ocean. The sound of traffic was drowned out by the howling of the wind.

I dropped the roach in the toilet and flushed it away, then sprayed the bathroom with strawberry-and-cream-scented toilet spray.

The following morning, while Victoria was cooking breakfast I went back to the bathroom and got stoned again. But the kitchen window had been open and the wind blowing flat against the building, so all my smoke had blown straight up her nose.

'You feeling better now?' she asked me.

'Why?'

'Byron. God, you're such a . . . Byron!'

We'd only been seeing each other for about ten days, but whenever she knew I was stoned, she started treating me like a ten-year-old child. And for some reason, I'd play right into her scheme and start acting like a fucking moron. A fair number of people had commented on the fact that marijuana and me did not gel too well. It made me a little slow at the best of times. But around her I'd turn into a gibbering fool. I'd become self-conscious, feel like each move was being watched. To avoid total paranoia, I became very quiet and completely withdrawn.

'We're taking your car, Byron. Or are you too stoned to drive?'

'No. No I'm not.'

I sat on her couch eating breakfast with an exaggerated smile on my face. My clothes smelt of weed, I'd forgotten to bring a change with me. When I'd finished scraping the egg yolk up with my fork, Victoria took the plate off my lap.

'Thank you,' I said. 'Very yummy!'

She shook her head and walked out the room.

Sitting in the driver's seat I looked at my face in the rear-view mirror. My eyes were still red. I unlocked the passenger door for her.

'We going to Cavendish, Byron. Do you know how to get there?'

'Yeah.'

'You won't get lost, will you?'

'Uh-uh.'

I avoided using my car when Victoria was with me. I'd made a secret compartment under the driver's seat by slicing a long line across the material and fixing Velcro to either side. I'd taken to visiting her in the evenings after work, and to avoid a trip home I'd hide the skins in the compartment, and seal it up. I didn't want her to find out that I was really still a translator. Before leaving work I would also lift up the felt that lined the boot of my car, and place the shield and spear on top of the spare tyre, before shutting it down again.

But I was in enough trouble already. If I started dreaming up excuses not to use my car I risked sending her over the edge. So we drove along High Level Road. It was what most people would describe as a glorious day. The sun was up and all the little cunts who like tanning were probably flocking to the beach. Anyway, it was the end of summer, and these happy bright days would soon be behind us.

'Maybe we should go to the beach later,' Victoria said, as if reading my thoughts.

'OK,' I said.

'You could get a tan. Maybe then you can get a better job.'

'What?'

'I'm only joking.'

'Oh.'

We stopped at the robots opposite the Waterfront. To our right was the convention centre. It was supposed to look like a ship, but looked more like the back of a boot. It's surrounded by a collection of exclusive hotels and the handful of high-rise buildings the city has.

I turned left into the Waterfront.

'What are you doing, Byron?'

'Oh shit,' I said. 'I'm sorry. I forgot. I thought we were going . . .'

'We meant to be going to Cavendish, Byron!'

'I forgot.'

'You're a pothead moron!'

I'd promised myself that I wouldn't do stupid things today. I wanted to get some respect from her, but it would never happen if I kept doing things like that. She sighed loudly and made a show of taking her cellphone out of her bag and looking at the time. Then she looked at me again, and smiled.

'I'm sorry,' she said. 'I don't mean it, you know, like that.'

I smiled a stupid smile. I really hate myself sometimes.

On the other side of the mountain it was quite a lot colder. I knew this without opening my window, because I was unable to shut the air vents in my car. Victoria also seemed to feel the difference in temperature and put her hands in front of the vents then rubbed them together.

'Are you still, I mean, you said you might at the beginning, are you getting a car allowance?'

'What?'

'You said. From your work, you know, now that you're a manager.'

'Oh. It's in the pipeline. Ja.'

Black clouds were coming down over Devil's Peak and into the thick forest below. I was very stoned and imagined for a moment that I was in Africa. Then remembered that I was.

I opened my window. The cold air came blowing in. I lit myself a cigarette, looked down at my feet and noticed that the scuff mark on the top of my right shoe had been coloured in with something too dark to be soil. I wondered if it might be dog shit, and where it would have come from.

'Byron!'

'What?'

'You nearly drove into that car.'

I'd misjudged a corner. A car next to me, with about five people in their mid-twenties, had slowed down. They were all giving me hand signals, pointing at their eyes, pointing at their heads.

'You must be careful!' she said to me.

'Ja.'

We finally made it into the Cavendish Square parkade.

Victoria pulled down the sunshade in front of her, expecting to find a mirror in which to examine her face. But there was none.

'Oh,' she said.

Without hesitating for more than second, she turned sideways, pulled the rear-view mirror toward her, looked at herself – coldly, as a surgeon might look at a patient – touched her pointy chin, tucked a strand of hair behind her ear.

'Come!' she said, then unlocked the door and hopped out.

I walked behind her. She never once turned around to see if I was following. She walked past the large mirror at the top of the escalators, paused for a second to look at her reflection, again coldly, hopped on the machine and began the descent. I followed.

The escalators are right in the centre of the mall, in a large chasm of space filled with sunlight. In front of me was a Muslim family. The father was dressed in a robe, as was his young son. The woman's entire body was covered, with only a small slit for the eyes. I was very stoned and suddenly realised I'd been staring at her for too long. And staring is wrong. We embrace diversity and barely notice minor differences like that. The truth was, I envied her. I was starting to get paranoid and would have killed to hide myself inside a full body veil. Perhaps I should invest in one.

Then I was at the bottom of the escalator standing in front of a Levi's shop with all the pretty models smiling at me. Victoria had already rounded the corner and walked into Truworths. I ran after her. She was winding her way through the women's clothing section. I noticed that the mannequins were getting slightly chubbier, and yes, some of them were charcoal coloured. I wondered if veil shops invested in mannequins.

I started moving faster and nearly bumped into a trendy black girl of high-school age. She was with a large group of friends and they were holding up clothes against their bodies and giggling. And Victoria was climbing onto the escalator. I ran toward her and grabbed hold of her arm.

'Byron. What are you doing?'

'Sorry,' I said.

It had been such a long time since I was last in the shoe section of a shop. Nothing had changed. A pop song was playing over the stereo. There were countless mirrors and large pictures of men kicking balls and girls sitting on haystacks and smiling. And then the shoes. There they were. The sevens with the sevens. The eights with the eights. All paired up and matching. They seemed to be staring down at me and laughing.

'Can I help you, sir?' A short woman with greasy black hair

pulled back so tight it looked as if it were about to be ripped from her skull was standing behind me.

'Umm . . . ' I said.

'Are you looking for anything?' She smiled.

'Yes,' Victoria said. 'We are looking for shoes, of course, that is.'

As she spoke her bag slipped off her shoulder and landed in the V of her arm.

'For?' asked the shoe lady

'Him,' said Victoria. 'We are looking for shoes – white shoes, nice, bowling sort of shoes. For him.'

'Well, would you like to come with me?' The assistant seemed amused by us. She had a smirk on her face.

'What is that you're laughing at?' Victoria asked her.

'Nothing,' said the shoe lady. 'Over here!' She pointed with her right hand at a shelf full of boxes.

'Stop sniggering' Victoria said. 'We've come here to buy shoes.'

I stood silently.

'Would you like to look at them?' The shoe lady was now doing her best not to snigger. She was in fact overcompensating, to the point where her expression looked like a stick-on serious face. At this stage I didn't know what she found so funny.

'These are some Levi's,' she said taking a white pair out of the box. 'They're on special. As advertised in our flyer.'

I saw all the boxes sitting there. The numbers: 8, 7, 11, 12.

'They're nice,' Victoria said, running her hand along the white leather, and holding them up to her nose.

'What size would you like?' the shoe assistant lady asked Victoria whilst looking down at my feet.

I slid the right foot back.

'We have to try on various sizes' Victoria said. 'We can manage by ourselves now, thank you.'

'Just shout if you need help,' said the shoe assistant lady. She walked away, the sniggering face prying its way out from underneath.

Victoria's handbag was still resting in the V of her arm. She looked up and down the rack of shoes. Her face had that same possessed intensity as when she took photographs.

'What sizes?' she asked, without looking up.

'Eleven,' I said.

'And?' She said the word so casually.

'Seven,' I said.

She took the two boxes out of the shelf, carelessly, and carried them over to the try-on spot. She placed the boxes on the floor. I stared at them for a second. She kicked the size 11 box toward me.

'Come on,' she said.

'I know.'

'Try them on.'

'I will,' I said.

In the distance, prowling between the shelves and the tills, greasy head emerging here, and there, and there again, was the shoe assistant lady. And yes, now she was talking to one of her shoe assistant lady friends, a fat white girl with straw-coloured hair and acne vulgaris. What a revolting creature, I thought. I felt angry at her for being so sif. Then I suddenly became nervous again and longed for a Muslim veil.

'What's wrong?' Victoria asked.

'Nothing.'

'So then, Byron, try on – I know, OK – just try them on, both.'

I opened the box with the size eleven shoes in it and took them both out, placing them on the floor.

'Why you taking them both out?' she asked me.

'No!' I said.

I picked up the right shoe and placed it on my lap. The leather was white and felt smooth beneath my fingers. I thought of the cow that laid down its life for these shoes. I was pleased.

'Come, Byron!' Victoria said.

I opened it right up and fumbled about, trying to undo the ridiculous knot that's always tied into new shoes. When I had it undone, I slipped my foot inside and tied it back up, then waggled it about in the air and put it back on the floor.

'It fits. I'll buy them.'

'But Byron, the other – what about the other, the other set of shoes.'

'They're fine.'

'You have to – I mean, you will be wasting both your money, and our time – Byron, you have to. Just try it on.'

'I know my size.'

'We've come all the way, Byron. Just do it.'

'Fine.'

The shoe assistant lady seemed to have been absorbed into another conversation. Victoria kept looking at me.

I first took off my right shoe, and tucked it away neatly in the box. Then, at super high speed, whilst pretending to look around the room at other things, even whistling a tune under my breath, I pulled out the size seven, and, without bothering to undo the ridiculous knot, slipped it onto my left foot.

'It fits. Let's go.'

'Aren't you, Byron, are you not going to walk around in them, to see, just to know, how they feel?'

'They're shoes.'

'If you don't want it – my help that is, Byron – then you can just say so.'

'Fine. I'll take them. Come.'

'Both pairs?'

'Yes.'

'And you're not going to walk?'

'Why?'

'To know.'

'I know. Come. I need to draw money.'

'I thought, Byron, can't you put it on your credit, or debit, whatever card?'

'No.' I shook my head.

'It's fine then. I will get them for you.'

'No. Why?'

'Because you have – in the last week or so spent money on me. So it's fair.'

'No, no!' I shook my head again, placed the size seven box on top of the size eleven and scampered off through the centre to find an ATM. I only had five thousand rand left in my account. Ten days earlier I'd had twice as much.

By the time I got back Victoria had already bought both pairs of shoes and was standing outside the store waiting for me to return.

'No,' I said.

'Yes, Byron.'

'No, I said I would. I can afford.'

'So can I, Byron, so can I afford.'

'I'm a manager. I'm a manager and I can afford my own shoes.'

'Oh, Byron, you really are, you are really so very silly. Sometimes. You are silly. You can buy them from me if you want!'

'Fine.'

'Or I'll give them away.'

'To who?'

'To someone else. There are, Byron – actually, in case you didn't know – there are other people.'

'With what?'

'With feet, Byron. With feet.'

And suddenly as I stood there in the centre of the shopping mall drenched in sunlight and surrounded by strangers, a thought occurred to me. A thought that stayed with me the whole drive home. Somewhere, perhaps not too far away, there must indeed be someone else with feet: my type of feet.

I dropped Victoria at her flat and went home. It was late afternoon when I pulled into my driveway and parked underneath the old carport. The driveway looks directly onto my bedroom, and although the cover partially blocks the sunlight, at this time of day my room is well lit. It gets more light than the rest of the house, which exists in almost perpetual darkness. The long passage with the old thick wooden beams, cracked and lined with dust never gets a drop of light. The ceiling is three metres up and decorated with intricate designs. This theme runs through most of the rooms in the house, but not mine.

I dropped down on my bed and sent a cloud of dust floating into the air. I dropped the packet with the two shoeboxes onto my table and opened up my clothes cupboard. It was pretty much empty. All my clothes were lying in a pile in the corner of the room. It smelt dirty. But the afternoon sun was just right: not that furnace-like heat enjoyed by cunts who go to beaches. I took the right shoe out of the size eleven box and the left shoe out of the size seven. I put them in the lowest section of my shelf alongside the other pairs, then put the remaining two shoes in the same box and placed them in the other section of my cupboard alongside all the other unused shoes I've collected through the years. The boxes have literally been caked by a thick layer of dust which I now unsettled as I added the new arrival to the pile. I sneezed.

Then I set off through the streets to the Spar. It moved one building down about a year earlier and the old building still stands there, unused. The old delivery zone has become a favourite hangout for the large number of hobos who live in my area, Observatory. Behind the new Spar is a pay-per-month parking lot, a butchery and a second-hand clothes store. A lazy-looking car guard was sitting on a plastic chair beneath a gum tree. The world felt tired. Nothing much was happening: even the hobos were sitting in silence.

I bought myself a pack of cigarettes and a Cape Ads, then went back home and paged through to the personals section. No one had beaten me to it. Or at least not this week. I scribbled down the advert I wanted to place, phoned the Cape Ads, and dictated it to a lady at the call centre:

Byron: I'd like to place an advert in the personals.

Operator: OK, sir, have you used the Cape Ads before? Do you have a reference number?

Byron: No.

Operator: Name please, sir.

Byron: Byron.

Operator: And what is your ad, sir?

Byron: I have a right foot UK size 11 and a left foot UK size 7. I'm looking for someone who has the opposite problem to swap unused shoes with, or go shoe-shopping with. Contact Byron on 082 995 2381

Operator: OK, sir.

The operator giggled a little. I'd never have had the courage to place the advert if Victoria hadn't helped ease my self-consciousness a little. Not to say it was gone. But at that moment, at least, I felt OK.

I hung up. Rolled myself a joint, kicked off my shoes, and waited for a response.

* * *

A dozen guests who'd come independently of the German tourist bus were the last to leave. One of the underling chefs threw a container of dirty water on the fire, sending a thick cloud of grey smoke into the air and causing the coals to sizzle.

I sat at the bar beneath the palm overhangs sipping a Black Label and smoking the second-last cigarette in my box. From the parking lot I could hear Charlie starting up his motorbike. He hadn't bothered to say goodbye.

I wasn't sure if he'd made a mistake, or if it was a setup. It could have just slipped his mind; alternatively he and Vusi could be in cahoots, and the reason he'd told me we wouldn't be using praise routine number four was simply to lull me into a false sense of security. Whatever the story, I knew what awaited.

Lindi came walking toward me from the girls' change room; she was wearing a tight grey top that hugged her large breasts. She looked up from writing an SMS and said: 'Vusi wants you in his office, Byron! Cheers, babe!' she called out to the barman.

I knocked back the rest of my beer, took a long drag of my cigarette and stubbed it out.

The entrance to Vusi's office is next to the service bar. It's a simple security gate that he'd obviously just unlocked after stashing away the cash. I walked down the wooden stairs toward his office, which doubles up as a storeroom. As usual there were empty kegs, unwanted promotional goods strewn across the concrete floor. His desk is in the far corner, illuminated by a single halogen lamp. He was typing on a laptop that he now folded flat.

'Sit down, Byron.'

I pushed the skins between my legs, placed the shield on the floor. He'd undone the top three buttons of his shirt, he looked stressed. He ran his hand over his bald head, then started playing with the curly stubble on his chin. He always does this before lecturing me. He wants me to believe that I'm in the presence of a sage.

'Let me ask you something,' he finally said. He continued to play with his beard and stare over my shoulders at an invisible point in the distance. 'Where do you see yourself in five years?'

'I'm not sure.'

'Not sure. Do you still see yourself here? At Bhakhuba?'

'Maybe.'

'Wearing the skins? Translating praise poetry?'

'I don't really know right now.'

'You only have to remember five routines.'

'Charlie said we wouldn't use routine four tonight.'

'It's only a few lines. Why do you keep forgetting it?'

'I don't know.'

'He doesn't know.' He started scratching his head. 'Tell me, Byron, how I can help you.'

'I'm not sure. I'm sorry, it won't happen again.'

'If you can give me the solution, I'm willing to listen.'

'The solution to what?'

'To you, Byron.'

'I'm not sure what to say.'

'He's not sure.'

'Ja.'

'I'm going to ask you to stop coming here.'

'No, please. I need the money. I will work hard.' I leant forward trying to convince him of my desperation. But even I could hear that my voice lacked authenticity. Right then I didn't give a shit if he fired me. I just wanted to go home and drink the bottle of brandy I'd saved for myself and smoke the rest of my weed.

'Show a white man some mercy!' I cried out.

'Are you amusing yourself, Byron?'

I was.

'Not at all,' I said.

He shook his head.

'You can come in once in a while. If you're desperate, you can do a shift here. A shift there. If people ask for you. I realise some of the guests find you amusing.'

'Please! You can't do this to me! It just isn't fair!' I don't even talk like that. Who was I fooling? 'There's nothing here without me,' I said, and leant across his table.

'Yes, Byron. We'd be finished without you. Go home.'

I picked up my shield and spear and gave him a half bow, half curtsy as I made my way toward the door.

'And stop smoking dope. You'll be brain dead before thirty.'

Vusi's silver BMW X4 was parked in the lot. He reserves his place with an orange cone each evening. I was still dressed in my skins and so it was easy for me to take a piss on his back tire.

Brain dead before thirty, I thought as I sat in my lounge rolling myself a joint. You'll be dead before tomorrow if you're not careful, Vusi.

I still had a few good heads left in my stash. The last few weeks had been bad. I'd been smoking heavily with Roddy. Sometimes he brought his own, but normally we smoked mine. Like him, his stash is full of shit. I sometimes think it's actually mowed lawn. It seldom gets us high, and he always has some excuse. He's an old man, Roddy. Somewhere in his sixties, I guess. He has a long grey ponytail, wears dirty clothes. He lives somewhere in Salt River and stays alive by doing odd jobs. He's a shit talker. I don't mind him, but he smokes too much of my weed.

Maybe I'm too generous, I thought, as I slid down the back of my couch and blew smoke rings toward the dim yellow light on my ceiling. I felt like a diver sitting at the bottom of a children's swimming pool. I took some long swigs from my bottle of brandy, then made my way into the passage. Two of the lights had gone and I hadn't had a chance to change them. The passage is wide, high, always cold. The large wooden floorboards are chipped and offer an ideal refuge for dust. I flicked on my lighter, holding it up to the electricity meter next to the front door. At current usage, I had twenty hours left. I kicked open my bedroom door, pulled some dirty clothes off my bed. The sheet smelt of beer. I ripped it off and sent it hurtling across the room, climbed onto the bare mattress, pulled the duvet up to my chin, jerked off and fell asleep.

I woke early in the morning to the sound of gentle rain on my roof. I was glad it was there to keep the water off my face. My father had paid the house off in full when he left the country and transferred it into my name. I had never laid eyes on it before the day it became mine. It was more than five years ago now, when the property market in Obs was just starting to grow. He'd paid next to nothing for it a decade earlier. But despite this one piece of luck he was adamant that his time in Africa was up. He sold his other properties and packed all his possessions into a crate, which he loaded onto the same ship that took him to England. He didn't want to leave by plane. He said it was important that he went by ship, the same way his grandfather had come to the country. He said he wanted to complete the cycle, and that one day I'd understand. As far as I was concerned he was just a sentimental old fart. But I was glad for the house. No matter what happened, I'd always have that.

Now that I'd been released from Bhakhuba, I had nothing to worry about except the six marijuana plants growing in my back garden. They were certain to bring me enough income to buy myself food and booze for a month. After that? Well, we'd have to see. I'd bought some indoor growing equipment from the Grow-it-Yourself shop up the road from my house. I'd been meaning to transplant the crop into my cupboard but hadn't found the moment. Anyway, I'd worry about them later. I rolled over and went back to sleep.

When I woke again the rain had stopped. I summoned all my energy and climbed out of bed. I stumbled down the passage to the bathroom and took a piss in the toilet, dribbling all over the floor. I wanted to wipe it up, but I was out of toilet paper. I splashed my face. My eyes were red, with dark rings beneath them. My normally black hair had traces of brown caused by the dirt at Bhakhuba. I ran my fingers through it and held them to my nose. Whew! I needed to wash myself. But first, I had to take a look at my plants. I walked down the passage and when I reached the end, the part where it drops into the sunken landing that leads to the back garden, I stopped dead.

The entire concrete landing was flooded by a few inches of dirty water. Without hesitation I jumped into it, wetting the bottoms of my jeans. I pulled open the rickety wooden door with the stained glass panes and was greeted by a miniature mud slide. Thank God the landing was a few feet below the rest of the corridor, or my entire house would have been washed away. I ran into the garden.

'What the fuck!' I cried out to no one in particular.

I ran through the swamp. I could feel the mud between my toes, the cold water against my ankles and shins. The tree in the corner of the garden had been stripped of all its little yellow leaves; they were floating on the surface of the swamp, serving as rest points for drowning insects. And then I saw them.

'Fuck!' I screamed. I fell to my knees, then shifted onto my bum.

All six of them had been uprooted. I was sure that I'd planted them properly. They were meant to be resistant. I started running through excuses in my head before realising that there was no one to excuse the disaster to except myself. I was sitting amidst my own failed cash crop. I felt like a Zimbabwean farmer, the rain my Mugabe and his war veterans.

I sat completely still. It was a quiet morning and the rain had stopped. From my garden I can see the top of Devil's Peak, the chisel-shaped rock, which at that moment was covered in grey cloud and truly looked like the forehead of Satan. I put my hands on the ground to try and push myself up. They sank into the mud. At that moment I almost felt like giving up. But then, suddenly, I felt a very sharp point stick into the palm of my hand. It sent a shock of pain up my arm. I felt around to see what it was, but now it was gone.

I decided I had to find it. I was angry with everything that was going on around me, and I was channelling all this anger toward whatever it was that had split my skin. I dug around in the mud until I managed to locate the offender. I got onto my knees and started working my right hand underneath it. My hand was pain-

ful and the cold was making it worse. I took hold of it, leant back
and pulled with all my weight. Out it came, bringing with it an
explosion of water. I jumped to my feet, turned my back against
the white glaring sky. I wanted to focus on the mysterious object
in my hand. It was still covered with mud, so I dipped it back into
the water and rinsed it clean. When I held it up again I could see
that what I was holding was definitely a bone.

It was half the length of my arm, sharp on the edges and old
and worn in the centre. In parts it was turning brown from soil
that had been caked into it.

I ran inside, paused, ran back out, fetched all the plants and
threw them onto my shower floor. I was doing everything at a
pace to which I was unaccustomed. I moved into the kitchen so
fast I tripped over the linoleum floor covering that was peeling
in the corner. I dumped the bone on the rickety round table in
the centre of the kitchen then took a step back and rested my
weight on the old wooden counter that runs down the side of
the room. The cupboards behind me shook under my weight,
all the old china rattled. A ghostly light came in through the window, passing over the dishes, the yellow floor. The bone made
me feel self-conscious. It had a strangely awesome presence, like
a great man. I felt I had to be presentable around it. I looked
down at my jeans, they were thick with water and the backs caked
with mud. My armpits stunk. I made a fart and scratched my asshole.

I needed to tell someone about the bone. It could be a murder. Perhaps the cops would rock up any day now, search the
house and arrest me as an accomplice. I'd seen enough cop
shows to know. But no. The bone must have been there for some
time. Whoever it once belonged to is way forgotten. The case is
long closed. But perhaps it could be a collector's item. Maybe

it's worth something. Enough to see me through the next few months, a present from the gods. Yes. I had to tell someone.

In movies when people find bones, they always know who to tell. But not in real life. Not round these parts.

I needed to think clearly. I needed to focus. I went to my lounge. There's only one window in the room and it's covered by a curtain that looks like mosquito netting. The already pale light filtered through the netting cast the room in a light the colour of a corpse's skin. I picked the bankie of weed off my lounge table, an item I'd made myself by placing a stop sign on top of a crate. I mulled some in my hand and let it drop on the crotch of my jeans. I had a little bag of chronic in my room which I'd been saving for a special occasion. But it now seemed special enough to me. I put the mulled weed back on the table and ran through to my bedroom. I always store my chronic weed on the bottom shelf of my table. It was a luminous green and smelt of chemicals. I'd paid a hundred bucks for a dime bag's worth. I cut some up with a pair of scissors and mixed it up with the Swazi.

I picked up the yellow pages which had been delivered to my house a few weeks ago. I'd been using the covers as girrick paper for my joints and there was barely any left. I pulled off a final strip, rolled myself a fat joint and got unbelievably high.

In my now stoned state I was struck by a thought. I knew at once where I'd be able to track down the people who'd be able to deal with the bone. I put the coverless Yellow Pages on my lap, it flopped about like a dead fish.

I flipped to the index and looked under B: Bird Seed Merchants, Boatyards, Body Building, Body Piercing, Bodyguards. But fuck all about bones. Was this not a common enough problem? Then I remembered something else I'd been using as girrick paper in the last while. It was a flyer advertising the Observatory Fair that was being held this week at the community hall. Various groups would have display tables with information and whatnot. Surely there would be some group that would show an interest in a bone found in a garden. But what sort of bone was it? It must have been fairly deep underground. I know this because I broke the worst sweat I'd had in years trying to dig the trench into which I'd transplanted the baby plants when I'd first started growing. So it wasn't a murder. And if it were, coming into the open about it would clear my name. But more likely it was an antique, something of value. I could sense money.

I went through to the bathroom and washed my hands. In the little freestanding round mirror I could see that my eyes were red. I went back to the kitchen and opened up all the old wooden cupboards looking to find some eyedrops. Somewhere I had eyedrops! But no sign of them. Just dust, old ashtrays, bowls I'd never used. I rubbed my eyes with the back of my hands, then splashed them with water from the sink. I needed to wash my dishes.

I sat down in the corner of the kitchen, smoked a cigarette and tried to remember if there was anything I had to do with my day. But of course there wasn't.

I'd go up to the fair and ask around. I'd play it cool. Someone would have the answer. I was so stoned that the walls of the kitchen appeared to be breathing. You get what you pay for.

I showered, and just before walking out the front door remembered that Pete was coming later that afternoon to check out the setup in my cupboard. The setup I'd told him was ready for use. The setup that wasn't really there.

During our first meeting he'd said that he might have some business for me. But if he learnt that my entire harvest had drowned in the garden, and that I still hadn't set up the system, I was sure his offer would be reversed.

I started getting paranoid. I walked up and down my corridor running my hands through my hair which still felt dirty. I was disgusted by myself.

I scrambled into my room and began emptying out my cupboards, starting with the shoe section. I had more shoes than at any other point in my life. This was, of course, because of Pete.

* * *

It had been a full week, maybe ten days, after placing the advert in the paper that I got the phone call. I was stoned at the time too.

'Byron bro. Is that you bro?' the voice asked.

'It is.'

'I read your advert in the Cape Ads bro. Says you got a big right and a baby left, is that the case bro?'

'It is.'

'No ways bro!' He laughed a deep laugh that came from his belly, and picked up phlegm as it passed his chest on the way out. 'That's so mad bro. You got an 11 and a 7 bro, is that right?

'Ja.'

'I'm seven and a half, and a ten. But bro, I don't reckon it'll matter bro. Such a small difference. That's so lank weird!' He laughed again.

We made a plan to meet at Obs Café. I hit a bong before I left and strolled up Trill Road to Lower Main. A couple of trendy gay men were sitting at a table on the pavement, having cocktails and laughing deliberately gay laughs. Next to their table was a fern in a pink pot. On the far side of the road a hobo had passed out underneath a large signboard advertising beer. I crossed over the dirty road and walked past the bottle store.

A couple of rough-looking guys were buying themselves bottles of brandy.

In Obs the roads are narrow and cars park all the way along the left hand side of the road. Traffic can't go in both directions at the same time and drivers have to wait their turn. A frizzy-haired woman in a Beetle, who'd been waiting for too long, was banging her steering wheel in frustration as I crossed in front of her. In the big glass windows of Obs Café were some posters advertising upcoming shows in the side theatre. And there through the windows I saw a man, and knew, without introduction, that it was he.

I pulled open the glass door and entered the non-smoking section of the café.

'You looking for a table sir?' a waiter asked me.

'Uh-uh.'

I made my way across the narrow alley that divides the smoking from the non-smoking section of Obs café. He was at a table in the corner, his body sunk backward and downward into the black leather couch, his knees stuck up high like exaggerated A-frames, his pants were torn at the knee. His hair was big and dirty, not dreadlocked, but almost. He hadn't shaved in months, and his beard grew out in uneven tufts like the grass on the maintenance road at Bhakhuba. His tattered pants were tucked into knee-high black boots, clearly of different sizes. Underneath his thick denim jacket he wore a red T-shirt with Che Guevara's face in the middle of it. He didn't stand to greet me, but simply extended his long gorilla-like arm. As we sat and spoke he sipped an iced cool drink with a straw. On the glass table in front of us he rolled himself a joint, and for mixer used the tobacco from the butts of self-rolled cigarettes that he'd kept in his tobacco pouch.

'You want a drag, bro?' He held the joint out across the table.

'OK.' I took three long drags and held the smoke in my lungs as I handed the joint back to him.

'Excuse me!' A perky waitress with nice tits came walking up to the table. 'I'm afraid you're not allowed to smoke that in here.'

'It's cool, bro, I'm lank buddies with the manager,' Pete said, while holding the smoke in his lungs.

'Who?' she asked.

'Stefan, bro.'

'Stefan? I've never heard of him. Come. Settle up and leave. Or I'm going to have to call my boss.'

'Chill, lady. We chucking.' He took another few drags, then passed it back to me.

The waitress shook her head and walked away.

I took a drag and put it out. We left.

He led me through the streets of Observatory, past a couple of hippies making their way out of an esoteric crystal shop, past a tattoo parlour with a Harley Davidson parked outside, and into his friend's shop, the Grow-it-Yourself shop: specialists in hydroponics and indoor growing.

The floors inside were made of smooth cement and shone under the overhead fluorescent lights. The walls were lined with shelves covered with chemicals and trays. In the far corner was a vault with a nuclear sign painted on the door. He introduced me to his manager friend, a guy named Brad. We walked past his desk and outside into the service alley.

It was mid-morning and deliveries were still coming in: we watched men dressed in sterile white uniforms unhook the skinned bodies of dead animals and felt the cool, urine-infused breeze blow against our skin. We sat there on the steps for a few moments, unsure how to proceed. I felt slightly self-conscious, and so looked away, pretending not to know the next move.

But Pete was more confident. With his brutish fingers he started unlacing his thick leather boots. I proceeded with caution, undoing one lace at a time and bashfully bringing my little left foot out into the air. He too, had taken the left out first.

When both his were out, he leant back and held them up to the blue sky. I laughed a nervous laugh. He looked at me and said 'Come on, bro. Let's see them.'

I slid onto my back and held my feet up to the sky.

Pete probably had the ugliest feet I'd ever seen. The toenails were black and chipped and the toes were covered in thick hairs. Compared to his, mine looked like film stars. He didn't seem to care about his feet's appearance, and laughed like a man sick in the head, because, appearances aside, it was clear that we had the same problem, in reverse. As we lay on our backs, feet up to the sky, the order went as follows: big, little, little, big. It looked like a half-pipe for skateboarders.

'Wo-ho, bro!' he bellowed. 'I can't believe it, bro.'

I too began to laugh.

Pete ran off the steps, and down onto the alleyway. He jumped up and down, raising his knees to his chest, and slapping them with his hands. 'Woo-hoo. Ha ha' he kept screaming. His thick dirty hair bounced up and down as he shook his body around. No one took any notice of him.

'Come bro. Byron! Hey, bro!' He came and sat down next to me, putting his arm on my shoulder.

'This is so weird, bro. What the chances?'

'Slim,' I said.

'We'll be friends, bro. Is that cool?'

'It's cool,' I said. And, without really knowing why, or even knowing if I wanted to, put my arm around his shoulder, and gave it a pat.

We sat there, silent for a few moments, looking out across the alleyway, our naked feet resting on the lower steps.

'Would you like a smoke?' I asked him.

'Sure thing, bro. Save me the mission of rolling.'

I took my arm off his shoulder, and pulled out a pack of cigarettes.

'Did people use to give you shit, bro? When you were at school?'

'Ummm. Not really. You?'

'Bit. But I never gave a shit, bro. I just thought it was funny.'

'Ja,' I said. 'Never gave a shit.'

'It's the only way, bro. But it's expensive. Nothing you can do 'bout that.'

'That's why I put the ad.'

'For sure, bro, for sure. I haven't kept all my shoes, for all the years. But I got a fair whack. I can't believe, bro. I still can't believe! I'll go to my house and fetch some of the boxes, bro. Is that cool?'

'Yeah, it's cool. I live at 48 Trill.'

'Sure thing, bro. I'll be back there later on.'

An hour later he pulled up outside my house on a dirty off-road motorbike. He was wearing leather riding gloves and a helmet that he tucked under his arm as he walked up the path to my front door.

'Come in,' I said.

I led him through to my room. He dumped his helmet on the table, shoved the gloves into a side pocket of the bag, then emptied the main content onto floor. Somehow he'd managed to stuff eight shoes into the bag. Then from another side compartment he pulled out a bottle of cheap brandy, which he placed on my desk. The bag was old and worn: it looked like it'd served its time.

'You got glasses, bro?' he asked me.

I rinsed out two mugs in the sink and brought them through to the bedroom. He filled them up to the brim and we both drank fast and in complete silence. When we were halfway through our first glass, he filled them up again and rolled a joint. When we'd finished smoking we finally got down to discussing the matter at hand.

'So, bro, for years you've been having to buy two pairs to own one?'

'That's right,' I said.

'Crazy, bro. So you end up with all these extras. I never thought I'd find another ou.'

He laughed.

The forehead was the only visible part of his face. It was kidney red, underscored by wide black freckles and blemishes. He had the look of a man who seldom changed his clothes. The khaki pants, the military jacket, the black boots. They felt as if they enjoyed staying put. He was like a kid's action figure; a standard-issue GI Joe: clothes boots and man, all one.

'Show me what you got.'

I took out all the boxes of unused shoes. He pulled them towards himself, then emptied the contents onto the floor.

'Nice, bro,' he said.

I looked at all the mismatched pairs of shoes that I'd never been able to use, these big lefts and baby rights. And here was a man who could use them. And all the pairs that had been sitting unused in his cupboard, would now see the light of day from the bottom of my legs. What a great guy I was for initiating the meeting.

We spent a few minutes admiring our newly acquired shoes. From a financial point of view, he was the definite winner. Besides the Levi's I'd just bought, he'd also won himself a pair of Nike cross trainers and some Oakley slip-ons. They were from back in my school days when I still got a spending allowance from my father, but my feet hadn't grown since then. As for me, I was getting myself three pairs of shoes that either came from Pep or Mr Price, and a single pair of smart evening shoes. I doubted if their twins even got used. I couldn't picture Pete in a suit.

We each tried on a newly matched pair, and sure enough, the minor difference in size didn't matter. They fitted just fine.

'So, bro,' he said. He had a big smile on his face. I'd packed my new shoes into the cupboard, and he'd crammed his into the bag. I made no mention of the fact that he was scoring big time: there was nothing else I could do with the shoes, and at least now all the pairs in my cupboard could be worn.

'Show me around the place, bro,' he said.

I took him out to the garden and introduced him to my plants, which, at that stage, were four weeks old, had just been planted in the soil and were looking fine and healthy.

'Look strong, bro,' he said, running his thick fingers over the leaves. The backs of his hands, like his face, were red and spotted.

'You ever grown indoors, bro?' he asked me.

'No.'

'Checks like your garden's in a bit of a sink, bro.'

'Might be.'

'Tell you what, bro. Those guys up at the store, my one buddy runs the place. I'll introduce you proper. You can get a nice kit. Then you grow indoors, and don't worry about the weather.'

'Sounds good.'

'Listen, bro. If you do get a setup going, I may have some business for you. Not definite, bro. But maybe. But shoosh about it, bro. Lank quiet.'

I hadn't heard another word from him until the morning of the day I got fired. He phoned and said he wanted to come visit.

So I attached the ultraviolet light to the inside of the small section at the top of my cupboard. I set up the HP globe in the lower section: the section where I used to keep my clothes. I shoved my clothes and shoes under my bed. I filled up six little pots with mud from the garden, and planted a seed in each. I placed them under the UV light, just as the man from the Grow-it-Yourself shop had instructed me to. Then I got the bone and wrapped it in the plastic bag and just before heading out, decided to change into one of the pairs of shoes I'd received from Pete. Although they were cheap, they were pretty fucking comfortable.

*   *   *

I took another hit from my bong before wrapping the bone in a black bag and heading off to the fair. I walked through the park that surrounds the community centre. Bodies were scattered here and there. Hobos seem to spend most of their time asleep. It's no wonder they're on the street. I wondered for a moment if I might end up like them one day. But no, I was a land owner. They were peasants.

I was revoltingly stoned and nearly stood in a dog shit. A drunken hobo wrapped in a filthy blanket and sleeping against a tree shouted some curses at me, but I ignored him and carried on toward the centre.

I leant against the fence for a few moments to see what was

happening at the fair. A couple of braais were going, people were selling cool drinks and chocolates. Children were playing on swings and screaming at one another. It all felt a bit stagnant, and just looking at it made me feel depressed. I began wondering why it was that I'd actually come to the fair. It'd seemed like a very good idea when I was freshly stoned, but now I doubted that any good would come of it.

'Are you coming in, sir?' the lady at the gate asked me.

It was a middle-aged coloured woman. She looked terribly righteous. She'd seen me watching the children and if I said I wasn't coming in she'd think I was a paedophile.

'Ah, yes' I said.

'It's ten rand please, sir.'

'Umm. OK.' I dug around in my pockets for some coins, making sure not to pull the bankie of weed out by mistake. I really should've left it at home.

She didn't ask me what was in the black bag.

I walked through the play area. The general murmur of little people screaming and big people talking hung about the air. The grown-ups stood in groups, exchanging opinions, nodding heads, biting boerewors rolls, wiping mustard off moustaches.

'Would you like to try some delicious homemade fudge?' a plump girl behind a grey table asked me.

'No. Where are the display tables?'

'Excuse me?'

'They said in the advert there'd be display tables.'

'You mean the community projects section? It's all through the buildings there.' She pointed at what looked like a small school block.

The idea started to make sense to me again. The weed was coming in waves. I'd sober up for a few seconds, and think it was all over, then a second later be completely fucked again. Yes, someone here would know what to do with the bone, and be impressed by my initiative.

I turned around and walked away, hopping up onto the concrete corridor that ran past drainpipes and doors painted in different colours. I walked up a flight of dark grey stairs onto the upper level and was accosted by a female. She was posing as human, but could easily have been a bull.

'Are you here for the drama class?' she asked.

I shook my head.

'We starting in fifteen minutes, hey!'

I looked over her large shoulders into the classroom behind her. All the desks and chairs had been moved to the side of the room, but there was no one inside.

'Ja!' she said. 'I'm not waiting. It says on the pamphlet we start at half past one. So we start at half past one. Come on!'

'I'm not here for that.'

'We do classes in Woodstock as well. Let me give you a flyer.'

'I'm looking for somewhere to take my bone.'

'What?'

'I found one. I don't know what to do with it.'

'Excuse me!'

'I found a bone in my garden.'

'And?'

'Well,' I said. I suddenly felt like a complete idiot. What was I doing?

'I was just wondering if anyone at the fair might know what to do.'

It seemed like a normal question, for a few seconds. Then, as I ran it over in my head it sounded completely ridiculous.

'I'm going,' I said, and turned to walk away.

'No, wait. Are you all right?'

I spun around. The woman had very thick eyebrows. Her face looked as if it had been moulded under extreme pressure. She could see that I was stoned, and was about to call the police. Only a stoned person would do something like this. I still had some weed in my pocket, it was higher grade and they'd think I was a dealer. The police would organise a search warrant for my house, find my setup. I'd spend the rest of my life behind bars.

I started to move faster, but then stopped. I had to try and redeem myself. I had to convince her I was normal.

'It was just a thought,' I said.

'Let me see it.'

I unwrapped the bone and held it out toward her.

'So you just came here to see if maybe . . ,'

'Well, I didn't know what to do. But I'll go now, if you want.'

'What sort of bone is it? Human? Animal?'

'I don't know. It came from my garden.'

'Let me hang on to this. I think I might know someone.'

I could barely believe what I was hearing. Perhaps I wasn't so stupid. No, suddenly it all seemed to make sense again.

'Who?'

'They're an organisation. They were meant to have a stand here. But something happened at the last moment. They're ar-chaeological students. They're called, something about restoring, to lost groups. Shit. I can't remember. Do you have a number?'

I gave her my phone number and address.

'So it looks like we should get the class under way.'

'No. No. I have to go,' I said, and started walking away before she could force me to participate.

What a strange woman. I was relieved that she wasn't a police informer. Whenever I became paranoid I could literally feel the muscles in my body tensing up, and then when the paranoia passed I could feel them relaxing again, as I did now.

I started to enjoy being stoned. The sky looked beautiful, so did the trees. There was a general sense of failure about the fair. A band whined away in the hall, but no one paid any attention. The sellers sold things half-heartedly as if they didn't really care. It was all rather melancholy. But at that moment the melancholy seemed poetic.

Then I noticed a man in a bear suit watching me as I made my way across the playground. Could he be an undercover policeman sent to look out for suspicious characters like myself?

I started to speed up. But now he was forcing the children off his legs and following me. I was terrified. I felt the muscles in my chest begin to tighten. I looked down at my feet and tried to pretend that nothing was happening. But then he was standing right next to me, looking at me with his big black plastic eyes.

'Byron,' the bear said.

Shit. They'd already built up a profile on me. They'd been watching.

'Sorry,' I said.

'What for?' the bear asked.

'Umm . . .'

'It's me. It's Roddy,' the bear said.

'Roddy!' I screamed. I knew he'd done a lot of strange jobs in his time, but I'd never known him to dress as a bear.

'Yes. Come. Keep walking out of here. I'll follow you.'

I didn't feel any relief. This could all be a part of their plan. But I kept going, out of the gate, past the lady with the tin and into the park. The bear continued to follow me. I started to pick up pace. I would run home and slam the gate behind me.

'Slow down, Byron!' the bear shouted again.

'What do you want?'

'Do you have any weed on you?'

'No! No, no!' I tried to run away, but the bear picked up pace.

'It's me, Roddy. Come here.'

'What do you want?'

'I just want to smoke with you.'

'I don't know what you're talking about.'

We were standing in the middle of the park, under a low tree. The bear kept scraping its head on the top of the branches.

'Come to the bathroom,' he said, and pointed to a public loo.

'Take your head off,' I said to the bear.

'I can't. Not here. I don't want to be seen like this, man!'

'I've got to go.'

The bear took hold of my right sleeve and gently tugged me toward to toilet.

'I'll take my head off in there! Come to the bathroom.'

I cautiously followed the bear into the public toilet. It was made of dark bricks, and the inside hadn't been cleaned in months. The toilet seat had been ripped off and the urinal stuffed with newspaper. It smelt of shit and urine.

The bear took its head off.

'It's me, Byron' said Roddy.

Sure enough, it was him. His puffy white face was red and dripping with sweat. His long grey ponytail was hanging down his back. He's a dirty man, Roddy. I'd been to his flat a few times, and I knew that he washed himself and his dishes with the same bar of soap. He smelt strongly of sweat, and greasy onions I think, but I was so relieved it wasn't a cop that I didn't care. He put the bear's head down on the floor.

'You'll make it stink, Roddy,' I said.

'How you doing, Byron?' he asked me.

'I'm all right. The head.' I pointed at it.

I could feel my heart slowing down and my muscles relaxing.

'Ag,' he said. 'Times a bit tough at the moment. Waiting for my payment on the Beatles royalties. Then I'll be set. For now, having to do this kind of shit. You got some weed?'

'I do,' I said.

I took the little dime bag out of my pocket and picked a few heads off the plant.

'We'll have to smoke it in a cigarette' I said.

'OK with me man.'

I emptied some tobacco out of a cigarette, and stuffed the bright green weed in its place. I removed the filter, then lit up. We finished it in a couple of minutes.

'Thanks, Byron. I'll come see you sometime.'

'OK.'

He put the head back on, and walked off to the fair.

I made my way through the park to Station Road. The hawkers on the far side of the street were selling single cigarettes and orange chips to passers-by. Underneath the old Spar, groups of hobos were sitting about shouting curses regarding the others' mothers' vaginas, and I fancied I could smell some rather rancid genitals in the air. I think it was the smell of the extractor fans.

I walked past a barefoot man in a tie-dyed top, and then straight into a young woman dressed all in black. The books she'd been carrying fell out of her hands and crashed onto the floor. She muttered as she bent down to pick them up. She had piercings all over her face, and as she bent down I could see the tops of her pale breasts. And she was scrambling to pick up all the books, but paused for a moment too long on my right foot. I was convinced that she was examining it and so kicked the book away and carried on walking.

'Hey!' she shouted at me. She had a boyish harshness in her voice. 'What the fuck's wrong with you?'

'Nothing!' I said. I started jogging. I really couldn't handle another second of the outside world.

'Fucking cunt!' she shouted after me.

I scrambled into my house and pulled the lock behind me. I'd had enough of the world for one day. I really did have to stop smoking weed. I made myself a promise that as soon as I was finished the current bankie I would give it a break for a little while. If I was going to get respect from people I had to stop acting like a moron.

I went into the kitchen and searched through the shelves for my teapot. I couldn't find it anywhere. I'd used it recently to make myself some weed tea, but right now all I wanted was a cup of Five Roses. I'd never really been a tea person. But when Victoria came to stay at my house she brought her teapot along with her, and when she left said I could keep it. Since then I'd developed a liking for Ceylon tea, and had discovered that if you add a few heads of higher grade weed into the mix you can preserve the taste and still get fucked. Of course I hadn't told Victoria that her teapot was put to such use. It made her happy to think of me sipping tea on my balcony like an English gentleman, and I didn't want to ruin the image for her.

* * *

Victoria had arrived unexpectedly in the middle of the night. I'd been drinking a bottle of cheap wine in my lounge, and when I opened the front door I was expecting to see Roddy or a beggar from the street. Instead her long black car was parked on the pavement, the engine still running, the bright headlights lighting up every car and drunken sidewalk sleeper on the street. And there she was, standing at the gate. She was dressed in a long flowing skirt, wore a hat on her head, carried a bag in one hand and a box in the other.

'Hello, Byron,' she said.

'Hello,' I said, and buzzed the gate for her to come in.

'The stuff, the other stuff of mine that is, is in the car still.'

I opened the gate, and she parked her car behind mine.

Into her big black 1978 Mercedes, she'd packed another suitcase, a box, and a large folder. I frantically brought them inside while she made some tea in the kitchen with the pot she'd brought. Then I ran into my lounge and hid the bong I'd been smoking behind the couch, collected the weed off the table and threw it out the window.

I sat down on the dirtiest chair and let her have the couch. Although I was horribly stoned, I promised myself that I was going to act like an adult.

'I couldn't,' she said, after sitting down with a cup of tea in her hand. 'It's just the craziest thing,' she said.

She took the large straw hat off her head and placed it next to her. She frizzled her hair with her purple-gloved hands, tucked the curls behind her ears, and took a long sip of tea. The dress covered her entire body, down to the feet, which were naked. She ran her left toes along the arch of her right foot. She did it so smoothly that I felt myself going hard. I raised myself slightly off the couch and stared at her feet. They were beautiful, pale and perfectly in proportion.

'What's wrong?' she asked me. 'Are you stoned, Byron?'

'No,' I said. 'I was just wondering if I could give you a foot massage.'

As the words were leaving my mouth, I could tell they were strange. She would now know for certain that I was stoned!

'Never mind,' I said, trying to redeem myself.

'No. That would be lovely,' she said.

'Really?' I could barely believe my luck.

'Yes. Really.'

I hopped off my chair and dragged the stop-sign table across the room. I could see tiny pieces of green still scattered across the surface, but the lounge was so dark that she wouldn't notice.

I dropped to my knees and brought her right foot up to my face.

'Are they smelly?' she asked, and giggled a little.

'No' I said. They were a little smelly, but I really didn't care. I took the right one in my hand and moved my fingers up and down the sole. Then I moved onto the left. They were so perfect. How I envied her. But if they couldn't be mine, at least I could play with them.

'That's nice,' she said, and slid down on the couch.

She put her cup of tea on the floor, and pushed her dress down between her legs so I was unable to see the prize that lay at the top.

I looked up for a moment and saw that her eyes were closed and her fingers were gently stroking the side of the straw hat lying next to her. For a moment I considered slipping my head underneath her skirt and going in for the kill. But then I pictured the way in which she'd pressed the skirt down between her legs. If she'd wanted me to go there she would have left the path unobstructed. Perhaps she was put off me after our first fumbled attempt in her bedroom. As I rubbed her feet they began to sweat a little and stink a bit more, and the toes were a bit dirty. But they were still beautiful, and for now they'd suffice. I'd leave the rest for later.

'That was wonderful, thank you, Byron. You've got quite.' She laughed. 'You've got quite strong hands.'

'Thanks,' I said.

The room was dusty and as she straightened herself on the couch she sent a cloud of dust toward my nose. The sneeze came so suddenly that I was unable to get my hand to my face in time and I covered her ankles in little spray droplets.

'Oh,' I said. 'I'm sorry.'

I ran straight out of the lounge into the bathroom and unravelled some toilet paper, but on my way back realised I was overreacting and so put it in my pocket and re-entered the room casually.

'Sorry about that,' I said, in an unnaturally deep voice. 'Would you like me to wipe it up?'

'No, Byron. Don't be silly.' She pushed herself upright on the couch and picked her teacup off the floor. 'They were working there night and day,' she said.

'Where?'

'That's the reason. That I came here, I mean. That's the reason. The people next door are renovating. And they make drill noises, Byron, and ladders scrape. All the time. All the time! And they leave the security gate open. Which is – I mean at the best of times, foolish. But that Dutch woman, her poor family. She was murdered. Recently. In my area. It isn't safe. All over. Gangs and all sorts.'

'I know.'

'But do you know? Because, Byron, the truth is, people always think it's someone else. And it is, of course, until the time when it isn't. And that time it's you. Or me. Or both.'

'I've never had a problem.'

'We must just be sure. All right.' She took a long gulp from her teacup and climbed off the couch. I followed her through to the kitchen.

'There are quite a lot of dishes.'

'I know,' I said.

'I will be useful, you know.'

'I know.'

'While I'm here, I mean. I will be useful.'

'OK.'

'These windows are big, Byron,' she said looking out the kitchen window onto the overgrown alleyway that runs alongside the house. 'Not to mention, Byron, the thick growth. Anyone could hide out there.'

'They don't.'

'Ah!' she said, and walked past me. She had that same psycho-possessed look she'd had when taking photos and searching for shoes. I stayed out of her way.

She hopped into the sunken landing – which at that stage was perfectly dry – and rattled the old wooden door.

'Broken in an instant!' she shrieked, emphasising the ins. Then she walked along the corridor, her legs landing softly, her feet wanting to take flight on each up-step. She turned to me, pointed with both arms 'And you live here alone mostly! Is there an alarm?'

'No.'

'Byron!'

'We don't need one,' I said.

'Ah, Byron,' she said softly.

'I can protect you,' I said.

'Oh yes!' she said. 'Thank you, Byron, for putting me at rest.'

She walked into my room, took her toothbrush and paste out of her bag, took her face wash, her cream, and went down the passage.

'Let's just *hope*,' she said on returning.

She climbed into my bed and rolled over to the far side, wrapping herself up in the duvet. By this stage the weed had worn off and I was in the mood for loving. I gently pulled her toward me and kissed her on the cheek.

'I'm sleeping,' she said.

When I woke up the next morning she was gone. I jumped out of bed, and noticed the large pile of laundry that, for the past two weeks had been building up in the corner of my room, was also gone.

I ran into the corridor. The floors where still wet and smelt strongly of lemon. I walked into the kitchen, and there she was, standing at the sink washing my dishes.

'You don't have to,' I said.

She spun around. Her hands, usually covered in silky purple gloves, were now clad in plastic yellow ones. They were dripping with foam. It was a cloudy day outside and she hadn't turned the light on.

'Do you always, Byron, sleep so late?'

'Only sometimes. What's the time?'

'It's nearly midday. I bought some cereal, if you want.'

'Thanks,' I said.

Each day she would wake up hours before me. She'd sweep beneath the cupboards and the beds and open up the curtains and let light into the dark house. She spent hours on the floor scrubbing the skirting boards and lower parts of the walls. Her knees began to chafe, but this would not sway her from the task. She started wearing jeans instead of skirts.

One morning I was woken by the sound of something heavy being dragged along the floor. I sat up and there was Victoria sitting on my boxing bag. Her face was red from dragging it from wherever she'd dragged it.

'What, Byron, on earth, is this?'

My dreams were still swirling in my head.

'It's a boxing bag.'

'And why on earth, Byron, why, did I find it, where I did find it? I found it in one of the cupboards. That is not where a boxing bag should be.'

'It fell down. I think.'

'And so, Byron. And so you never, just, never put it up again?'

'It was long ago.'

She spent hours that afternoon trying to hang it from the tree in my garden. I'd watch her from the landing for a few minutes then go back inside. I'd come out again, and she'd still be trying. She stood on a chair and hoisted it up with rope. Then she'd place it on top of the tree trunk and try hold it there as she tied the knot. But it would always fall.

Eventually she gave up and came and found me in my lounge.

'Thanks, Byron!' she screamed. 'Thanks for helping me!'

She burst into tears and ran through to my bedroom. She sat on the edge of my bed and cried for about an hour. I tried to comfort her but she pushed me away. So I told her I was going to the shops, walked off to the park and got stoned on the swing.

We shared the same bed, but nights passed and still we did not touch each others' bodies. I started going crazy. I would jerk off three, four times a day. Sometimes five. I longed to unroll the little ball she curled into at night. I longed to devour her like a hungry wolf.

She went to bed a few hours earlier than me every night. I'd spend the time alone in my lounge, sometimes hitting the bong, sometimes smoking joints or cigarettes, always trying to think of new ways to get her to open her legs. It just didn't seem right that someone should sleep in your bed every night and not have sex with you. Was there not someone to whom I could complain? One night after smoking a thick joint of pure hydro I paged through my tattered Yellow Pages to S. Seaweed, Second-hand dealers, Sewer cleaning, but fuck all about Sex complaints. What good were the Yellow Pages really?

I decided that I was far too keen. I had to cool down a little, hold off. So one night, after smoking my sixth bong I went through to the room, which I now thought of as hers. I carefully opened the door. She was asleep in the far corner of the bed. The light was off, but the curtains were open and the moon was shining in over the carport straight through my window and onto her head.

I climbed into bed fully clothed. That will do the trick, I told myself. If she thinks I don't want her, she'll have to open up.

But no. She just lay there. I could feel her uninterested torso rising and falling. It made me upset. And trying to sleep in jeans was simply impossible. I slipped my hand into my boxers and rolled my balls around in circles as I contemplated my next move. I unintentionally made myself hard and so started playing – very carefully – with the tip of my dick.

'What are you doing?' She rolled over and put her hand on my chest.

'Umm . . . ' I said.

'Hey?' She pulled her body against me. She was wearing a long T-shirt, no pants, but a very silky pair of panties. I rested my hand on her naked leg, hesitantly at first, uncertain as to the tone of her question.

'Are you feeling?' she asked and climbed on top of me. Her long hair fell down onto my face and she started kissing me. In the moonlight I could just make out her eyes, and they had that psycho look in them. Her hands moved down my chest and frantically got to work on undoing my belt.

I realised that my hand was still holding my balls. But I whipped it out, and ran my fingers up the front of her body. She leant back and let out a groan as her hair fell back and she threw her T-shirt off. Now she was just wearing underwear and ripping off my jeans, and the metal belt buckle hit the floor, and I grabbed her and rolled her over. We were like wrestlers, and by fuck I was still stoned, and the moonlight was playing ball. And then her hand was taking hold of my dick. This time she got a good grip. She was still wearing her gloves, and the feeling of the silk on my cock was like getting a blowjob from an angel. I ran my hand up her thigh, she was wriggling out of her panties. I stopped just short of her groin and could feel the heat coming off her pussy. I rubbed the entrance for a few seconds, then slipped my fingers inside. They went in with such ease and my fuck it was smooth. I moved my fingers around in little pulse motions and could feel her warm breath against my neck, her feet moving slowly at the bottom of the sheets.

'I want you inside me,' she said.

'Sweet,' I said, then realised my response was a little childish and tried to compensate with some new – more adult words - as I climbed on top of her.

'I must be on top,' she said.

I rolled back over again and lay on my back. She climbed on top of me, and with faultless movements took hold of my penis and moved it inside her.

'You must be careful,' she said.

I was. I rolled her off me and came on the freshly washed sheets. She moved her legs in frustrated little twitches, indicating that she was not yet finished. I continued to massage the inside of her body until I felt her heartbeat race, her lungs fill, hold, then empty with a satisfied shudder.

She told me that she couldn't go on the pill because it had a bad reaction with her body. Neither of us enjoyed using condoms and so I had to practise the ancient art of coitus interruptus. This meant that I had to finish her off with my hands, and so I often found myself watching her as she had an orgasm. Her orgasms varied in style. Sometimes she would close her eyes, bite down on her lips and stay absolutely silent. I felt like a bit of a loser then, and would often go and get stoned immediately afterwards. Then I'd get paranoid and think that I should go back and give her another one. The second time round would usually be more theatrical, and I'd be able to fall asleep with my pride intact.

If we had sex when drunk it was a totally different story. She would scream and shout so loudly that I'd be convinced she was having me on. But one night she pulled herself up to me and said, 'Thank you. That was amazing.' She put her leg over mine and I could feel that she was still wet. I must be pretty good, I thought.

When she'd fallen asleep, I gently pulled her leg off mine and went outside. I sat on the swing seat on my front veranda, smoked a joint and watched the moon through the branches of the mulberry tree in my garden.

One evening we were lying on my bed. I had not yet penetrated her. She was not touching me, but I had my fingers inside her
and was moving them in little pulse motions. I started to get a
cramp in my arm and drew my fingers out for a moment so that I
could rearrange the position of our bodies. She seemed irritated
at me for stopping and forcing her to move slightly down the
bed. When she was in position, I slipped my fingers back inside,
and watched the expression on her face as I moved my hands
more aggressively in and out. She enjoyed the increase in pressure, and placed one hand on her breast and started moving her
hips up and down in order to increase her pleasure. I slipped
a third finger inside her, and she placed her hands up against
the wall behind my bed, and screamed from right down inside
her. The scream subsided. She opened her eyes. She dropped
her body. My hand was positioned in such a way as to prevent
the fingers from sliding out naturally, so as she came down I got
a slight twist in my upper arm and had to move my body to the
side to ease the pain. I slipped it out, and saw that I'd hurt her.
She pushed my hand away, grabbed the duvet and wrapped it
around her body.

'What was that?' she said.

I could smell her groin on my fingers; I ran my moist hand
through my hair.

'What was what?' I asked.

'The noise,' she said, and jumped off the bed.

She frantically wrapped the duvet around her body, and
started fumbling on the floor for her clothes. Her panties were
curled up and wrapped around the inside of her pants. Her top
was at the far side of the room, next to the closed door.

'Byron!' she said in a stage whisper. 'Go and look. You said
you would.'

'OK,' I said.

I'd heard nothing, was slightly drunk, and not in the least afraid. I found the whole scene rather amusing.

When I reached the door, she screamed after me 'Don't leave me here alone!'

And so I picked up an empty brandy bottle that had been lying on the floor. I put it over my shoulder like a baton and tried my best not to burst into laughter as we moved around the house.

'Byron,' she would say when we'd enter a room 'What was that? I heard something.'

The noise would suddenly be coming from the other end of the house.

We locked all the doors.

We checked all the windows.

There was nothing.

We went back to bed, but there was to be no more touching for the evening.

We spent hours between the sheets. I would always come before her, and so I could feel that as I finished her off the look on my face would be pretty dull. One day she opened her eyes. I had two fingers inside her, she lay, legs spread wide open on the bed, hands twirling the covers, eyes shut, her pleasure crippling. My right hand – the one at work on her groin – started to cramp, and so I was forced to swap hands. I did so, and rested the now free hand on her naked left leg. It was then that her left eye popped open. I was unable to hide the vacant look in my eyes, and judging by her reaction she must have noticed it right away.

'What?' she said, and pulled her left leg inward.

'Nothing. I was enjoying myself.'

'Oh,' she said, and gathered the sheet around her naked

groin, and left it there as she went to the bathroom. When she returned, she dropped it quickly and stood naked in front of me. I looked at the shape of her bush while I scratched my knee. She tried to pull on her pants with the underwear still wrapped up inside them and nearly tripped herself up.

'I'm going to get some food,' she said and walked out the room.

I farted.

When she came back she said 'We have to do something. Else. That is. I was thinking now while I was walking.'

'What?'

'I don't, Byron. Know. What do you do?'

'Not much.'

'You sit. On the seat. The swing seat.'

'Ja.'

'Well, come.'

We went and sat on the swing seat at the front of my house. It overlooks my road, Trill – a thoroughfare to the train station – which is always busy in the early evening.

'So?' I asked her.

'So, Byron. So. So what?'

'What do we do?'

'I don't. OK. Know all right.' She pulled herself close to me and rested her head on my shoulder. I wasn't really sure what to do with it, but gave it a little pat. Dissatisfied with my display she sat up straight again and the two of us were silent for a few minutes.

'Look,' she said eventually. She was pointing at a strange man whose body was all twisted and contorted. He was having enormous difficulty walking down the road.

I started laughing. Then suddenly realised that she would

think I was cruel. So I shut up. But she was already laughing herself. So we laughed and laughed. The contorted man hurried off down the road trying to avoid our laughter. I felt bad. But not that bad.

After Victoria caught me watching her with the blank look in my eyes, I didn't really know what to do. I still came before her, and still had to finish her off with my hand. I'd close my eyes, but then want to open them to see if hers were open. Mostly they weren't, but sometimes they were. Then she'd shut them. After a while we learnt to keep our eyes open, and I discovered that it's actually quite nice to look someone in the eye when fucking them.

After discovering that the two of us shared a passion for laughing at passers-by, Victoria and I spent more time on the swing seat watching the world. When sober, I always felt relaxed around her. But whenever I was stoned a sick feeling would rise in my chest. The feet. Had she noticed them? I knew the answer was yes, of course. But there was the prenuptial understanding. They were there, and normal, and fine. But perhaps they weren't. Perhaps she'd been laughing at them from the start. Perhaps she had a confidante, someone with whom she laughed about my deformity. When she'd seen me at Bhakhuba, she and the journalist had made a pact. She was acting out a dare.

'What's wrong?' she asked me one day. I was sitting in silence, not laughing at her jokes. The paranoia was intense.

'Nothing.'

'Not nothing.'

'Nothing!' I said and walked down the passage to the kitchen.

'Don't ever,' she screamed from the kitchen doorway. 'Don't ever walk away while I'm talking to you!'

'Come on,' I tried to walk past her but she blocked the door-way with her body.

'What's wrong, Byron?'

'I can push you out the way!'

'I'm asking you, Byron, nicely.'

'I could,' I said, and pushed past her.

'Don't!' she screamed, pulling me toward her. Without saying another word she dropped to her knees, and started undoing my belt. Suddenly my pants and boxers were sliding down my legs, and I was standing half naked in the middle of the corridor. She ran her hands up my legs and started fondling my balls until I went hard. Then she took my penis in her mouth, and start-ed sucking, her mouth making squelching sounds. At the same time, her right hand crept up the back of my leg and took hold of the hairs growing in the area behind my knee. She would pluck, then stop. Then pluck. I tried to focus on the pleasure, and found it easier to do so if I kept my eyes open and looked down at the top of her bobbing head. The door at the end of the passage was open, and so I was well aware that we were perfectly visible from the street. I noticed then, that standing at the gate was a woman with a child on her back. She had a letter in her hand and had come to beg. Beggar women with babies always walk slowly, and so Victoria must have known she was coming. She knew she was watching us.

I closed my eyes and pretended the beggar woman wasn't there. I concentrated on the pleasure and even when the door-bell rang I did not move, and Victoria did not stop sucking.

When I came she pulled a final chunk of hair from the back of my knees, stuck her nails into my flesh, and without looking me in the eye, climbed off the floor and went to sleep in my bed. She'd left a gooey lump of semen mixed with spit lying on the floor. With my bare left foot I worked it into one of the cracks between the boards. The beggar woman was still standing at the gate staring blankly down the long passage.

* * *

I finally found the little house-shaped teapot I'd been looking for. I'd grown rather fond of my teapot. The lid was made to look like a roof, and the body like a house. There were even little tufts of grass growing around the edges.

I boiled the kettle and made myself a cup of tea, then went and sat on my swing seat on the front porch. The porch is only a few metres long and to its immediate left is my driveway. In front of it is a shin-high brick flowerbed. A year or so back I planted some marigolds in it, and they seemed to be doing pretty well. In front of that is the small front garden and then the green fence that surrounds the property. It's high and spiked.

I was still rather stoned, but felt far more at ease now that I was back on home ground sipping a cup of tea. I sent Pete an SMS, and told him that I was ready for his visit.

I waited for about an hour, smoking cigarettes and reading pamphlets that had been left in my postbox. He eventually pulled up on his old scrambler, sending a thick column of black smoke into the sky. He had the same backpack on his back, and held the helmet in his left hand as he strolled up the path.

As with the first meeting, he patted my back. His arm was so long and flexible that he was able to do so without entering my personal space. He was more awkward than I remembered. His current dress confirmed my earlier suspicion. He was wearing the same jacket, the same army pants, the same black boots. He put his helmet and gloves inside his backpack.

'Should we go inside, bro?' he said, making his way in. He walked with his hands facing backwards. If his arms were any longer the knuckles would drag along the floor. The palms, like the knuckles, were a deep pink, but unlike the knuckles were not covered in black spots.

'So, bro,' he said standing in the centre of my room.

'So,' I said.

'You enjoying your new shoes?'

'I am. You?'

'For sure, bro. They fit alright?'

'Perfect.'

'Same here, bro. They all lank comfortable.'

I wanted to ask him why then he was still wearing the same black boots, but decided to let it go.

'How did those crops you were growing in your garden do?' he asked me.

'Umm . . . ' If I told him I'd let them drown, he'd walk straight out the front door.

'Do you have any left? Maybe we could sample it.'

'It's all gone.'

'No ways, bro!'

'Harvested early. Me and my friends smoked it in a few days. I sold some too.'

'OK, bro. Did you ever buy the indoor growing shit from my buddy's store?'

'Ja.'

'Sweet. Can I check it out.'

'Up there.'

He pushed some clothes and a plate to the side of my table then dragged it across the room and climbed on top of it. He opened up the top cupboard and picked up one of the pots that

I'd placed there earlier that morning. I hoped there was no way of telling that I'd just set the system up.

'Why's your ultraviolet turned off, bro?'

'It isn't.'

'Bro. It is.'

I looked up at the ceiling and noticed the light in the centre of the room was also off.

'My electricity. Finished. I'll get some more.'

'Not good for plants, bro.'

'I'm going to get some more. I'll be back now. Just wait.'

'Bro – .'

'I'm coming.'

I only had twenty rand in my pocket and I wasn't willing to draw any money out of my account. I ran toward the Spar. I think it must have been lunch break for people who work. The car guard was running up and down the street trying to get money from people who'd parked for a few seconds to buy themselves lunch. The inside of the Spar is in huge contrast to the streets of Obs. It's all clean and shiny, all the food is packed away neatly in rows. I stood for about five minutes in the queue, and when I got to the front gave the lady my account details and handed her twenty rand.

After the seven rand ninety cents government charge, I only had twelve rand ten left to load onto my electricity meter. I punched in the numbers. It would, at the very least, last for a day or two.

I went back to my room and found Pete sitting on my chair smoking a cigarette and dropping his ash into a coffee mug he'd found on the floor.

'It's bad for the plants, bro.'

'I know. I'm poor at the moment.'

'And the HP light, bro. Did you find your plants grew well under it?'

'Definitely.'

'Thing is, bro. Look. Remember I said last time that I may have some business for you?'

'Sure.'

He opened up the bag on his lap and took out a bottle of brandy. Only a third of it was left.

'You got cups, bro?'

I rinsed out two mugs in the sink and brought them through to the bedroom. He filled them up, and we each took a long swig before continuing our conversation.

'If you going to help me out on this, you going to have to make sure shit like that doesn't happen.'

'Like what?'

'Like the electricity running out and shit.'

'I know,' I said.

'OK. I'm going to show you something, bro. But it remains a secret. You understand?'

'Sure.'

'I got this buddy from North Africa, bro. Walked down here, all the way. Brought these seeds with him. But listen, bro, no one is to know. All right?'

'I got you.'

'Cause me and my other buddy had a kif setup at his place. In a garden cottage. Anyways, bro, his landlord, this fat Iti ou, busted us. Turns out, bro, he knows my landlady. He tells her. She searches my room. Finds my stash. Basically my place is out. And he's disappeared. So I need a spot.'

'No one will know.'

'Listen, bro.' He undid his left boot and placed it on his lap.

He stuck his hand inside it and fiddled around with a zip for a few seconds before bringing out a small object, which he placed on the palm of his other hand. I moved my face toward it to see more clearly what he was holding. It looked like an old-fashioned ladies' pillbox, white, porcelain I guessed, with a gold-rimmed lid. On the cover was a picture of a rose. He moved his palm toward my face so I could get a better look. I made to pick it up, but he shut his hand and held it against his chest.

'I'm serious, bro. I'm showing this to you, under secret.'

'Whom I going to tell?'

'That's not the point, bro.'

'No one will know.'

He put the box out again, this time sticking his thumb into the mechanism that opened the lid. It popped open, and there I saw, resting in the centre of the gold-lined tin, six little seeds rolling around the corners. They were perfectly oval and dark green in colour with tinges of purple on the edges.

'What are those?' I asked.

'These are the seeds. From North Africa, bro. They fully grown in four weeks under light. No jokes. It sells two-fifty a gram.'

'No ways,' I said.

'No lies, bro.'

I stuck my hand out to pick one up, but Pete snapped the pillbox shut.

'I want to see them,' I said.

'No, bro. We can plant six, as I see from your setup. Four weeks, bro. Each crop gets about two-fifty grams. I have buyers. Once you've tried this shit, there's no turning back. You do the maths, bro.'

'Yeah!'

'But no fuck-ups, bro. Like with the lights.'

'No mistakes. I need the money.'

'We have to share with Isaiah. So three ways. You'll buy yourself a new car, bro, no fucking jokes.'

'Please, I'm in.'

'That's fine, bro. I need you to buy one thousand rand electricity. That's your side. Cause I'm bringing the seeds. I also need some surety. There're people who after this shit. They'll kill for it, bro. No jokes.'

'So they going to kill me too?'

'Not if you keep it secret.'

'I will. That's enough. Whatever. Surety.'

'Not quite, bro.'

'Why!'

'Women, bro. Women.'

'Ag.'

'Delilah, bro.'

'No, Pete.'

'She got Samson to cut his hair. He lost his strength.'

'I don't have long hair.'

'You bring home a floozy, you do the thing. Then she says, what's in the cupboard, Byron?'

'I'll say nothing.'

Pete noticed something resting on the shelf, and half-stood up off the chair, stretching his long arm toward it and picking it up.

'You got a chick, bro?' he asked me. He was staring at a self-portrait Victoria had left at my house.

'Give it here,' I snatched it from his hand.

He got off his chair and stood silently, staring out the window, his arms hanging limply at his sides. Then he sat down, interlaced his fingers and hung his arms in a hoop shape between his

open legs. He sat up straight, ruffled his dirty hair, then stared
at his freckled wrist.

'OK, bro. Tell me her name.'

'I'm not!' I put the photo face down against my knees.

'Just the name. What harm?'

'No.'

'Tell me the name, and we plant them right away. No questions. Just the name, bro, it's just cause I'm curious. Pass it here!'
He grabbed the picture off my knee, and stared at it again.

'No!' I took it back from him.

'This is your floozy, right?'

'What does it matter? Do you want to hurt her?'

'Bro!' He laughed. 'We said we'd be friends right? When we
checked out our feet. We said, bro, we'd be friends.' He leant
over and patted me on the knee.

'I'm not telling you.'

'OK, bro. Suit yourself.' He stood up, placed the picture on
my table, walked toward the door, then paused and looked back
at me. 'Not to speak around the point, bro: that is the cost.'

'I don't understand.'

'People will kill for this shit.'

'So you're threatening her?'

'You'll only be silent if there's a reason, bro.'

'You said I'd be killed. That's enough.'

'Look, bro. That is the price. Give me a call in a few days.
Think it over.'

He buzzed himself out and started the motorbike without saying another word. Perhaps I'd totally misjudged him. What sort
of a man threatens another man's girlfriend?

I went through to my lounge and started mulling some of my
Swazi onto the table. I'd promised myself that as soon as the cur-

rent stash was finished I'd give it a break for a while. So I rolled myself a really fat joint. The faster I got through it, the sooner I could quit.

I lay down flat on my bed and rested an empty cup – the one from which I'd drunk the brandy – on my chest. I dropped the ash into it as I made my way through the joint.

A quarter of the way through I was already unbelievably stoned. But I pushed on, telling myself that it was for my own good.

By the time I finished I was so completely fucked that the only thing for me to do was go to sleep. I closed my eyes but could not get the image of Pete climbing onto his motorbike out of my mind. Perhaps I'd completely misjudged the man. He could be dangerous. He'd already seen a picture of Victoria. What if he decided to track her down? By showing me the seeds he'd made himself vulnerable and the only way to bring the scales back to balance was to get to Victoria. That's what he meant to do! That's where he was headed!

I sat up straight and ran my hands through my hair. I needed to warn her of the imminent danger. I jumped off my bed and started shuffling through the clothes that were strewn across my floor. My phone had to be in one of my pants' pockets. I threw them frantically across the room, they all stank and I couldn't find the phone. Then I remembered that I'd used it to SMS Pete earlier. I must have left it lying on the swing seat.

Thankfully no one had seen it from the street and hopped over to steal it. I felt a moment's relief as I held it in my hands, but then remembered why I'd been looking for it in the first place. I no longer had the nerve to phone Victoria. If I did she'd know I was stoned and leave me.

The only thing to do was plan the conversation in advance. I found a piece of paper and scribbled down what I'd say.

Hi, Victoria.

Yes, it's Byron.

I was just phoning to.

But fuck, what if her responses were different from what I planned?

I must just do it.

I picked up my phone, scrolled down to her name and pushed the green square. It rang for a few seconds then cut out and went to answering machine. I felt my chest tighten up and my heart rate increase. Everything seemed to go blurry. I fell backwards onto the bed. It was too late. He'd already found her.

* * *

I walked outside and sat down on my swing seat. The sun was bright, the world vibrating. I was too fucked to deal with this. I went back inside and splashed my face with cold water. I felt sober for a few seconds, but immediately went back to paranoid. I must phone Pete and tell him that the picture was of someone else: a random picture frame model. But I must try her first. I scrolled back to her number. Again the answering machine. I sat down on the swing seat and slapped my temples. The thought of her dead made me feel ill. I went to the bathroom and held my face over the open toilet bowl. I looked at my reflection in the water and wondered what I'd wear to her funeral. I pictured myself trying to give a eulogy and being too fucked to remember what I had to say. Again I pictured her white face, but then my pants started vibrating and I sat up straight resting my back against the toilet. I fumbled for the phone and read the SMS: *Hi, Byron. Sorry, my battery's dead. With my dad at the mo. See you later. Vics.*

Oh, thank Jesus! I lay down on the bathroom floor, put my hands in my pants, cupping my balls, and brought my fingers to my nose. Musky. As long as she was with her father no harm could come to her. Harm itself went to great lengths to keep out of his way.

* * *

I'd met him for the first time a week after Victoria had moved out of my house. She invited me to dinner at her parents' place. We drove in her car to their little villa neatly tucked away in the hills of Constantia: away from the commoners. The garden was darkly, densely green, and in the middle of the dark stone path was a concrete water feature of a cherub taking a piss. The whole thing was covered in moss: but the moss looked elegant, as if it were paid to cling to the statue. The edge of the roof had traces of this elegant green fungus too. And beneath the eaves stood the man. He had a thick nose that bulged toward the tip: it looked Jewish, but he, I knew, was not. His eyes were a light blue, almost white like concrete in bright sun, and seemed to end right where they started. His head was bald, except for slight strands around the sides and on the back, which he kept shaved to the skin, but showed an afternoon shadow. His skin was coarse: he looked like he'd spent years fighting in the desert. He took my hand in his, and although he'd doused himself in aftershave he could not hide the stench of his greed.

'Regereman.' He only gave me his surname.

'Umm. Byron,' I said.

He nodded.

Her mother was far gentler. Her hair was long and flowed loosely down her shoulders like the white dress that drifted sweetly from her body. She led me into the house and placed her arm gently on my shoulder, and said how nice it was to meet me, and that she'd heard so much about me, which I knew, of course, was a lie. She had a peaceful quality about her and seemed to float above the ground with that angelic pleasure experienced by women in constipation adverts after they've finally cleared their bowels.

The floors to the large entrance hall were tiled and the walls covered in family pictures. There was an image of Victoria, a good few years younger, smartly dressed, her arm looped through a strange-looking man dressed in a suit. Her mother smiled as I took in the surroundings. A carpeted stairwell led to the upper area of the house, and the walls, too, were lined with large framed posters. Her mother again smiled at me as she placed her body behind mine and directed me, gently, but certainly, toward the kitchen, which opened into the lounge which opened onto a patio which opened onto an expansive dark garden. There was a large cabinet to the right of the lounge area and a small cabinet to the left. There were decorative plates hanging from the walls of the kitchen: a dinner plate paired with a side plate. Big and small.

Then Victoria and her mother, also Victoria, slipped out of the room with wine glasses in their hands and went and seated themselves outside. I was alone with Regereman.

He offered me a beer. He walked to the fridge: his body rigid and upright. There were grey hairs beginning to show on the back of his neck: it made me feel slightly at ease. He came back and placed a long tom Black Label can next to a common-size Windhoek on the granite table. I felt as if he were sending me a secret message. He knew. He'd keep silent; but whisper loudly and insultingly behind my back. I shifted my right foot backwards. He shuffled around the kitchen then opened up the beers. He handed me the long tom.

'You work at Bhakhuba.'

'That's right.'

'You translate from Xhosa to English.'

'I used to.'

'Now?'

'I'm a manager.'

'A restaurant manager.'

'Yes.'

'So you obviously speak Xhosa.'

'Obviously.'

'Why did you learn Xhosa?'

'Not sure.'

'You're not sure? What, did you learn it by mistake?'

'No. I learnt it because. I had to learn it.'

'What else do you do? I assume you're not planning to work at a restaurant for the rest of your life.'

'Of course. I plan to do other things in the future.'

He went to check on the food and spoke to me as he took a large duck out of the oven and stuck a skewer into its flesh, then placed it back inside.

'Of course we all plan to do things in the future,' he said. 'I'm planning to take a trip up through Africa early next year.' He spun around and looked at me. It was early evening and a light rain was falling. The ceiling and the roof were one: the top of the room was thus in an A-shape, creating the illusion that one was in the house of God; the steam rose up from the stove like incense. And there stood Regereman with the skewer in his hand.

'Have you ever been through Africa?' he asked me.

It is the attitude one expects from these types of men. The quasi-explorers who see Africa as their little garden, and *traipse* through it all kitted out with their fancy cars and tools.

'No,' I said

'Pity. Do you play any sport?'

'I rowed.'

'And now?'

'Well . . . I'm going to start boxing again.'

'You were a boxer?' For the first time I saw a smile appear on the man's face as he looked me up and down. 'Not a heavyweight.'

'No, not a heavyweight.'

'And neither a flyweight. You look welter to me. Middle even. Come let me show you something.'

My ears and the back of my neck turned cold as he led me up the stairs into the upper section of the house. The walls were all made of light, varnished wood, and sloped inward. The house was all angles and slopes. The floors were carpeted with soft fluffy rugs, the types soft fluffy dogs sleep on in carpet adverts. He led me into the main bedroom. It was surprisingly unpretentious. Large, of course. A bathroom at the far end, a walk-in cupboard, an exercise bike in a little corner that looked out over the garden, lit up now by a large lamp. The raindrops were getting thicker.

'Here!' He pointed to a set of pictures on his wall. It was of a young Regereman, dressed in blue boxing shorts, his hands clad in gloves, and his arm around an equally powerful, yet slender-looking black man.

'Shanghai Blowshark' he said. 'Me and him used to box together back in the seventies. Illegal. He's one of the most successful men in the country now. You've heard of him.'

I nodded.

'The two of us recently opened a new boxing gym. We both train there. Mostly businessmen. Older crowd, but a couple of youngsters. People with experience. How many years did you box? Show me your hands.'

I could taste blood running down the back of my throat.

'Stretch out. Nice. You should come train some time.'

I nodded.

'You ever been hunting?'

I shook my head, then swallowing softly, trying to hide my lie, said 'But I've always wanted to.'

'Let me show you something else.'

I followed him into his walk-in cupboard. It smelt of Regereman's aftershave. There were rows of suits, and shirts, cotton and silk. On the floor were boxes and boxes filled with shoes. And on the white railing that ran at eye level were a variety of brushes and polishes. He signalled that I should stand to his left and then pulled one of the railings in the other direction, to reveal a safe door. He turned around and stuck his hand into the inside pocket of one of his suit jackets and took out a key. He looked at me as he unlocked the safe. He wanted me to know that he knew that I knew how to get into his safe.

'Don't go talking to people about this. They're not all licensed,' he said, then finished opening the safe door. An overhead light came on in the safe and lit up a small arsenal of weapons. He leant forward and brought out a heavy-looking hunting rifle with a scope attached to the top.

'This is a .48 calibre. You can kill a buffalo with this if you know how to shoot right. I'm going hunting early next month. Shanghai's coming.'

'That sounds . . . ' I stopped mid-sentence, uncertain of what adjective to use.

'Look at this,' he said placing the hunting rifle back down and pulling out a fat handgun. 'Do you know what this is?'

'No.'

'It's called a Smith and Wesson. .48 calibre. The most legendary pistol you're going to find. Here, hold it.' He handed it to me.

My hand, totally unprepared as it was for the enormous weight of the gun, sank down. It was cold and heavy, and holding it made my muscles tighten. I wanted to get rid of it.

'Huh!' He laughed. It was the kind of laugh an aristocrat would make with his boot on the neck of a peasant.

'You never went to the army. None of your generation did. It's tragic. Those were the best years of my life. I was there for seven years. They couldn't get rid of me. Here!' He stuck out his hand. I placed the weapon in it, and as I did so immediately missed the feeling of the cold steel against my palm. I almost asked for it back again. I'd never held a gun before. I suddenly understood why men liked them.

'Friends you make in the army are friends you keep.'

The walk-in cupboard was feeling a lot smaller than it had when we'd first entered. I still hadn't become accustomed to the smell of Regereman's aftershave. It was making my lungs feel tight. The clothes were pressing up against me. The light was bright. I was so hot that I started getting those strange chills that are both boiling and freezing.

'The guys I met in the army are my business partners, my friends,' he said. 'I trust them. How do you make friends nowadays? You been in the army with someone for seven years, you know what sort of guy they are. Now you meet a guy he could be a *softy*.' He said the word the way an evangelist might say *Satan*.

He was facing me now full on, spitting out his words. I smelt on his breath, for the first time, something other than beer. He'd definitely been consuming some hard alcohol before I'd arrived. Plenty of it.

'What do you do if you don't know how to use a gun?' he asked me. 'What do you do if someone comes and you need to defend yourself? Vics told me about the Dutch woman near her flat. What if someone had come while Vics was at your house? Huh? I begged her to take a gun with her. But she refused. She's trained though. I trained her from when she was girl to use guns. You're not safe without them.'

'Yes,' I said.

'Let me ask you something.'

'OK.'

'Victoria tells me your father's left the country.'

'It's true.'

'Where's he gone?'

'To England. He has family there.'

'England! It's too wet. There's no space. Why did he go?'

'I don't know.'

'He was successful?'

'He was quite rich.'

'He doesn't trust darkies. Or what?'

'It's not that,' I said, looking away from Regereman. My father was from the old school. He used to call black people natives. He had a gardener he'd referred to as boy. But he started getting paranoid that the boy and the boy's friends were plotting to kill him. So in the end he left.

'You going to come hunting some time?' Regereman asked me.

'That would be nice,' I said.

'Vics doesn't like it any more.'

'I can believe that.'

'What do you mean by that?'

'I just mean . . . she doesn't like violence.'

'She lacks ambition?'

'No. I just mean, that, well, she doesn't like to kill things.'

'Who does?' he said, and winked at me.

He paused. His leathery skin was red. The suffocating smell of his aftershave was mixed with the liquor coming from his pores. This was his scent: an odour of greed that hung about him like flies around a corpse. The way he sweated, the way he spoke. He wanted to keep everything for himself, even his words, his sweat. And he was overcome now with a sense of grief at the loss he'd caused.

I slowly stepped away from him, out of the cupboard and into his room.

'Ja,' he said. 'We'd better check on the duck. Don't tell my wife I was showing you the guns.'

I nodded.

* * *

The next time I saw Regereman it was as if our previous meeting hadn't taken place. Victoria had taken to running along the Sea Point Promenade. I was at her flat, waiting for her to return. From my house I'd brought a few quarts of beer, a pack of cigarettes and of course my weed. I'd just finished smoking a joint out of her bathroom window and was watching some stupid programme on television and sipping a beer, when the doorbell rang. Assuming it was Victoria I jumped off the couch and opened the gate, the quart still in my hand.

When I saw Mr and Mrs Regereman standing there I felt a surge of icy fear run through my tendons.

'Where's Victoria?' he asked me.

'Umm . . . She's taking a run.'

'On her own?'

'Yes.'

'Let us in.'

I did.

'Does she have her pepper spray with her?'

'I think so.'

Regereman had a packet of peanuts in his hands. He'd pour a generous helping into his right palm, throw them into his mouth and savage them, as if punishing them for some wrongdoing.

Victoria senior went straight to the bathroom, and when she came out she sat down on the green couch, placed her hands in her groin area, crossed her legs, and stared dreamily out the window. Regereman had found an old television guide and was reading the comics section, laughing to himself and crunching on the nuts.

When Victoria finally returned she was showered with affection. Her father asked a thousand questions about her safety.

Victoria and her mother wanted to buy some food to cook for supper, and Regereman decided that he and I would be in the way, so he asked his wife to drop us next to the ocean.

We started walking down the boardwalk. It was a beautiful, perfect day, five in the afternoon, the sun still two or three hours above the ocean, creating a bright strip on the water, which rose up like overpowered footlights on a stage and burnt my eyes. Regereman of course had on his sunglasses, which he wore arrogantly on his big nose. The hair around the sides of his head was shaved short, freshly so I assumed, and the top shone like a globe. He surveyed the heavily peopled boardwalk as a king might survey his land. Or as Hitler might have surveyed a crowd at one of his rallies. Or as Hitler might have surveyed a cattle truck crammed with Jews. I couldn't see his eyes – his glasses were totally black – so I wasn't entirely sure. We passed ladies in tight elastic black shorts with bubbly thighs, speed walking to whatever tune they had selected on their I-pods. We passed ladies wheeling babies, and couples with young children, and lovers holding hands. We were silent. Neither spoke a word. The beer I'd drunk was overriding the weed, so I felt slightly light-headed and a little more secure than I would have otherwise. The traffic was noisy, but not unpleasant. We passed the light-house, and the ancient rundown putt-putt green. People were out in kayaks, and a strange old lady was sitting by the rocks in the alcove beach clutching an old dog that looked as if it'd risen from the depths of a mythical ocean. Regereman was wearing brown shorts that stopped just above the knee, brown leather shoes with hidden socks, a white shirt that he'd undone to ex-pose the gold chain he wore around the neck. He had plenty of rings on his fingers and a fat gold watch on his wrist.

We passed some public toilets. I said I needed to take a piss. He said he did too. This was unexpected. I was feeling that strange hazy drunk one feels during the day, my mouth was dry, and the beer was pounding away at the inside of my bladder. We stood next to each other at the urinal and a single beam of light shining through a crack in the window cut through my piss. It danced on the urinal and made sparkling patterns on the steel. I watched this phenomenon with amazement, and thought at first that Regereman was watching it too. Then I realised that he – without any doubt – was watching my penis. He'd put his glasses on his forehead, so when I glanced up I could see his eyes. It wasn't a homosexual stare. Rather a stare of intrigue. He knew that I stuck the beast in my hand inside his daughter. *He knew it!* He knew she liked it too. But we could never speak about that.

I shook it off with pride, and walked the rest of the walk until we reached the end, the public pool. He asked me if I'd like an ice cream. I said I would. He bought us each one from the Milky Lane, and without confirming my preference had mine dunked in chocolate. Then we sat on a bench and looked out across the sea. When we were finished he wiped his mouth. My legs were sticking out in front of me, and I'd crossed my feet, right over left. I could smell him: the greedy odour, like the seaweed rotting on the rocks a few hundred metres down the walk. Out of the corner of my eye I could see him sweating and wiping the moisture up with a serviette that came with the ice-cream. He didn't want to lose anything. Retention; greed. His eyes, with the same intensity with which they'd watched my penis, locked in on my feet.

'Interesting,' he said.

I nodded, as I continued to look out across the ocean.

'Where do you get them from?'

I shrugged my shoulders and pulled my feet underneath the bench.

'No. Don't. They're fascinating. I've seen this sort of thing before. I've always wondered if it was genetic.'

'I don't know.'

'You must know.'

'I don't know.'

There was a long silence.

A stray poodle came wandering down the boardwalk. It stopped when it reached my feet and began to sniff them. I took my big foot back a few inches, then lunged it forward into the dog's nose.

The animal rose into the air, its body doing a ninety-degree flip. It screeched as it rose up, and I immediately saw the little trail of snot it'd left on my shoe. It ran away with its head twitching slightly, its body bent to the side.

'What the hell was that for?' Regereman snapped at me.

A distraught-looking woman with a large tangled mop of brown hair came running towards the dog.

'Boris!' she screeched as she bent down to pick it up. Her sunglasses, which had been placed in the thick mop of hair, came falling out onto the concrete. Regereman rose from the bench and walked toward her.

'I'm terribly sorry,' I heard him say. He bent down and picked up the dog. He rubbed its head, and held it to his face.

I couldn't make out the rest of their conversation, but they kept turning and looking at me, the woman making deliberate glare motions with her eyes, Regereman responding with a shake of the head. A little tut-tut at my behaviour. People love to pick someone out for tutting. It unites them in their common disapproval.

Fucking Nazis!

In between their stares they'd pass the dog back and forth, Regereman kept holding it to his face like a little baby.

The whole time I sat still, my feet tucked under the bench. After a few minutes the woman put the dog down on the boardwalk, and started walking it again. She gave me a final look.

'What was that for?' Regereman asked me again. The anger had gone from his voice; he sounded disappointed.

'Sorry,' I said.

'No, that's not what I asked you.'

'Sorry.'

'Let's go.'

I followed him at a distance, then when I realised he was paying no attention to me, slipped into the public bathroom and
rolled myself another joint and got stoned. When I knew that he
was gone I hailed a taxi and caught a ride to the central rank. It
was at the busiest time of day and there were literally thousands
of people waiting to catch taxis home.

The central taxi rank is directly on top of the bus station in
the centre of town, but does a hundred times more business. It's
an enormous concrete lot, and from one end to the other is a
covering that looks like a long carport. Below it there are concrete dividers that split up the lanes, above which the names of
various places are written: Nyanga, Delft, Gugulethu. I needed
to catch the one to Mowbray and hop off early.

I forced my way through the thick crowd. There's a long row
of stands where they sell single cigarettes, packets of chips, ap-
ples. The hawkers were screaming out the day's specials. A dark-
coloured man wearing black glasses came up to me and asked
if I wanted to buy some Tommy Hilfiger perfume from him. He
stank to shit, was missing most of his teeth, and wasn't exactly a
good advert for his product.

'No,' I said, and kept walking.

It was a beautiful afternoon. To the one side I could see the
mountains lit up in pale yellow sunlight, and to the other side the
buildings in the centre of town. I kept forcing my way through
the crowd and eventually joined the queue that was waiting for
Mowbray. I stood for about half an hour. Everyone was packed
too tightly for my liking. I could smell cheap food and petrol.
The ground was dirty and people were screaming. Victoria kept
trying to phone me to find out where I was, but I didn't answer,

fearing my phone would be stolen if someone saw me speaking on it. In the end the crier directed me into an ancient taxi but directed me to the front seat where I got extra space. Being white sometimes counts in your favour at the most unexpected times.

The taxi ride was bumpy. The driver had installed a subwoofer under the front seat and played R 'n B music so loudly that nothing was audible except the bass. My balls vibrated with each note. Sitting next to me was an enormous coloured woman with boobs the size of watermelons. I couldn't help staring at them, and she noticed this but didn't seem to care. I think the vibrations of the subwoofer were turning her on, and she raised her eyebrows at me seductively as we sat at an intersection. I pretended not to notice, and felt uncomfortable for the rest of the ride. When I finally got out she blocked my way and forced me to rub myself up against her breasts. She pinched my bum and the taxi driver laughed. And I smiled with them because I'm white and love everybody.

When I got home I SMSed Victoria and told her I'd come down with a fever and she was please not to visit me.

*　*　*

I'd tell her the same thing now. I picked my phone off the bathroom floor and SMSed her, saying I'd come down with a stomach bug and wasn't in the mood for company. I didn't want her coming around until I knew exactly what was happening with Pete. He could be staking the place out, waiting for her to arrive, then bam! That would be that.

I went to my kitchen and made myself a pot of tea, then went through to the lounge and hit a bong of hydro to send me over the edge. Now that I knew Victoria was all right, I had nothing to worry about. I went and sat down on the swing seat and watched the world pass me by. I fell asleep, and some time during the night I must have gone to my bedroom, undressed and come back to sleep on the swing, because in the morning when I was woken by the sound of a strange woman calling my name, I was dressed only in boxers. When I finally opened my eyes, I sensed that she'd been standing there for a long time and that each 'Byron!' had been a single step on a long stairwell to consciousness.

'What!' I shouted at her.

'Hello, Byron' she said. 'Wakey! Morning! Can I come in please? I have some things to talk to you about.'

It was a bright morning, not a cloud in the sky. I climbed off the swing seat, went inside and buzzed the gate. She came walking up the path. She was dressed in a tight pink top and a long denim skirt that went down to her shins. She bulged slightly around the waist, but only slightly. Her tits were fat. Her hair was revolting: like a bramble bush. It'd been pulled back tightly and tied in a knot, but I could see that if undone it would spring open and stand out in a thousand different directions. Her face too, was unfortunate. Her skin, like her hair, had the look of the bramble. It also appeared to be pulled toward a central point at the back of her skull. As she moved past me, I expected to see a spot where the skin was tied in a fleshy knot, the kind one finds at the end of a traditional sausage.

'Is there somewhere I can put this stuff down?' she asked. In her left hand she held a leather briefcase, in her right, a metal one.

I walked past her, down the passage and into the lounge. I pointed at the couch, then went to my room and fetched a pack of cigarettes. Still dressed in my boxers, I seated myself in a chair in the corner of the dark lounge. She placed the metal case on the stop-sign table, and the leather briefcase at her side.

'So. You're Byron!' Her voice was at odds with the rest of her: sweet, smooth, angelic almost, rising up from her like musical notes from a church organ. There was something sexual about its pureness, and although she truly was a vile creature I felt the blood flowing toward my penis.

'Ah,' I said.

'You're friends with Liz?'

'What!'

'She teaches drama. She said you brought her this bone.' She opened up the metal case and took it out, placing it on the table.

'I found it yesterday, I really didn't know what to do with it.' I felt like such an idiot, how could I explain my stoned behaviour to a normal human being?

'You so did the right thing.'

'What!' The shock in my voice was obvious, I even shocked myself. The chances!

'My name is Susan. Susan Ridge. I'm at the University of Cape Town you see. I belong to a society that we set up a year or so back. It's called RDFM, Restoring Dignity to Forgotten Minorities.'

'What?'

'We're a sort of an action group. It's all official and licensed.'

'OK.'

'I really want to show you something. I think it will change your perception of things.'

I leant forward and dropped my smouldering cigarette butt into a half-finished bowl of cornflakes. She was shuffling through pages in her leather briefcase, and on finding something, shifted up, leaving a space in which I was meant to sit. She held the briefcase down firmly against her lap, indicating that her genitals were locked away, not coming out for the party. I moved toward her. In the air between us there was tension, but it was dirty, like semen and shit and motor oil.

She further shifted her weight to the edge of the couch until her body was rubbing against the armrest.

'How much do you know about the history of this area?' she asked me.

I shrugged my shoulders.

'Can I show you something?' she asked.

I nodded.

'This is a map of Observatory in 1901. You see here where it says Bellevliet? That is what the area you live in was originally called. Well, when I say originally, I don't of course mean in the very beginning. But when white people first subdivided the land into privately owned farms.'

Her angelic voice continued to float upward, symphonic, pure, but *white*, the word, was hit like a flat note.

'Now you see over here, Byron?' She shifted toward me, I could smell her. Her perfume was musty. It didn't hide a stench; rather a feeling. There was something greasy in her aura. 'Over here you see the Malay cemetery. Then here the TR church cemetery. Yes? And then here the St Peter's cemetery. You see don't you?'

'I can see them labelled there.'

'But you see how close they all are to Bellevliet. The farm that was subdivided to form your property.'

'I see that still.'

'Let me ask you a question, Byron. How much do you know about the Khoi people?'

'I've heard of them.'

'You know more about the Xhosa people, don't you?'

The look that accompanied this question must have been learnt from the television: the type one secret agent gives another when he reveals that he knows the agent's real name.

'Some,' I said.

'I've been to Bhakhuba a few times' she continued. 'I used to know Vusi. RDFM actually held their annual bash there at the end of last year. I knew you worked there. I remember you translating the poetry.'

'I took the job at Bhakhuba cause I needed work.'

'I'm the last person you need to hide your passions from. I'm an archaeological student. I love the past. And all sorts of cultures. They fascinate me.'

'That's great. Do you think there are more bones in my garden? Or what do you want?'

'Can I talk to you a little bit?'

'You are.'

'I must just tell you something. It may seem a bit shocking. The Khoi, as I was saying, yes. They were a one-time prolific people that lived all over the Western Cape and established themselves along the banks of the Liesbeeck River. In 1713 there was a smallpox epidemic. It was terrible, Byron. It arrived on the ships with the Dutch. The Khoi people had built up no immunity to this sort of disease. It was new to them. It took them out. I mean nearly all of them. Ninety per cent. It was tragic.'

'OK.'

'OK, Byron? No, not OK.'

'Not OK then. Why are you telling me this?'

'Well no one knows. Of course no one knows, exactly, what became of all of them. Their bodies that is. Many were burnt, some buried – .'

'And you think they're all in my garden?'

'You're jumping the gun here, Byron.'

'1713 was a long time ago.'

'Yes it was, Byron. I'm not saying that they are or that they're not. All I'm saying is, we need to look into it.'

'And how do you plan to do that?'

'Well, Byron, to do that, we'd have to take the bones to a lab. And perform tests. But I'm sure you're not in the least interested in that.'

'Ja.'

'What you do need to ask yourself is: what is my part? Where is Byron's place in this whole thing?'

'Oh, Jesus Christ.'

'What, Byron?'

'I really just thought. Oh fuck. I took it to the fair cause I didn't know what to do with it. I thought it might be important. Like a murder or something. I've seen TV shows and I didn't want to be an accomplice or a suspect. Ah fuck! I was bored. I wasn't expecting this nonsense.'

'Byron!' she screeched, as she stood up. She was highly skilled in the art of anger display.

'I'm offended by that remark!'

Ah! And a master at taking offence. This sort of performance doesn't just come naturally. It has to be worked at: each facial movement, each tug of the skirt, each mild click and tut of the tongue. Watch the way she picks up her briefcase, notice that look in her eye. This woman has it! She knows how to take offence!

'I'm going to leave now,' she said.

Poetry!

Poetry!

She packed the bone into the metal case.

'It's clear that I came too early. You're not even dressed. Hardly ready for something of such importance.'

'I didn't think you were going to talk mumbo jumbo.'

'I'm not talking mumbo jumbo!' she screeched. 'That's the whole point. I have a very practical way to go about this.'

'What?'

'Here' she said, taking a card out of – I could not quite see. It might have been her underwear. I held it to my nose.

'What are you doing?'

'Nothing.'

I read the card.

'Live action museum. What is that?' I asked her.

'We've never done it before. But we really do want to.'

'And?'

'There's money to be made.' She picked the two cases off the desk. 'Do you have an e-mail address?'

'I think so.'

'I can e-mail you a proposal. Or I can come again when you're slightly less,' she looked me up and down 'Or should I say slightly more decent. I can't stand immaturity. That's one thing I really can't stand. Immature people.'

She walked into the corridor and stared at me for a few seconds.

'How much money are we talking?' I asked her.

'A lot. If it works the way it should.'

'OK.'

'Well look, Byron,' she continued to eye me with disdain. 'You've got my number on that card. Call when you're ready to make up your mind. To be a little more serious about the whole thing. You do have a place. You are involved, whether you like it or not. Goodbye, Byron.'

'Cheers.'

She plodded off down the corridor. She could let herself out. I went back into my lounge and mulled some of the Swazi onto the table. I was getting close to finishing it, then I could start sobering up and taking life more seriously. I was using my favourite bong. It was made from a Black Label bottle, a hosepipe and a stone chalice. There was no clutch on which to place your finger which meant that you had to pull the entire hit through before the smoke would rush from the chamber into your lungs.

I packed the hit tight, and mixed in some hydro, and as I blew the long line of smoke toward the ceiling and sank down onto my couch looking forward to another uneventful day, I heard keys jangling in my front door. Dear God, the only person with keys to my house was Victoria.

I jumped off the couch, and scraped the leftover weed into my hand and ran to the window. I was about to throw it out when I realised that some of it was hydro and had cost me a fortune. I wanted to drop it into my pocket, but was wearing only boxers. So I ate it. I hid the bong behind the couch and walked into the corridor trying to look as natural as possible. Weed smoke came drifting out behind me.

'Morning,' I said, trying to sound together.

'Why are you coughing? Byron!' She'd smelt the smoke. 'You said you were sick!' She was holding two shopping bags in her left hand. 'I can't, Byron, believe. What is this?'

'It helps with stomach cramps.'

'Oh, yes, right!'

'I bought some bread for you and stuff, Byron, stuff for your fridge.'

'Thanks,' I said, following her into the kitchen. She dumped the two shopping bags onto the rickety table in the centre of the kitchen.

'So many dishes, Byron' she said. 'I bought you a newspaper. Look here,' she said slamming it down on the table. There was the usual picture of a cordoned-off crime scene, flashing lights, police officers. Above that there were the faces of two young white men in small block frames.

'Do you recognise these two?' she asked me.

'No.'

'Do you know, Byron, who they are?'

'No.'

'They're *you*, Byron! That's who they are. They're *you!*'

'What?'

'Shot. Point blank. In the back of the head. Gang initiation, that sort of thing. That's what it is. They kill for fun, Byron!'

'OK.'

'No! If you just wander around stoned and stupid. No security, Byron. Dead. Boom! It's coming to you! I doubt you even care.'

'I'm sorry. I'll be more careful.'

'Fine. Well, I'll see you, Byron, later on. I guess.'

'Where you going?'

'My display is just round the corner. Plus I am, Byron, contracting. At the moment. I just came to bring you stuff and see, just check, how you were. You said you were sick. But clearly . . . '

She walked out the kitchen, turned around, looked me up and down.

'And put on clothes, Byron. Clothes. Not just boxers. That's not how it works. And you need to shave. You're going to get fired from work. What is – Byron – what on God is that?'

She was staring at the marsh in the landing.

'It isn't really anything. It only came yesterday.'

'Not, Byron, anything! Are you, completely insane? Your house is going to flood and you are going to die.'

'You're exaggerating.'

'I am not, not one bit, exaggerating. Look at that! How did that happen!'

'It's just from the rain. It's not so bad.'

Before I had the chance to convince her otherwise, she'd gone to my room, changed into a pair of shorts and marched into the centre of the garden. The water level had dropped, and what remained was no more than thick mud. Barefoot, she walked right into the centre, stood still and stared at the sky.

The water in the landing was trapped by the doorstop, I stood staring at it for a few moments. She's never going to have any respect for a man who can't even keep his own house in order, I thought. I ran into the kitchen. I was terribly stoned. I turned the kettle on, and thought for a moment that if I took her a cup of tea it might make things better. But no. I had to swing into action. I fetched a broom from my pantry and ran through to the landing with a look of forged determination on my face.

I started sweeping the water into the garden with exaggerated motions. I worked up a deliberate sweat, continually wiping my forehead with the back of my hand, and saying, whew, whew. This ought to convince her, I thought. But she just stood in the garden staring at me, her hands resting on her hips.

'What is "whew", Byron? Hmm? What's this "whew"?'

I continued to wipe my forehead with the back of my hand, and then looked back down at the broom. I thought again of the Muslim women in their veils. How I wished, at that moment, that I could cover myself in one of those.

'Hey, Byron?' she asked me again. 'Whew. Whew whew whew!'

She grabbed the broomstick from my hand.

'Hey?' she asked me again.

'What?'

'Whew. Give us a whew, Byron. Give us a whew!'

'What do you want?'

She prodded me in the chest with the sweeping end of the broomstick. I stumbled through the door into the garden. She followed me.

'How could you let this happen?' she shrieked, as she continued to prod me in the chest. 'Whew!' she screamed with each blow, 'Whew! Whew!'

'Please, Victoria!' I held my hands up. I wanted to burst into tears. I felt so stupid standing there in the middle of my sunken garden. I was dressed only in boxers, and the morning air was cold. I could feel my penis shrivelling.

'Look,' I said, raising my hands. I couldn't tell if Victoria was playing the fool, or if she intended hitting me over the head with the business end of the stick.

'What has happened here, Byron?' She kept walking toward me, never changing her pace. The prodding had stopped, but a beating seemed imminent.

'I found some things in the garden. That's all.'

'And so you just let it!' She lunged toward me and slammed the broomstick into the mud. 'You just let it rot like this! Fine. Don't expect anybody's, Byron. Don't expect any help. Because you are an idiot! A stoned fool!' Each word was pronounced slowly, deliberately.

She ripped the broom out of the mud and hurled it in my direction. I jumped out the way and it crashed into the garden wall behind me.

'Victoria!' I screamed. But she was already turning around and walking away from me. I stood still for a few seconds, then decided to chase her. I had to spin this somehow. Surely, I wasn't as stupid as I looked.

.I followed her into the house. She was leaving muddy foot-prints all the way down my passage. I caught up with her, put my hands on her shoulders, physically preventing her from moving any further.

'Get off me!' She violently wriggled her body, but I wasn't let-ting her get away.

'Please,' I said, holding her firmly. 'It just happened yesterday, I haven't had a chance to fix it, and I was sick . . . '

'Just shut up!' she said, pulled my hand off her shoulder – I didn't try to stop her any more – and walked out the front door.

From my corridor I watched her climb into the big black car. I walked on to the balcony, and stood with my hands behind my back as she examined her face in the rear-view mirror, started the engine and drove away.

I stood on my patio for a few moments overwhelmed with anger. But then I could feel it morphing into pathetic self-pity. I hated myself right then. Everything about me seemed revolt-ing: my hair, my hands, my stupid mismatched feet. There they were, sitting at the bottom of my legs, covered in mud. I looked down the passage and sure enough, there were two distinct sets of muddy footprints running from the back door to the front door. The one set belonged to a normally proportioned human and the other to Byron. I got down on my knees and stared at one of my print sets, the large right and the baby left. I smudged it with my hand. I needed to get more serious!

There was only a little bit of weed left, so I smoked a joint and made a pot of tea. Soon life was going to get better.

Victoria returned early in the evening. I was smoking a cigarette on my swing seat, and didn't even get up to greet her. She had a large pizza box in her hand and she placed it in between us.

'Do you like this one? It's got chicken and avo.'

'Ja. I like it.'

Although I couldn't tell her, I had terrible munchies, and the food tasted amazing. We sat in silence for a few minutes enjoying the pizza. When Victoria ate, she never took a full bite but picked pieces off and nibbled at them, never taking more than a peck out of the dough, and leaving behind pieces of mutilated base.

'When I arrived, Byron, early this morning, that is, a girl was leaving here. Who was that, Byron?' She was deliberately keeping her tone consistent with the earlier question about pizza. She wanted me to think she didn't care.

'She was just some girl. Her name is Susan Ridge,' I said through a mouthful of pizza.

'Susan Ridge? That's not a real name, Byron.'

'Yes it is.'

'No. Byron!' She always had difficulty maintaining the uninterested act. Once, a few days after my stroll along the boardwalk with Regereman we were watching television in her flat. Without turning from the television, as if asking me to pass her a chip, she'd said, 'Why, Byron, please tell, why did you kick that poodle?'

'I said I was sorry.'

'That day you went for a walk with my dad. Then disappeared and came down with that mysterious fever. He told me, Byron, my dad, that you'd kicked a poodle. The lady was very upset, Byron.'

'I know. And I said I was sorry, I didn't mean anything by it.'

'Didn't mean anything? Didn't mean anything?' She started getting angry. 'How do you say you didn't mean anything! You kicked the poor dog in its face.'

'OK. The reason is. I was a bit drunk at the time.'

'But hurting animals is a bad sign, Byron.'

'Fuck!' The next line I was certain would get me boundless sympathy. 'I thought Regereman would like it,' I said.

Instead it sent her into a rage.

'You thought my dad would like it? What sort, Byron, of a sick idea is that!'

'He was showing me his guns. He said he was going hunting.'

'Oh, Byron – dear me, please, oh me – Byron! There is a difference between hunting and kicking poodles.'

'Is there? How's there a difference?'

'There is! And if you think; if you actually think this Byron, if you think my dad would be impressed!' By this stage she was screaming at me 'Then you have him very, very wrong, Byron. Very wrong!'

'OK. I realise this now.'

'Oh, you realise! If only you could learn to see things, Byron! I don't know what's wrong with you.'

'Sorry,' I said.

'Byron!' She was screaming at me again now. 'Please look up at me when I'm speaking to you. Don't mumble. Take the food away from your mouth when you speak!'

'What do you want to know?'

'Who is she?'

'Her name is Susan Ridge – .'

'I've heard that bit already.'

'I found a bone in my garden yesterday morning. That's what

I was trying to tell you this morning, but you wouldn't listen.'

'And?'

'Well. I don't know.'

'You don't know. How did she get to hear about it?'

'It's a bit strange, I realise now.'

'Always realising too late.' There she went again, treating me like a fucking child, and there I was playing straight into it.

'Listen!' I snapped at her, trying to assert some authority. 'I found it in my garden. I didn't know what it was. I thought maybe there'd been a murder or something.'

'So you should have gone to the police then!'

'It was so old. I thought maybe there might be someone there. I don't know what I thought, OK!'

'Well, Byron, whatever. You were probably stoned. What did she want?'

'She was talking about some museum project thing. I really wasn't paying much attention.'

'Do you have her number?'

'It's on a card on my desk.'

'I'm going to call her, you can finish the pizza.'

She went inside. I kept shoving pieces of pizza down my mouth. I loved sharing pizza with Victoria because she'd buy the family size, nibble at two pieces and leave the rest for me.

'Why's this card all torn up?' she asked as she came back onto the patio.

Oh fuck! I'd used the card Ridge had left me as girrick paper for my last joint.

'I don't know,' I said.

'Well I phoned her anyway. And I'm meeting her just now.'

'Just now?'

'In about an hour. I assume, Byron, that you can't make it.

Because – shouldn't you already be getting ready? Work, Byron. They'll demote you again, back to translator. You don't want to have to start wearing the skins again.'

'Oh ja. No,' I said.

'What, Byron?'

'No nothing. I'm just going to get changed.'

Fuck! I went into my room and closed the door behind me. As far as Victoria was concerned I was still employed at Bhakhuba. I was meant to be getting more respect from her, not less. If she discovered on the same day that I'd allowed my house to flood and lost my job, she would leave me for good, or start treating me like an infant.

I got changed into my suit then looked around for something I could carry to make me look more professional. There was a collection of pages on the table – I'd used them to mull weed onto earlier that day. I dusted them clean, then tucked them under my arm and walked out the front door.

'Are you going to be late, Byron?'

'No. The managers can get in a . . . bit later.'

She took a step toward me, put her arms behind my neck, fixed up my collar, then brushed my hair off my face and kissed me on the forehead.

'You look so handsome in a suit. Better than your skins.' She giggled as she continued to touch my collar gently. 'Will you come to my place later on? After work. I'm going to meet with this girl, find out, you know, what on earth is going on.'

'OK. I'll see you later,' I said and walked through the front gate, climbed into my car. I struggled to start it, and gave her a final wave as I drove off.

I had no idea what I was going to do for the next six hours. I hardly had any money. I assumed that she'd leave my house in a

couple of minutes. Then I could return and hang around until
the time I'd normally knock off.

To kill some time I drove through to Rondebosch, down the
Main Road past the video store, the hairdresser, the brightly lit
fast food joints. I turned up a dark side alley and parked my car
on a solid red line, hoping no traffic officers would pass by. I
went into the Hussar Grill, the oldest-looking place on the street.
It's a dark bar and I found the darkest corner, ordered a draught
and lit up a cigarette. I was nervous and made my way through
the complimentary bowl of peanuts with such haste that I drew
a funny look from the waitress.

I tried not to let my thoughts carry me away. Sometimes, recently, I'd think about everything at the same time, and feel like
I was being sucked away down a wild river, dragged underwater.
But things weren't too bad, I told myself as I sipped my beer. I
didn't have that much money left, but that was fine. I was going
to stop smoking weed soon, any day now. Then I'd start thinking
more clearly. The thing with Pete, maybe there was something
there. Otherwise I could get another job, there must be something. Victoria never had to know about the Bhakhuba situation
and by the time I saw her later, I'd have thought of some way to
spin the sunken garden story.

I paid the bill and made my way home. I parked my car a few
blocks away just in case Victoria was still at my house. I slunk
through the back streets. It was dark now and groups of people
were walking from their cars to the local night spots. I tried not
to make eye contact with anyone. When I reached the corner
of my block, I crouched down and looked over the fence of a
corner house. Her car was gone and the patio light had been
switched off.

I ran across the street and let myself in. It was eight o'clock now. I normally knocked off at midnight, but sometimes earlier. I'd hang around the house until half past eleven, then make my way through to her place.

I walked up and down my passage, which at night was terribly dark. I didn't know what to do with myself. I had a tiny bit of weed left. Not much. I could probably finish it right now. It would be a large full stop in my life. The next sentence was bound to be better.

I went and sat down in my dark lounge and rolled a fatty: a mixture of Swazi and hydro. I got terribly stoned, and immediately started getting nervous. I wondered if it were possible to view oneself objectively. I didn't think it was. But when I was stoned, I felt like I was seeing myself from the outside, and I didn't like what I saw. But was that just the drugs? What had I been telling myself in the Hussar that had sounded so good? I ran over the same things again, but where earlier they'd relaxed me, they now tightened my chest. Nothing made sense. I had to go to sleep.

I set my alarm for eleven o'clock and remarkably fell into a deep slumber. When I woke to the sound of my phone vibrating on the floor I climbed straight out of bed and went through to the bathroom. My eyes were red, there was a terrible taste in my mouth. I was no longer freshly stoned, but still had the haze hanging over me. Stupidly I'd gone to sleep in my suit and no amount of dusting could get the creases out.

On the way to Victoria's house I stopped at a petrol station and bought myself a Red Bull and some chewing gum. I parked outside her house, and spent a few minutes staring at my face in the mirror, blinking quickly and trying to clear the redness from my eyes. But it wouldn't go away.

I walked across the road and rang her doorbell.

She opened the door and stood in front of me without saying

a word. She was wearing pyjamas and had a bowl of popcorn in her hand.

'Hey!' I said, and made to kiss her. But she turned away from me and went back to the couch.

'Just going to the toilet,' I said. I shut the door behind me and looked at myself in the mirror. My eyes were still horribly red. I splashed my face with water, and tried to neaten up my hair. My jacket was creased and smelt of weed, as did my shirt. I took the jacket off and sprayed myself with strawberry-and-cream-scented bathroom spray. I hung the jacket in her room and went to sit down next to her.

'Very smoky at Bhakhuba tonight,' I said, and tried to put my arm over her shoulder and kiss her face.

'I can smell the wood smoke on you,' she said as she put another handful of popcorn in her mouth. There was an infomercial on the television. A blond woman in her late forties was coming in her pants as a fat Italian man explained to her how a vacuum pack machine worked.

'So exciting,' I said in a sarcastic tone, hoping to engage her in a humorous conversation.

'What?' she said.

'You know. They always seem so excited over these things.'

She looked at me for a few seconds, pulled her hair behind her ear and took another mouthful of popcorn. I shifted my weight slightly toward her and placed my hand on her knee. Her body did not respond lovingly, nor did it recoil.

'OK,' I said. 'What happened with Ridge?'

'I met her.'

'OK.'

'I met her, Byron. We had some drinks. She told me about her plan. I don't like her, she seems like a slut.'

'What are her plans?'

'She works for that RDFM thing, like it says on her card. They want to turn your house into a museum. A live action, she calls it. Live action museum. I don't trust that slut.'

'Me neither. So am I going along with it?'

'We haven't decided yet. There's money in it. Lots, so says the Ridge girl. But I guess you don't really need money, hey?'

'Of course. No. Where would I sleep?'

'You get to keep your room. She's going to call you.'

'Thanks.'

She took another mouthful of popcorn and folded her legs up against her body. I shifted my hand down toward her naked ankle. She looked at me, sniffed, and looked back at the television, flattened her hair against her head.

'Was it busy tonight?' she asked me.

'Yeah. Lots of Germans.'

'Where were they?'

'All about. You know. They like the place.'

'Not the upper section. Hey, Byron?'

'Umm. I think maybe not.'

'Not where I was sitting.'

'What?'

'There were some Japanese tourists there. I think there were even some, yes, I think there were Italians. Yes.'

'What?'

'Just thought I'd be friendly. Pop in. Say hi. "Where's Byron?" I asked the one waitress. What's her name, Byron? Lindi, I think. "Oh, he's not working here any more."'

'It's not that,' I said.

'Of course, Byron. Not. You were just, what? Taking a very long fucking smoke break! Hey!' She screamed at me and climbed off the couch. She employed that I'm-leaving-the-room-now march that girls learn at eight and use to their advantage for the rest of their lives. She went straight through to her bedroom, but left the door open, deliberately I think, so that I could hear her crying.

I didn't know what to do. I rearranged my balls, took another mouthful of popcorn and carried on watching the infomercial. I could hear her sobbing down the passageway like a little child who'd lost her ice cream. And I was the bad man who'd knocked it out of the cone. I felt a fart coming on. I pushed it out, then stood up and walked down the passage. I stood in her doorway and watched her sitting on the edge of her bed, pillow pulled up against the stomach, hair hanging loose in her face. She'd been crying so hard that the tears were dripping off her chin and falling onto the duvet. A truly pathetic sight.

I felt removed from the whole situation. The taste of popcorn was still in my mouth and I could easily believe that I was in the movies watching the scene unfold before my eyes on a large projection screen. I knew that the best thing to say was something cliché. If I said anything too out of the ordinary, I'd probably make the situation worse. What would an actor say in a situation like this? Maybe something like: *I didn't know how to break it to you.*

So I stepped toward her and said, 'I didn't know how to break it to you.' I sat down next to her on the bed and could smell the tears on her face.

'You don't have to pretend, you know,' she said. 'You don't have to pretend to be someone else. I like you cause. Just cause you're you. OK, and you're funny and stuff.'

I pushed her down against the bed, and started kissing her face. I kissed her on the nose and pulled her close to me.

'Sorry,' I said again. I was finding it remarkably easy to play

the part of the boyfriend begging for forgiveness. 'I'm just a moron. I'm sorry.'

'You're not a moron,' she said.

'I am.'

'No, Byron.'

I rolled over onto the far side of her bed and buried my face
amongst her teddy bears. She touched my back. I rolled over,
covered my face with one of the bears and made it talk.

She started laughing, so I dropped the bear, sat up and started
undressing her. We fucked three times and I fell asleep rushing
with happiness. But when I woke in the morning, alone, I felt
disgusted by myself. What she felt for me was pity, not love. She
saw me as a caring child sees a bird with a broken wing. She was
meant to start taking me seriously. I needed to be feared, not
pitied.

I lay very still imagining what it would be like to be feared by
all who knew me. Even Regereman should fear me. He would
warn his daughter to tread carefully around me, but never dare
tell her to leave me. Not even a man such as Regereman would
oppose my will.

Indeed, it was time for a change.

Wealthy, powerful men put aside personal sympathies in their
quest for control. And so should I. I would phone Pete that instant and tell him I wanted in. I didn't care what the price was.
In fact, I would offer to put Victoria down as collateral. Soon I
would be mighty!

I climbed out of bed and looked around for my phone. I
scrolled down to Pete's name and gave him a call. But a voice
told me that the number I'd dialled was not available at present.
So I climbed back into bed, jerked off, pulled Victoria's teddy
bears close to me and went back to sleep.

* * *

I spent the rest of the day in Victoria's bed. I got up twice to go to the bathroom. I didn't shower. I SMSed Pete and told him I wanted in. I'd give him whatever he wanted.

He didn't reply.

I tried to call him, his phone didn't ring.

By nightfall Victoria had still not come home. I got out of bed to watch the news. A couple of people had been murdered. A few cash in transit heists. The odd rape. They'd arrested some of the gang members who'd been involved in the murder of the two young men who'd been on the front page of the paper the day before. But a magistrate had already let one of them go because the police had held him for an hour too long. A woman stood crying outside a burnt shack. All in all a decent nightcap.

She returned while the weatherman was giving his predictions for the following day.

'Where you been?' I asked her.

'This lady's house in Camps Bay. We taking photos – for the magazine that is. You know, of course,' she said. She spent an hour lying in the bath, continually running the hot tap and causing the pipes in the walls to scream. I tried to go in and talk to her, but she'd locked the door. When she came out she was dressed in pyjamas and climbed straight into bed. I tried to get cosy with her but she resisted my advances with force.

The following morning she'd already left when I was woken by the sound of my cellphone ringing in the pocket of my jeans, which were lying on the far side of the room.

'Hello?' I said.

'Byron. It's Susan here. Ridge.'

'What?'

'Where are you, Byron?'

'I'm at. Why?'

'I'm outside your house. I need to speak to you.'

'I'm not there.'

'Victoria said you would be.'

'I'm not.'

'Can you come here now, please?'

'No'

'I'll fetch you.'

'No. Come tomorrow.'

'Byron, this is . . . '

I hung up.

She tried to call again; I didn't answer.

I must have fallen asleep again, for at some point I was startled by footsteps on the wooden floor. I sat up expecting to see Victoria standing in the doorway. But they continued, straight past my door, and into the bathroom. Someone was running a bath.

I lay still, holding my balls for comfort. Twenty minutes must have passed before I heard the bathroom door open and the footsteps come back down the passageway. They paused outside the door. The handle turned, the door started to open.

'AAAH!'

I sat up pretending to have woken from a deep slumber.

'Oh,' I said, rubbing my eyes with the back of my hands (the way only people in adverts for breakfast cereal and cold medicine wake up. I must have given myself away!)

'Mrs Regereman!' I said.

'I'm so sorry,' she said, and looked it. With her right hand she held the towel against her breast, with the other, she balanced the turban-like contraption in which she'd wrapped her hair. Her scream had shocked me into doing something rather peculiar. I found myself holding the duvet cover over my chest, and yet I was fully clothed, and had no breasts besides.

'I'm sorry,' she said again, but looked, this time, slightly less.

'It's um . . . ' I dropped the duvet.

I realised that the towel around her body was only being held in place by the clasp of her fingers. One wrong movement, a momentary loss of concentration, a cramp in the hand, and Mrs Regereman, Victoria senior, would be standing before me in all her middle-aged feminine glory. She had her daughter's authoritative chin, but otherwise her features were less pointed, flowed into one another with a certain grace.

'Did I wake you?' she asked me.

'Sort of,' I said.

Without fastening the towel around her breast, Mrs Regereman, with her graceful, careless walk, made her way across the room and carelessly sat on the edge of the bed. I obediently shifted up, and lay my head down on the pillow, like a sick child.

'I got caught in the rain. It came down quite hard and sudden. Unusual for Cape Town really. I was walking on the boardwalk.'

I could feel the heat coming off her body, smell the soap on her skin.

'I have a key for Vic's flat. We're the same size. Would you believe? Mother and daughter.'

'Hum,' I said.

She had an aura of sympathy. Everything about her was sympathetic. The way the towel hung loosely on her body, the way her skin clung carelessly to her face. To be sure, she was beautiful. Her breasts were larger than her daughter's, gravity and time appeared to have taken only a mild toll on their firmness. Feeling down and dark as I was, there was no creature in the world

I would rather have had sitting on the edge of my bed. I wanted to take off her towel, open her legs, and for a few moments just look. It would not be a look of perversity, or even arousal. It would be like looking at the colour blue when you're feeling enraged. Then I'd touch her pussy – no that's the wrong word: vagina (that's more suited to a woman of her design) – I'd touch the outside with the top of my head. Then I'd push harder, and slowly make my way through the canal and into her uterus, where I'd curl up into a little ball and suck my thumb, safe and peaceful in womb à la Regereman.

'Byron!'

'Yes,' I said. I think I'd closed my eyes.

'Do you want to sleep more. Are you feeling sick?'

'Yes, Mrs Regereman. Sick.'

'Please sweetie, call me Victoria.'

'Umm.'

'I know. All of her boyfriends find it strange at first. But Mrs Regereman makes me feel too old. Clive's mother is Mrs Regereman. Not me.'

'Who?'

'Clive. My husband.'

Clive, hey? So the fucker's first name is Clive.

With her left hand she continued to hold the towel around her breasts, with her right she touched my forehead. I could not discern the intentions of her fingertips. Was it motherly or sexual? Or both perhaps. Could it be both?

A gentle grey light came through the window above the bed.

'You're feeling hot, Byron,' she said.

'Yes.'

'You might have a fever.'

The steam had stopped coming off her shoulders, the turban

stayed put of its own accord and the soapy smell rose off her body.

'I must just put on some clothes. I'll see to you now.'

She climbed off the bed, and for the first time adjusted the towel around her breasts and removed the towel from her head. From Victoria's cupboard she selected a long white dress, crinkled like crepe paper. She paused now, and watched me. Perhaps she knew that we were thinking the same thing. The underwear. What of *them?*

But no, there was to be no underwear wearing around these parts.

A mother and daughter sharing clothes has a certain charm to it. When thinking of a mother and daughter sharing underwear, however, the word charm does not spring to mind. We seemed to agree on this.

She smiled at me, slipped out the door, and when she returned moments later was dressed in the flowing crinkle dress, her wet hair resting on her shoulders. Her hair was very dark, and there were no traces of grey. The gentle wrinkles on her skin were pleasing to the eye. None ran too deep. Her skin was pale, her eyes green. And in the gentle grey light, as she stood there, robed in pure white, I was convinced, truly convinced, that she was an angel. An angel without underwear.

'Would you like some Disprin? It will help you sleep.'

'Yes.'

She returned with a glass of bubbling white liquid. I drank it in one go, and handed her the glass.

She touched my forehead again.

'Vic didn't tell me you'd be here,' she said. 'I spoke to her on the phone just before I came.'

'I see.'

'She, um, was working in Camps Bay, for that magazine she takes photos for sometimes. You mustn't take it personally.'

'What?'

'Her neglect. She really likes you. I think.'

'What neglect?'

She sat back down on the bed and put the empty glass on the floor.

'Well she's working on that photographic project. I think she's told you about it.'

'Yes.'

She flicked her hair with the backs of her hands, it cracked like a whip.

'She takes it very seriously. She hasn't told me that much about it, but she talks to Clive. He has an art gallery out in Hout Bay, did you know?'

'I think so.'

'Well she's going to have her display there maybe. The theme has something to do with people being out of place. At odds with the landscape.'

'OK.'

'I've never asked Victoria how the two of you met.'

'She wanted to take photos of me.'

'Oh!' She sounded rather shocked. 'Well then I suppose you know already. About her project.'

'I do.'

'She's been like that since she was in school. She gets involved in something so intensely that the rest of the world disappears. She would become like a ghost in our house. Just have meals, but then not even speak. Not even answer questions. Really I mean. Not really answer them. It used to bother me, but then I found out that she was really talented and good. At what she did, that is. And I think, you have to be a bit obsessed to do well.'

'I agree.'

'But then she comes out of it, loses the obsession for a while, and obsesses over people. She's very caring. Always has been. So she'll come out of it.'

'OK.'

'Maybe you should get some sleep, Byron. I'm just going to sort things out around the house.'

'All right.'

She leant over and kissed me on the mouth. Her lips were not open, but neither were they sealed. There was a slight gap, just enough for a tongue to slip through. A moment's howl of hot breath filled my mouth.

* * *

When Victoria returned that evening, she was indeed ghostly. She left her equipment at the front door and went through to the kitchen. There were chopping sounds, followed by the clicking of a boiled kettle. She walked through to the lounge and turned on the television. I decided to make my presence known, and crept slowly from the bedroom into the lounge.

She didn't seem surprised to see me, nor that interested. I hadn't left the house in two days. My hair was standing out in shocks and tufts, my clothes felt wet and heavy, there was a bad taste in my mouth, I knew that I stank.

'There's some in the pot – food, I mean,' she said with a tone of indifference, as she watched the e.tv market indicators.

Once, a few weeks earlier, I'd stood in the same spot watching Regereman watch the news. On e.tv the market indicators are accompanied by a customised, rather cheesy, house tune. It starts off with a simple doo doo doo doo. And builds ultimately to a doo doo do dooooo, do doooo doooo dooo doo doo doo. Not knowing that I was watching him, Regereman bobbed his head as the doos built to the climax. Noticing plenty green arrows, he slapped his knees with his hands.

I went into her kitchen and found a plate in the small cupboard. Her kitchen was small and always perfectly ordered. As I dished myself some vegetables and rice I thought about the greedy odour that hung about Regereman, then went and joined Victoria on the couch.

'She's been trying, Byron, for two days. To get hold of you. Ridge that is.'

'OK.'

'No, Byron. You must phone her.'

'I thought you didn't like her.'

'That's not, Byron, the point. I don't see you going to work. It's not easy for a white boy to find work in this country. Especially one that's always stoned. You need money. What else, Byron? Are you going to sell things made out of wire and beads? Hmm?'

'No.'

'She's offering to pay you. It's just a few months. Just speak to her.'

'There might be something else.'

'What?'

'That I can do.'

'To make money?'

'Yes.'

'What?'

'It's hard to explain.'

'I'm sure it is. You really need to bath, Byron.'

'OK.'

'I'm very tired. I have a long day. Tomorrow will be a long day.'

'All right.'

'I think you must go home. You were snoring again last night. I can't sleep then.'

'OK.'

I finished my supper and went back to the kitchen. I washed my plate and stacked it in the metal dish rack next to her sink.

'Bye,' I said to her. I kissed her on the head as she typed an SMS on her phone. She raised one hand to wave at me as I walked toward the door.

'Can you unlock?'

She came walking toward me, still typing a message on the phone as she unlocked the door.

'Cheers,' she said, and locked it behind me.

I walked across the dark street and down a side road to where I'd parked my car. There'd been a strong wind the night before and my car was covered in leaves. I opened the door and climbed inside. Weed smoke had sunk deep into the material of my seats. It smelt acidic, like urine. I tried to start the car, but the engine sounded unhealthy. It rattled, then choked, then cut out. I tried to start it again. And again the same thing. I climbed out and locked the door. I felt too embarrassed to tell Victoria and so started walking along High Level Road back toward my house. But after a few minutes I realised that there was no way I'd get home alive. Someone would mug me and rip out my intestines.

I walked back to her flat. One of her neighbours was leaving as I arrived and held the gate open for me. I walked up to the front door and rang the bell.

She opened the door and was visibly shocked to see me. She'd changed into pyjama pants and slippers.

'I thought you said you were leaving,' she said.

'I can't.'

'What? Byron, why not?'

'I need a lift.'

'What! Why?'

'Umm. Car won't start.'

'Jeez, Byron. OK, come. Quickly.'

I climbed into Victoria's car. It smelt so good compared to mine. She hung one of those things on her rear-view mirror that constantly released a pleasant odour. Her seats were made of nice white leather. The steering wheel was solid black, and the dashboard was done in classic finishes.

'Thanks for the lift,' I said to her.

She didn't respond.

We drove in silence. There was a thick mist coming in off the sea and the lights of the ships in the harbour turned the white clouds yellow and orange. The wind was blowing hard and although Victoria's car was heavy she had to compensate so as not to be blown across the lanes.

She dropped me on the street outside my house, and drove off into the night. Through the bare branches of the mulberry tree I could make out a fingernail moon in the black sky. The overhead streetlamp spluttered and lit up a bergie shit left as a gift outside my gate. There were brown smears up the wall, from where the mystery shitter had evidently wiped his filthy asshole. The thick smell sat in my lungs like smoke. I coughed as I made my way up the path to the front door. Inside I flicked up the light switch, but the corridor remained dark. I took a lighter out of my pocket and held it up to the meter. I'd run out of electricity.

The freezer had defrosted leaving a large puddle on the kitchen floor. There was no hot water. I found a candle in the cupboard, and stumbled through the house looking for titbits of marijuana. I held the candle to glasses and cereal bowls in which I'd snuffed out the ends of joints. I managed to find a few roaches which I slipped into my back pocket as I continued my journey around the dark house. In my bedroom I found an almost full joint floating in a bowl of milk and soggy cornflakes. I stuck my hand in between the cushions in the couch, but any weed I found was mixed with dead skin cells, hair, grey dust. After about an hour's searching I'd found enough to make a joint. I couldn't be expected to quit now. I then realised I'd run out of Rizzla and I couldn't drive anywhere to buy some. I had to smoke it through a bottle neck.

Feeling more stupid than stoned, and overwhelmed by the smell of my own body, I retired to my cold bed, and pulled the cold sheets over my body.

In the morning I was woken by the sound of the doorbell. Standing outside my front gate, overdoing the *disgusted by human shit on the pavement* act, was Susan Ridge. The sight of her, combined with the smell of my own body was enough to make me nauseous. I buzzed her in and she wobbled up the path, her sweet voice rising from her flabby jowls like notes from a church organ.

'We're worried about you,' she said, and paused in front of me. As on her first visit, I was dressed only in boxers. My unwashed body provided the ideal grounds for bacteria. I was alive with it. My own ecosystem.

'What?' I said to her.

'Victoria and I. We are worried about you. I just got off the phone with her.' She made a sort of grumbling sound, indicating that I should step aside and let her in.

I did.

She half-pointed at the muddy footprints left by me and Victoria, and made a slightly different grumble.

Her frizzy greasy hair was pulled back tightly to a point on the top of her head. She'd tied a jersey around her waist. If it was – as I assumed it to be – an attempt at hiding the enormity of her behind, it failed miserably.

'Look, Sue,' I said.

'Don't call me Sue!' she said, turning into my lounge. Sue, the word, was hit like a flat note; the way she'd said white on her first visit.

'There's no electricity,' she bellowed from the lounge.

I know, you stupid fucking bitch, I wanted to say, but settled rather on 'Yes, I know.'

'Why not?' she asked me.

By this stage I was standing next to her in my lounge.

'We're really worried about you,' she said again. 'Me and Victoria. She says you're not going to work. I really want to help you. That's all.'

She plonked herself down on the couch, and rested her hands on her thighs.

'This is the third morning I've come here. In a row. You haven't been answering your phone.'

'What do you want? I need to put on clothes.'

I put on a dressing gown and some slippers, emptied one of the chairs in my lounge of its contents, which included, amongst other things, a pair of underpants, a bowl with dried Pronutro on the edges, some doodlings I'd done when stoned.

'Your house is not in a good way,' she said.

'I realise that.'

'You'll make money. I'll be responsible for cleaning it all up.'

'What do you want?'

'It'll be called a live action museum. It's been a dream of mine, of ours, for such a long time. RDFM has been looking for this sort of opportunity, and we really need to grab it while we can. The space is perfect.'

'What do I get?'

'We'll split the profits fifty-fifty. We'll charge thirty to fifty rand at the door. I must still do some calculations. We'll sell meals. We'll sell T-shirts. All the profit we'll share. And I know it will be a hit. I just know it will! Look at the Robben Island Museum. The District Six Museum. It's the thing, Byron. You should be overjoyed to be a part of it. I'll pay the electricity. Clean up the house. We're going to turn each room into a different display area. With information about the Khoi. Then what we'll do is put a tarpaulin over the garden. For the rain. Then people can watch the excavation as it happens.'

'But you don't even know if these are Khoi bones. They could belong to a dog.'

'A *dog*,' she shrieked. 'That is what you think of these people!'

'No. I just say you don't know.'

'You don't care. The reason you're resisting is because you think of them as subhuman because they're not *white*.'

'I don't.'

'Then you'll let me open the museum.'

'I'm just saying you don't know. You can't have info about Khoi and whatever if you're not sure.'

'You think they're worse than *dogs!*' she shrieked.

'No! When will you know if they're Khoi bones?'

'I do know. I know in *here!*' She pointed to her heart.

'Are you going to send them to a lab?'

'Afterwards. Later.'

'How much are we going to make?'

'It will run for a few months. Then it goes. We leave. You'll make thousands. I know it. What else are you going to do for money? Sell wire animals at robots. Hmm?'

'You *have* been speaking to her!'

'Who?'

'Victoria. Whose line was that? Yours or hers?'

'I don't think I understand you.'

'The wire animals thing.'

'I don't know.'

'She said the same thing to me. Who thought of it first?'

'I really don't know what you're going on about. I'm leaving now. I'll be here tomorrow. By then I need a definite answer, and I'm going to start cleaning out your house. If you say yes, I'll put in electricity. And start cleaning. I'll bring help. Goodbye, Byron.'

'Bye, Sue.'

'Don't call me Sue!'

* * *

Roddy arrived at my gate a few hours later, still dressed in his bear suit, the head in his hand.

'I got some weed,' he called out to me.

'Good.' I let the little guy in, he came and sat down next to me on the swing seat.

'It's rubbish,' he said, as he mulled the weed in the palm of his hand. 'Total rubbish, man. The Stones still owe me money for the first album. I told you that I wrote all those songs.'

'You told me.'

'Yo, Byron man. So I'm working at this other place now, dressed up in this nonsense costume!' He kicked the bear's head off the verandah and it rolled onto the grass. I watched him mulling the shitty weed and considered telling him that I was trying to quit, but decided that one little joint couldn't harm.

We smoked together – the weed was the cheapest shit available, I felt more stupid than stoned – and every few minutes I'd get up and phone Pete's phone. But still I got nothing.

'What's wrong, Byron?' Roddy asked me. His face was beginning to lose its pink colour, but whenever he moved a strong humid odour would come rising up from inside his bear suit.

'I need to get hold of this guy,' I said. 'I need money so bad. Otherwise, I'm going to have to let this other lady have her way here.'

'What lady's that, Byron?'

'He's the only chance I have at being able to stop her. I need money!'

But when she arrived the next morning I got the distinct feeling that nothing could stop her.

'Hi, Byron,' she said to me. Again I was dressed only in boxers.

With her was a white man of about my age. He was so tall that his head would have peered over the top of the fence, if it weren't for the fact that it hung constantly to the side. He had a thick mop of twisted black hair which – in the minute or so that I stood watching him – fell into his face twelve times. He looked like a Muppet who'd been stretched on the rack.

With her also were three black women. They reminded me of a set of babushka dolls. The largest, and first to enter, was forced to turn sideways so as not to bring the building down with her powerful hips. The next was slightly smaller, she'd straightened her hair and pulled it tightly back, exposing a Regeremanesque intensity in the eyes. She viewed my house with the enthusiasm of a conqueror admiring new territory, and when she set to work cleaned it with force. The third was a petite woman who avoided eye contact.

'Make yourself some tea ladies,' Ridge called after them as they made their way to the kitchen.

'They must be careful with my teapot!' I said. 'What's going on?'

The Muppet man offered me his large hand.

'Hi,' I said.

'Hi, man. My name is Damien.'

'Great. What's going on, Ridge?'

'We're going to clean your house. You can't live like this. What's your electricity number? I'll get you some right now.'

'Should I . . . ' The Muppet man moved cautiously and questioningly.

'Yes,' said Ridge. He obediently walked into the lounge.

'What's happening, Sue?'

'Susan!'

'What's happening?'

'You're going to give me your electricity details. Damien's just getting measurements, so we know the space we're dealing with.'

She noticed an old receipt resting on the top of my electricity meter.

'Oh,' she said, and picked it up. 'I'll go get some for you now. You know, Byron,' she said, taking my keys out of the door, 'It would really make our lives easier if I had my own set.'

'Ridge!'

But she was gone.

Fifteen minutes later she rang the doorbell and I let her back in.

'They'll be ready this afternoon. I'm getting a few pairs cut. In case Damien needs. Or one of the other people. I got you three hundred rand electricity. Now that should last you for a while. I'm just going to type it in. What's wrong, Byron?'

'Ridge. I really –'

'It's true what she says. I wasn't sure if I agreed at the time.'

'What?'

'You really think everyone's out to get you. It's from smoking pot, Byron. It really is.'

'Who told you this?'

'Victoria. That girl of yours. She's really very sweet, Byron. You're lucky to have her.'

'Am I?'

'Don't be sarcastic.'

She loaded the electricity onto the meter.

'There we go. That should do for now. What's wrong, Byron? You're staring at me like I've just crawled out of a block of cheese.'

'Well, you have,' I said, and walked past her. I sat down on the swing seat, buried my head in my hands.

'You really are ungrateful.' She was standing on the verandah. 'After all we're willing to do for you. This is how you respond.'

'Ridge.'

'Do you have a CD player?'

'Yes.'

'Well, I'm going to get some nice music from my car, and put it on your stereo. Then I'll get you some nice white wine. Ice. This is how it's going to be. It'll be like living in a hotel. And getting *paid* for it!'

'Aye, Ridge. You have . . . a way.'

I saw, for the first time, a smile on the face of Susan Ridge. She stood in front of me with her hands on her hips, the edges of which hung over her sides like saddle bags. She wasn't actually all that fat. But just as inner beauty can shine through, so can inner ugliness. And Ridge was glowing!

'I have a way, you say?' she said, and tilted her head to the side.

With the sun to her back, and a smile on her face, the round, undefined features, even the masculine jawbone had a cuteness to it. 'What sort of way is that then?' she asked.

'You're persuasive.'

'I have my moments' she said, and smiled some more.

As promised she went and bought a bottle of white wine. She put on a Celine Dion album, and sat down next to me with a glass of her own.

'What's going on in there?' I asked.

'Well, Damien's still measuring. The ladies are cleaning. They'll be a while still.'

'OK.'

She was wearing a blue top with little shiny beads. It was cut so that when she sat, the material sagged slightly and exposed a good deal of cleavage. Her breasts were large, and somewhat saggy. She was wearing pedal pushers, and so I was able to see the bottoms of her legs, which were surprisingly thin. I was fascinated by this body of hers. Not in the manner that men are usually fascinated by the female form. It was a different urge: the scientist's urge to discover, the artist's urge to know. The same drive, I assumed, that, through the ages, has sent men down to the paddock after a hard night's drinking.

'Sooo,' I said to Ridge, and stretched out my arm to pick up my glass off the floor.

She smiled at me.

My God, you're ugly, I thought.

The jawbone looked like that of a strong fish, a barbel perhaps. Thankfully she wasn't wearing any make-up and so the whiskers were less obvious.

We chatted: conversation came naturally. Like most physically unattractive women she had the desire to tell me about her sexual conquests. Like a master weaver, she wove these tales of lust and satisfaction between our other topics of conversation with graceful ease. How this man had her. And this one wanted her. How this one was buying her drinks. I nodded and smiled. She spoke of the ladies inside, and how much she just *absolutely* adored them. In a hush she mentioned Damien's supposed long-term crush on her.

Eventually her minions finished their work.

'I must take the ladies to the station, and Damien home.'

'All right,' I said.

'Then. I must come back here. To discuss something with you.'

I walked through my house. I could smell the lemon fresh detergent. The ammonia-clean bathrooms. They'd disposed of my dead plants, and even cleaned the garden. They'd wiped the muddy prints off the floor. I was a little drunk, but still the thought of Ridge returning was an unpleasant one. The morbid fascination with her body had vanished. I knew what she was coming for. It was obvious. I would go down as one of history's great fools if I was unfaithful with – with what? Ridge! No!

But then she was at the door with two bottles of wine in her hands. She placed one in the fridge and some Andrea Bocelli on the CD player. She sat down next to me on the swing seat outside and saw to it that my glass was always full. She did most of the talking, I listened, passively, nodding now and then to assure her

that I hadn't fallen asleep. By the time we'd finished the second
bottle of wine, the dark fascination of the soul had re-arisen.

'There's still one more she said. It's getting a bit chilly.'

She came back with the final bottle and a blanket she must
have liberated from my bed. She threw it over both of us. The
street was getting dark. The evening was here. *Amore!*

Beneath the blanket I felt her fingers touch my own, I let them
wrap themselves around me. She was telling a story about one
of her lecturers and how he was just the most funny guy in the
world. And how he always forgot what he was talking about but
then covered up with a funny story. And I looked at her, for what
must have been a second too long. And the jaw came toward me,
like a fish going at its prey, the whiskers wobbling at the sides.
Her thin lips struck mine, and her tongue went right to the back
of my throat. Her mouth was full of saliva. I felt like I was drowning. Then, out of sheer courtesy, I placed my glass on the floor,
and ran my hand up her large leg. She pulled away.

'Should we . . . ' she said, and bobbed her head toward the
house.

'OK,' I said.

I kicked my glass over as I stood up.

'Never mind,' she said. 'Come!' She led the way.

Like a drunken farmer walking the well-worn route to his
barn, the face of his favourite sheep lighting the way, I followed
Ridge. She lay down on my bed. I lay down next to her. We carried on kissing and touching each other, like friends, almost giggling at the absurdity of the situation. But then I started taking
off her top, and there were her breasts. And then I was taking
off her pedal pushers, and her big white panties. And there she
was, naked. And so was I. I carried on kissing her, and held her
big boobs in my hands. They were soft and wobbly. And in a

moment, I had my fingers inside her, and they were making a squelching sound, and she was rolling about like a fat kid being tickled by Santa.

The way she tugged at my penis confirmed my earlier suspicion. The conquests had all been in her head.

'I don't normally,' she said, as if reading my mind.

'What?'

Why were we talking? I mustn't think about what I'm doing.

'No, but I do now,' she said. 'There's one in my bag.'

'What?'

'Condom.'

Oh, of course condom, I thought.

At some point she'd placed her bag on my table.

How optimistic I thought, that a woman such as Ridge should keep a condom in her bag. I shuffled through her private crap, and finally found it. It was one of those silver ones with red writing. The type they distribute for free in public bathrooms. I struggled to get it on. And as I was about to enter her from above, she closed her eyes, and tilted her head back slightly. I caught sight of her nasal hairs, and realised my penis wasn't fully erect. But hell, I sort of shuffled it inside her anyway. It all felt off. There was no connection. No timing. She didn't move her body that much, and I closed my eyes to try and focus on coming. It was difficult. It just wouldn't happen. And finally, as it did, the accompanying feeling was like that one feels after taking a really good shit. And as I retreated from her body, I realised why she didn't want to be called Sue. She took the condom off my penis, tied it in a knot and threw it onto the floor. She didn't look at me. Sue, I thought. Sue Ridge. Sewerage. Oh my God, I did all I could not to burst into laughter. I couldn't wait to tell Victoria about the name. She'd just laugh and laugh.

* * *

When I woke in the morning, I alone was lying in the bed. The sheets were tangled around my feet and the voice of Andrea Bocelli was coming from the CD player. He was blabbering his way through *Con te patriro*, which means, I do believe, *time to say goodbye*. The calculating Ridge must have set it going as she left. Fully conscious of the irony – the disc belonged to her, she'd be back (if for no other reason) to retrieve it – she must have laughed a villainous laugh. You haven't seen the last of me, Byron, she must have chuckled, as she pushed the play button and slipped out the door.

Naked, I climbed from the bed, retrieved my boxers from the floor. Resting on top of my bookshelf was the self-portrait of Victoria. As I held it to my face I could smell Susan's groin on my fingers. The smell intensified as I brought the picture toward my face, and the sadness in my girl's eyes seemed to deepen. All night her face had sat there, hair behind ears, eyes deep and sorrowful.

I remembered a moment a few weeks earlier when the two of us had decided to take a walk along Noordhoek beach. It was late afternoon and the sun was setting over the ocean, the clouds alternately golden and black. The green of the mountains behind us was so intense that although I'd been perfectly sober, I'd felt like I was stoned. All the colours stood out against one another in a super-real fashion. A proud-looking woman with an erect spine came riding along the beach on a black horse. The woman saw us and smiled. Victoria paused, turned around and looked at me for a few brief seconds. She was wearing a loose tracksuit top, her hair was flowing freely in the gentle breeze, her chin was soft. I had never seen her looking so beautiful. At that moment, she stepped forward, held my head in her hands and kissed me on the nose. She laughed for a second. The breeze intensified, she turned away and carried on walking.

Now as I stared at the picture of her in my hands I could not remember if, on that day, a light mist had been coming off the ocean, or if my guilty mind had summoned it to destroy a moment of perfection.

I put the picture face-down and walked through to the bathroom. I was physically ill and threw up in the toilet. I climbed into the bath and washed myself over and over again, my face, my hands, my balls and penis. But nothing made me feel better. I went to the kitchen and gargled with salt water. I dissolved Vicks in a tub of boiling water and breathed the menthol fumes through my lungs. I ate a banana I found lying on my table.

After returning from a walk that afternoon, during the course of which I decided to remove the night's events from the course of history, I found Ridge's purple Corsa parked behind Victoria's black Merc on my pavement. My heart rate trebled, the veins in my neck froze. I could smell blood in my nasal cavity.

My first thought was to carry on walking, down to the bottom of my road, climb onto a train and head to another city. Johannesburg perhaps. I would leave my life behind, start a new one. But even as I was thinking these thoughts, my hands were unlocking the gate and my feet marching toward the lounge. I expected to be greeted by horrific screams and shouts.

But instead I was greeted by a scene uncommonly civilised for my house. Two women – Victoria on the couch, Ridge on the chair – were sitting erect, sipping cups of tea. Ridge turned and smiled, 'Hello, Byron,' she said.

Victoria patted the space next to her on the couch. I sat down and kissed her on the cheek. She squeezed my hand. It appeared that Ridge, like me, had decided to erase last night's happenings from her personal history. And if we both agreed that sex had not taken place, surely then, it hadn't.

'I was just telling Vics here about last night,' said Susan.

My fingers went limp.

'Yes, Byron. I'm so very glad that you're accepting the proposition. As we were saying, what else would you do? Sell wire animals at the robots.'

Victoria burst into laughter. Susan burst into laughter. My relief was so intense, that I too burst into laughter.

'Chameleons seem to be popular these days.' Victoria patted my leg, and we all agreed to carry on laughing.

'And fish too,' said Ridge.

'Yes, yes,' said Victoria. 'I know, Susan, the ones!' She could barely speak through her laughter. 'I know the ones you mean,' she shrieked, and leant forward holding the cup away from her body so as not to spill on herself.

I looked back and forth between these two women, they were overcome with laughter and joy. I stood up, planning on exiting the room, keeping a gentle smile on my face to show that there were no hard feelings. But then Victoria took a cigarette out of her handbag and lit up. I had never known her to smoke. She threw the box over to Ridge who also lit up. The two women sent columns of smoke billowing toward the ceiling. A yellowish light came through the single window at the top of the room, and shone onto me like a dim stage light.

'Or,' Ridge leant forward as she said this, 'He could be one of those chaps who *sell*',' she made little rabbit's ear quotation marks with her free hand, 'Those jokes-for-change pamphlets at the robot.'

'Yes,' Victoria roared. 'That's perfect for him. That's just – exactly – what he should do. Yes!'

I smiled as best I could, pretending I was happy to be the butt of their humour.

I made my way out of the lounge and down the passage. Their laughter, I could hear, did not die as I left. Standing at the front gate, with three black men dressed in grey overalls, was Damien the Muppet man. He was unlocking the gate, and now giving instructions to one of the men, who obediently retrieved a large box from a white van on the far side of the road.

'Hey there, Byron,' Damien called out to me as he held the gate open.

'Hi,' I said.

One of the black men clad in grey overalls, walked up to me and asked 'Where must I put?'

'I don't know.'

'Oh, I'll show you. Come!' Ridge had come out of the lounge and was standing in the passage with a cigarette in one hand and a cup of tea in the other.

'When did you start smoking?' I asked her.

'Not now, Byron. Come, let me show you where to put the box. We're going to put everything in here for the meantime.' She pointed at the vacant room directly opposite the lounge. 'We're going to put things in here, and also in this next room. Then we'll sort it out later, I'm thinking that we might –.'

The mover man, not in the least interested in what happened with the boxes after he received his pay, paid little attention to Ridge's boring explanations, and placed the box on the floor.

'When did you start smoking?' I asked Victoria, as we stood on my balcony watching the men carry boxes and signage into the house.

'On, Byron, and off. On and off, I mean. My whole life. From when I was fourteen. My first boyfriend smoked.'

'OK.'

Damien stood on the far side of the street watching over the truck. Ridge was inside, presumably giving orders to the poor men.

'So she said, Ridge that is, that you two were getting along fine yesterday.'

'I suppose we were.'

'And that . . . ' She dropped her cigarette onto the floor and crushed it with the front of her shoe, as she blew out a thin line of smoke.

'And that?'

'And that, Byron. What more must I say? I can't remember. She said you agreed to the museum. Unconditionally, she said.'

'Is it?'

'Well, Byron, what, did you not?'

'I did. I suppose.'

'You suppose.'

People were making their way home along the street, birds were making their way home through the grey sky. Footsteps and caws.

'Cigarette?' I put my hand out to Victoria.

'OK.'

'Why'd you start now?'

Ridge came and joined us on the balcony but continued to bark instructions down the passage.

'I started cause I wanted to, Byron. Surely that's enough. I don't need to tell you everything I do. Do I?'

'No,' I said.

The three of us were standing next to one another on my balcony. Evidently the two women had not discussed last night's happenings, and so it seemed that somehow, I would escape the consequences of my actions. There had been a cause; there would be no effect.

In the evening when everyone else had left, Victoria and I lay side by side on my bed. Fully clothed, she placed her head on my chest, and rested her hand on my leg.

'I'm sorry,' she said.

'About?'

'About everything, really. We were laughing – we were laughing, but with; not at. Me and Ridge, it was just for fun. But then she was saying how lucky I was to have you. And I just thought, well I did, just think. Yes, you know. Probably.'

'OK.'

She pulled herself closer to me.

'Both Ridge and Damien have keys to my house,' I said.

'She said so. But we spoke, me and her that is, about security. And she is going to install. You have to be careful.'

'I know.'

'It is tomorrow. Do you know that?'

'What?'

'My display. I think that's why I've started smoking again.'

'You've told me nothing. About it.'

'I know. I – now only, I mean – I didn't really speak to anyone about it. I sort of feel that when you do speak about it – and this isn't because I don't love you. I do. It's just that when you speak about it, you kind of kill it.'

'OK.'

'So you'll be there, of course.'

'Where is it?'

'In Hout Bay. At my dad's art gallery. You, Byron, are going to be featured, and you must, really, must wear a suit.'

'I will.'

'We'll fetch your car in the morning.'

'OK.'

She moved her hand up my leg and started unbuttoning my jeans. I did the same to her, pulled off her pants, rubbed her stomach for a few seconds and slipped my fingers inside her. I moved them around, back and forth, up and down, and felt them getting wet.

* * *

I shook Regereman's hand for a long time. He gave me a wink. In my heart I was winking back. We were standing in the centre of his art gallery. I was dressed in my suit, shirt buttoned to the final button, tie, shining shoes, white smile. The floors of his gallery were made of thick, varnished pine boards that reflected the overhead lights. There were multiple rooms and skylights. Victoria's photographs adorned the walls, and the city's social- ites slipped from room to room, champagne glasses in hand, refined laughter and carefully selected banter bubbling out of their pretentious mouths.

I knocked back five glasses of champagne and took a sixth out- side with me onto the steps, where I found a seat, lit up a smoke and gazed at the city's lights reflected in the inky black sky.

'What you doing out here, By?' Victoria called to me.

I stood up to greet her. A sparkling blue dress, bought espe- cially for the occasion, clung tightly to her long thin body. Her hair was tied in fancy plait works on top of her head, sharpening her angular features to a degree as yet unseen by me. It was dark outside and there was light coming from the gallery. The tops of her eyelids were shadowed in blue dust, and this combined with the dividing light, gave her face the look of the yin and the yang.

The light dot of the yin level with that of the yang. On her hands she wore no gloves, and as I stood to greet her, I took her long elegant fingers in my hand and raised them to my face.

Every time we touched or spoke, the image of Ridge would rise in my mind. And although, to an extent I hated myself for what I'd done, I had, in the short time since the betrayal, become more attractive to Victoria.

As I held her hand now and kissed her fingers, I felt as if we were two different people, in another time. I kissed her on the cheek and said 'Mweo!' out loud. I hadn't been stoned in a few days and my head was feeling clearer than normal.

'Byron!' she giggled. 'You still haven't seen them. Of you. The pictures.'

'I know. I'm afraid.'

'Of what?'

'Did you tell him?'

'Who? What?'

'Did you tell Regereman that I still work as a translator? When I work at all. Cause I told him I was a manager.'

'I haven't told him anything. You look so handsome.'

I looked down at my feet. One of the pairs of shoes I'd received from Pete were smart evening leathers, and this was the first time I'd had the chance to wear them. 'And probably, Byron, you would never have bought it. The suit that is. If you hadn't been pretending.'

'I guess. So you've forgiven me?'

'I told you before. I just like you because. OK. You don't need to pretend to be anything.'

'But you still mustn't tell Regereman.'

'I won't,' she said, and stepped towards me. She held her face a few inches from mine, kissed me on the nose and smiled.

I was amazed at how easily she'd forgiven me for lying to her about my job. For an instant I considered telling her about Ridge. Perhaps forgiving easily was in her nature. But no, she'd already forgiven me for one thing, I didn't want to push my luck. She wasn't a Catholic priest. And anyway, lying about a job and fucking another woman are not the same thing.

'I'm quite nervous,' she said. 'About, you know, what people will think. I've never, well I've had a section once, but never the whole gallery.'

'I know.'

'Let's go and have a look at the pictures of you.'

'I'm also nervous,' I said.

'Just come!'

She grabbed the cuff of my jacket and pulled me up a few stairs and into the first room of the gallery. The ceiling was high above our heads. The walls were high, there was lots of glass, the shiny floors squeaked as I slipped over them. People stood in circles sipping champagne, and would turn to greet Victoria as we wound our way through. They'd take her hand, pause, smile. She'd have the perfect, polished response, all part of her rich-person upbringing. Some of the men held her hand for a few seconds too long, but none – not even the slimiest amongst them – dared hold it to their lips.

When introduced to me, there would be a pause, a nod, a brief smile. We reached a group of three men, two black, one white. They were in their mid or late twenties, smartly dressed, looking rich: the type of guys Regereman would probably have chosen for his daughter.

They all chatted with Victoria for a few minutes as I stood silently. One of the black men, turned to me and said, 'You the guy in the picture, right?'

'Yeah.'

'So what you do?'

'I'm a . . . ' I looked at Victoria. 'I'm a restaurant manager.'

'A restaurant manager. OK. Which restaurant?'

'Bhakhuba.'

'No ways. So you know Vus right?'

'I know him.'

'Me and him were in res together.'

The other two men walked away, leaving me and Victoria with this new guy. He wore a gold watch on his wrist, apparently his name was T.

'Really?' I said.

'Yeah.'

'What do you?' I started trying to ask him a question. I wanted to look like I was at home with the rich and powerful.

'What?' he asked me.

'What do you do?'

'I'm in investment banking these days. Do some work with old Mr Regereman.'

He had braids in his hair, held his chest out with pride. His nose was strong, his cheekbones were strong, his jaw was strong.

'OK,' I said.

'So what's up with those skins?' He directed the question at either of us. 'I'm not sure if I got the whole thing. I'm not like, much of an art critic or anything, so I always feel a bit dumb at galleries. Like I'm always missing the point.'

'Ha,' Victoria gave a crispy laugh. 'Not at all. It's really open to your own interpretation.'

'But what were *you* thinking, putting him in skins?'

'It's someone out of place, you know.'

'Ok, cause he's like a white guy, and he's dressed in African skins.'

'Yeah.'

'And has it also got to do with shifting of power, or what?'

'How do you mean?'

'Well, like, you know, the shifting of power in our society.'

'I suppose you could say that. It wasn't really the idea. It was born out of a very real situation.'

'Oh yeah?'

'I saw Byron one day, wearing the skins, and it just fitted, you know, with the overall theme of my project.'

'OK. People out of place. So that's why you got that girl in the suit, and the man on the stripper pole and stuff.'

'Exactly.'

'So tell me, my man, you've worn the skins before?'

'It was just a once off thing.'

'At Bhakhuba?'

'Yeah.'

'Last year OK, my grandfather lives in Natal, he's still like seriously traditional. So we had a ceremony to mark my sister's coming of age. So I wore skins for the first time. I felt a bit funny in them myself. So I admire anyone who can wear them. Lucky it was just a once-off thing.'

'Ha-ha.'

'And why did you have him holding the skins down like that?'

'Well, it's a play on the classic Marilyn Monroe image. And just to give it a feminine feel. More out of place, more disjointed.'

'All right. So you could even say that was another kind of shift in power.'

'I suppose. I hadn't really thought of that. You don't seem ignorant about art at all. You know more than me.'

They both laughed.

I joined in.

'I'm sorry I've got so many questions. But how did you disjoint the feet like that in the picture?'

'Hey?' she asked.

I slipped my right foot back.

'How did you make them look different sizes?'

'Oh. It's easy really. On a computer. Post-editing stuff.'

'OK. And the point of that?'

'Just for a bit of fun.'

He leant over and gave me a friendly, how-you-doing-buddy tap on the left shoulder.

I winked at him, and immediately regretted it.

I walked away from the two of them, turning around to give T a handshake. I walked past women and men leaning against walls, sipping drinks, exchanging opinions. Between the various display rooms were narrow corridors, the walls to the display areas were made out of what could only be described as designer prefab.

I slipped into a side room, and felt a surge of nervous jitters run up my abdomen. The walls of the entire room were covered with pictures of Byron. He didn't look too bad. His skin was fine, his legs not too hairy. He wasn't fat. In a few photographs his black hair was falling into his face. In some of them his feet were not properly visible, but when they were, they were clearly different sizes.

There was one picture, larger than all the rest, alone on a wall in the far corner of the room. It was of Byron standing up and holding the skins down against his knees. A crowd of five people, amongst them Regereman and his wife, were looking at it, discussing the merits. I tried to slip out of the room, but Regereman had seen me.

'Hey!' he said 'Come over here, my friend.'

He was a tall man, Regereman, and the top of his bald head glowed. 'This is the man himself. His name's Byron. These are some friends of mine.'

I shook hands. Names were given, but immediately forgotten.

'You're like a movie star. Tonight only. So enjoy it.'

'Ha!' I forced a laugh.

His friends, two women, one man, all middle-aged and white, laughed genuinely.

'So what do you think of it, hey? You satisfied?'

'I like it a lot,' I said.

'Ja. This gentleman here. Old friend of mine. Interested in hanging it on his office wall. Owns an advertising agency.'

'Nice.'

The advertising agency man looked at me. He had thick black hair, black eyebrows, saggy greying skin. He looked like he was rich and drank too much.

'People will see you,' Regereman continued, 'Like this.' He pointed at the picture. 'They'll see you. So what do you think about that?'

'It will be great.'

' "It will be great," he says. Hey. Great. That's what he says. Will it be great, Byron?'

'Yeah,' I said.

'How's this guy, John?' Regereman looked at his friend.

John nodded, and looked me up and down.

'So, Byron, you like the picture,' Regereman continued. 'Tell us what you do again.'

'I'm, I work, as a manager. At a restaurant.'

'At a restaurant. Get this, John. Which restaurant?'

'Bhakhuba.'

'The Xhosa place,' Regereman added.

John nodded his head, and smirked.

'So tell us, Byron. Where did you get the skins for this picture?'

'I, um, well. I used to have to wear them as part of my job.'

'How's that, hey? Wears these skins for his job. That must have been a popular job. Were people queuing up for it? Did you have to do a special degree? With honours.'

'Clive,' Victoria senior was gently tugging at her husband's white shirt.

'I'm just asking,' he said, and shrugged his shoulders. 'So what did this job of yours entail?'

'I had to um . . . '

'Listen to this, John. Go on,' He nodded at me.

'I had to translate from Xhosa to English.'

'What did you have to translate Byron?'

'Praise poetry.'

'What's that Byron?'

'Praise poetry.'

'Praise poetry. Byron. Hey. You had to translate praise poetry from Xhosa to English. Was it fun? Did you enjoy it?'

'It was all right.'

'It was all right he says. Hey. Was it all right Byron?'

'Ja, it was all right.'

'It was all right hey, Byron. It was all right. John over here, he owns a couple of restaurants himself. Maybe he could do with someone like you translating from Xhosa to English. Hey, John.'

John rocked his head back and forth, a smirk on his lips. He had a mild hunch in his back. I could imagine him playing the sheriff of Nottingham in a modern version of Robin Hood.

Victoria senior's telephone started to ring in her bag. She left the room as she answered it.

'Women and their bloody phones,' Regereman said, and winked at the two women left in the room. 'What do you say about that, Byron? Hey. Women and their phones.'

'Ja,' I said, and laughed.

Moments later Victoria senior returned. Victoria – my Victoria – was with her, still chatting to T. The two were laughing.

'Hey, hey!' said Regereman. 'The first couple.'

I took this as my cue to move over to Victoria, but Regereman was casually blocking my way.

'It's good of you to come, T. You two look good together,' he said as he admired T and Victoria.

'Nice to see you, Mr Regereman.' The two men shook hands, Regereman giving T a solid pat on the back.

'Come. I want you two over here.' He guided Victoria and T toward the large picture of Byron on the wall.

'Hey, Vic,' he shouted to his wife.

'I'm right here.'

'Fetch Leila for me. She's got the camera.'

A middle-aged woman with bushy black hair came walking into the room on Regereman's command. She had a soft face, and mouthed 'Hello' without any sound actually coming from her mouth, the way Anglicans greet people at church fetes.

'Leila! How you doing?'

'I'm all right thank you, Clive. How are you?'

'I want you to take a picture of these two.' He pointed at T and Victoria.

'OK.'

'You two. A bit of a pose. A smile. Look happy.'

They interlaced arms, looked at one another for a second, smiled, then faced the camera.

'Now raise your glasses. Come. Give us a smile.'

T turned and gave Victoria a kiss on the cheek, she giggled, looked at him, her eyes lingering on his for one-third of a second longer than was platonically acceptable. This gave Regereman a thrill, and he clapped his hands as the Anglican church fete woman snapped her camera.

Victoria senior turned to look at me, a sympathetic smile on her face. I in turn gave her one of those why-would-you-even-be-looking-to-see-if-I-cared sort of smiles.

'Byron,' she said, as I walked past her, making my way out of the room.

'I'm just going to the bathroom,' I said with as little emotion as possible.

I wandered around the gallery trying to find the toilet. I put my glass down on a concrete, hip-high ledge. The gallery was still full. The evening had come to the point where people were expected to place orders for photos that they fancied. There was an air of excitement, but at the same time I sensed a lack of interest. Not in the artwork, but in the other people.

One woman, I noticed, had undergone so much plastic surgery that her right eye was no longer level with her left. She stood alongside her husband, a man who was quite evidently a cunt. He was short, wore a jersey – I'm sure he'd call it a cardigan – and spoke in a fabricated British accent about a gallery he'd *recently bin to in Lundin*.

I made my way outside, down the stairs and off to the side so that I was no longer in the light. In the darkness I could make out a pile of scrap wood leaning against the side of the gallery and saw it as the perfect place to take a piss. And then an idea dawned on me. Regereman wouldn't be coming out any time soon, and his car had to be around here somewhere. I walked along the well-kept dirt road in the semi-dark. Grass embankments rose up on either side and luxury cars were parked at angles all the way along them. Eventually I came across his, the big green Jeep with the personalised number plate that read: REGEREMAN.

I whipped out Mr Johnson and took a long slash on his fat front tyre. It felt as good as fucking his daughter.

But she was inside talking to another man whom her father wanted her to be with. It wasn't right for her to do this to me. I walked back up the steps and wrapped my arms around my sides for warmth. I was convinced that if I were gone for long enough Victoria would be overwhelmed with guilt, and come running to find me.

Minutes ticked by. Groups of people, couples, threesomes, made their way out of the gallery and off to their fancy cars. People made their way around me, muttering as they passed. One woman nearly tripped over me. She offered an apology but, I felt, it was directed more at the step and possibly the underside of her shoe.

But still Victoria did not come. I got up and walked back inside, knocked back a glass of champagne and took another with me. I sipped my drink, smoked cigarettes, blowing out long lines of smoke mixed with steam. I stared at the city lights in the distance.

'Hey!' I turned around. Victoria senior was standing one step up from me. She was wearing a blue dress with a slit to the knees and was shaped in a U above the breast. It hugged her frame revealing a body remarkably well toned for a woman of her age.

'It's quite cold this evening,' she said, wrapping a scarf around her neck.

'Cold. Ja,' I said.

She gently tucked some strands of hair behind her ears, ironed them against the back of her neck.

'What did you think of?' She bobbed her head toward the gallery.

'It was good.'

'I think the ones of you were certainly the best.' She smiled and put her hands out toward me. I put the glass down and gave her my hands.

'It's just Clive and those friends of his left inside.'

'Yeah.'

'They'll be a good half hour. Vics is talking to that fellow.'

As she spoke she gently massaged my palms, then started tickling the underside of my wrists. Apart from a tiny bulge around the waist, her body had the curves of a woman half her age. I allowed my eyes to wander freely over her body. She noticed my gaze, and gave her consent by gently looking away with a light smile on her face. Again I sensed that her affection was not overtly sexual. I had the right to observe the body from which my lover had come. It was educational. I felt myself going hard, and the soft material of my suit pants allowed Mr Johnson to rise with ease. But I was not in the least embarrassed. Our conduct felt so innocent. Even if she'd fallen to her knees and started sucking me off, it would have been a gesture of goodwill: like sending someone a Christmas card. I'd never felt so peaceful in my life. Receiving the blessing for an inappropriate erection was heaven.

'I haven't had in years,' she said.

'Hmm?'

'Clive will kill me. Let's go round the corner, and have a quick
one. Have you got any left?'

'What?'

'Cigs.'

'Oh. Yeah. I've got.'

'Come,' she said and carefully made her way down the stairs.
The bright light at the top of the gallery cast its beams no further
than a few metres from the last step. Beyond that there was darkness. We walked across the gravel parking, Victoria senior half a
metre in front of me. Her heels were sinking into the gravel and
she moved her body from side to side to keep her balance. The
way she moved her thighs, her butt, she seemed free of worldly
constraints. That's why she could tickle her daughter's boyfriend
and smile at his erection. Nothing had set meaning for her. I
longed to have her for myself. Lucky Regereman!

She paused, turned around and waited for me to catch up,
then extended her arm. As I slipped mine through hers I could
feel the skin was not as taut as that of a young woman. And although her perfume was sweet, her smell had an aged edge to
it. But this in no way put me off. If anything, it made her more
fascinating.

'Come' she said, and led me off the gravel path. We were walking on grass, surrounded by shoulder-high trees planted in cir-
cular flower beds. They'd recently been covered in compost.

'Whew,' she said, commenting on the smell.

She stopped next to one of these trees. We both looked back
at the gallery. It was clear that no one was standing on the steps. I
put my hand in my pocket and brought out a pack of cigarettes.
I took out two and leant over placing one in her mouth. I struck
my lighter and held it near her face even after the cigarette was

burning. Her eyes were smaller than her daughter's. Gentle lines ran alongside her lips.

We smoked silently for a few moments.

'I feel like I'm being naughty. We must hurry,' she said, but made no attempt to follow her own instructions. 'I always feel like smokers have a little secret.'

'Ja.'

'It's like having an affair.'

I made a humph sound.

She dropped her butt into one of the flowerbeds and left it smouldering. I dropped mine alongside hers and put them both out with my right foot. I felt safe in the dark.

We made our way back toward the gallery. She started swaying again as her ankles bent trying to balance her body. She leant over and grabbed hold of my wrist, letting out a sudden shriek of laughter. I too started laughing. Just at that moment we came out of the darkness and were standing at the very bottom of the steps. Without our noticing, Regereman had come out of the gallery and was standing at the very top of the stairs with his friend the villain, his wife, Victoria and T. Everyone went quiet for a few moments, then continued to talk, not because the moment of shock had passed, but because they wanted to cover it up.

The villain and his wife came walking down the stairs, climbed into a silver sports car and fucked off into the night. T kissed Victoria on the lips, shook Regereman's hand and trotted off to his car, not bothering to say goodbye to me. All the while Victoria senior and I stood silently, a few inches apart, like naughty children waiting for our punishment.

Eventually Regereman came walking down the stairs, Victoria junior at his side.

'What a lovely evening,' Vic senior said, trying to sound as jubilant as possible.

'Of course,' said Regereman.

'Come, Mommy.' Little Vic walked over to big Vic and took her by the arm, leading her to Regereman's car.

'Nice night, Byron.' Regereman took a cigar out of his top pocket and placed it in his mouth. He turned to face the gallery, a look of ownership in his eyes. It was the greediest I'd ever seen him. He lit his cigar and sent a large puff into the night air.

'I'd say it was a success,' he said.

'It was. Yes.'

'You enjoy yourself?'

'I did.'

'Good. It's important to enjoy yourself when you're young.' He put his free hand on my shoulder. 'Hey?'

'It is.'

'It's fun to be young. Do as you please.'

'Yes.' I was barely breathing.

'Just remember something, Byron. Big dogs bite harder than puppies!' He took another drag of his fat cigar, then threw it onto the ground and crushed it with the back of his foot. He'd barely smoked a tenth of it, and I could see it was expensive. He wanted me to know that he could.

* * *

We'd decided to take my car to the gallery. We'd had to jump it from outside her flat, and I was glad that it started now without any trouble. Neither me nor Victoria said a word to each other as we drove along the dark winding road that led from Regereman's gallery to the highway. Then, as we took the onramp, as if she'd timed her little display for maximum effect, water burst from her eyes and streamed down her face. She heaved like a baby and wiped her face, smearing make-up all along the contours. Again, as I'd witnessed in the past, a big dark tear clung to the underside of her chin, robbing it of its power.

'I'm such a moron!' she screamed, pounding her hands against her thighs.

'No,' I said.

'I'm such a loser. Tonight was a disaster.'

'But you did so well.'

'Shut up. You know. So don't pretend that you don't. You know the reason!' she screamed.

''Cause you're good.'

'My dad, Byron. You fucking know that. So don't lie!'

'Not the reason.'

'He brings all his friends. They have money. They're doing him a favour. I worked so hard. He doesn't even care.'

'What do you mean he doesn't care? He put it on for you.'

'Exactly. So you admit. It was because of him!' She wept, and bent her body forward, resting her hands on her knees.

When we got home, she stripped down in front of the mirror, all the while crying so hard that at one point she had to rest herself against the doorframe. I tried to comfort her by putting my arms around her waist, but she pushed me away and said I was a liar.

'Fuck off then,' I said.

'Fuck off too!' she screamed through her tears.

'Fine.'

I went to the lounge and would normally have hit the bong, but I had no weed left. Again, I told myself it was a good thing. My thoughts were clearer when I wasn't getting stoned. I had a few cigarettes then went back to my room. She'd curled up into a little ball in the corner of the bed. I lay down next to her and started jerking off. She started crying even harder as the bed shook with my private passion. She tried to take over from me, but I pushed her hand away, rolled over and went to sleep.

* * *

In the morning she was gone. I jumped out of bed and ran into the garden. Damien, head drooped to the right, hanging gardens of Babylon hair tucked behind his right ear, was sitting on a deck chair in the front garden making a sketch of my house.

'Morning Byron,' he said, in his droopy timid voice.

'Where's Victoria?'

'What?'

'My girlfriend.'

'Oh. I'm not sure. Susan asked me to make a sketch of your house. For the poster. For the opening.'

'When's the opening?'

'We're planning to have it this time next week. Or rather yesterday a week. Friday. Yeah.' He looked up and nodded his head.

'Where's Susan?'

'Oh. I don't know. She'll be here later.'

I went back inside, showered and changed into some fresh clothes. Although I was hung over from the night before, I could feel that I hadn't been smoking weed. I'd been off it for a few days now, and already I could feel the porridge effect waning. I picked up the pair of pants I'd been wearing the night before to see if I could find my cellphone. I did, and was just about to dial Victoria when I saw a note she'd left for me on my table.

Hi, Byron

Please do not be angry with me. I had to leave early to do something with my dad. He came to pick me up. I didn't want to wake you. I'll see you later on.

Love, Victoria.

* * *

I went and sat on my swing seat, lit up a cigarette and stared intently at Damien as he tried to sketch my house. I realised that I was making him incredibly self-conscious, and this is exactly what I wanted to do. He kept sneaking a glance at me, then looked back down at his page, then me, wishing I would disappear.

'So,' he eventually said, 'I never found out what it is that you do.'

'Not much,' I said.

'Susan said something about Bhakhuba.'

'Yeah.'

'Oh. I'm still studying at the moment. I'm doing, um, architecture.' He kept trying to sketch as he spoke, but I could tell that he was feeling so intensely awkward, that he was unable to concentrate on anything. 'But before that. Well, I did a course in graphic design?' He ended his sentence with an upward inflection, as if asking if I knew what graphic design was, if I knew what a course was.

'Uh-ha,' I said.

'So that's kind of why I'm qualified to do measurements of the room, and design the poster.' He giggled. I did not.

My phone rang. It was a call from a private number. I considered not answering, but at the last moment gave in.

'Hello.'

'Bro.'

'Pete? Is that you?'

'It's me, bro. It's me. Have you been trying to get hold of me?'

'Ja.'

'Sorry, bro.' His voice was lifeless and empty. He sounded like an old man.

'Where you been?'

'You need to come visit me.'

'Where?'

'Groote Schuur.'

'Hospital?'

'Ja.'

'What happened to you?'

'Between twelve and two for my ward. G12, I think. Peter Baklava. Ask at reception.'

'OK, Pete.'

'And bro, bring a bag.'

The hospital was only a few minutes' drive from my house. I found a parking spot at exactly twelve o'clock. Something bad must have happened to Pete, and although I knew it was wrong, I was excited to find out what it was. I kept telling myself to act mournfully, to slow down a little. And although consciously I wanted him to be fine, there was a part of me that hoped for the worst.

The weather was playing ball. The enormous red turrets of the hospital rose up into the thick grey sky. There was a gap in the clouds just above the mountains, and a biblical light lit up Devil's Peak. The rain was coming down gently, and there were large puddles all over the parking lot. An ambulance came rushing past me, but unfortunately continued around the corner, so I was unable to see the injured person on board.

I stood outside the entrance for a few seconds, staring at the large chimney that must be attached to the incinerator. A light smoke was drifting into the air. It was all very exciting.

But when I stepped inside the smell made me feel sick. It wasn't so much the chemicals as the food. The whole place stank of food. Coming toward me was an old man dressed in a blue dressing gown, completely open, exposing his entire wrinkled body, covered in white hair. There was a scar that ran right across his stomach. The sight of this mixed with the smell of cheap food ended my fun for the day.

I looked around for someone I might be able to speak to. A very attractive young woman, of about my age, with blond hair tied on top of her head was walking toward me. I prepped myself for a moment. I had to seem professional, and at the same time rather concerned.

'Excuse me,' I said, putting on a dour look.

'Yes.'

'I'm looking for a friend. Peter Baklava.'

'What ward is he in?'

'G12, I think he said.'

'OK. To get there . . . ' She rattled off instructions and my journey continued. The corridors were wide enough to be used as roads. My feet squeaked on the shiny blue surfaces. I glanced into each ward, and saw pretty much what I'd expected to see. People struggling to get out of beds, families holding loved ones' hands. The smell of hospital food was thick and sickening.

Finally I found G12, and stepped inside. It extended for maybe fifty metres back, and was crammed with beds on either side. Coming toward me was a tall black man in blue overalls, supporting himself with crutches. His left trouser leg ended a foot from the floor, and below it there was nothing. But the sight of the empty space hit me hard, like a kick in the balls. I looked away; but knew I'd done it too quickly: the way you'd look away from a spastic dwarf. To compensate, I looked back again; then into his black eyes.

'Bro.' I heard the word I'd been waiting for.

There he was, using his elbows to prop himself up against the back of his bed.

'How you doing, bro?' he said. His voice was still very weak, there was a tiny smudge of yellow custard stuck to the corner of his mouth.

'How you, Pete?' I asked.

'Take a chair, Byron bro. There's one there.'

I turned around. A black man of about sixty, on the opposite side of the room, sat limply on the edge of his bed, his left leg wrapped tightly in bandage. I walked across the room toward him 'Can I take this?' I asked, and dragged the chair across the room.

'What happened, Pete? Are you all right?'

'How you been, Byron?'

'Fine. What happened?'

He licked his lips very slowly, and rubbed them against one another as if trying to awaken them from some paralysed slumber. Each movement cost him great effort, and it seemed that he calculated them with absolute consideration. He rubbed his beard with his right hand. The freckles on his knuckles looked darker than before; or perhaps it was just that his hands were now whiter.

'It was a crash, bro,' he said.

'What? Are you all right?' There was genuine shock in my voice. I felt terrible for having wished the worst on Pete. It'd all seemed fictional before now. I'd been excited as one would be before a slasher flick. But now it was all so real. I wanted to apologise for what I'd thought, but trying to explain it would only make the whole thing so much worse.

'I was on my bike. Some dude in a bakkie jumped a red robot. Into the side of my body.'

He closed his eyes. I watched his Adam's apple rise and fall as he swallowed. He licked his lips again. I looked across the room. Sitting on the edge of the bed, still hunched over, looking at his bandaged leg, was the elderly man. He saw me watching him and pointed at his chest. I did not respond, and so he tapped himself repeatedly, as if playing a game of charades and ensuring that I knew he was the subject. Then he lowered his arm and made a slicing action with his open hand just below his knee. Then he pointed at himself again and mouthed the word: tomorrow.

'So, bro.' Pete was speaking again.

'Yes?' I said.

'They took it.'

'What?'

'The big one.'

'What!'

'From the knee, bro. Downwards.'

'No, Pete.' I found myself involuntarily touching his shoulder.

'Yes, bro. Chucked her in the incinerator.'

'Pete.' I moved my hand onto his head. 'I'm so sorry.' I meant what I said. I felt somehow responsible for this. I started lying to myself, pretending I'd never wanted to see bad things.

He shrugged his shoulders.

'I really am so sorry,' I said again.

'Not your fault.'

'I don't know what to say.'

'You don't have to say nothing.'

'Is there anything. That I can do?'

He gently licked his lips, shifted himself upward with his elbows.

'There is something.'

'What is it? I'll do what I can.'

'The other day, when I was saying how you had to give me something and all that shit. And I was checking that picture of your chick, bro. I never meant nothing by that, bro. Swear, bro. Swear.'

'It's all right Pete.'

'I think I learnt it bro, from watching movies or something.' He shrugged his shoulders and tried to smile.

'It's all right.'

The skin on his face was so pale that I was able to see it contrasted against the darkness of his beard. It brought out the freckles on his forehead.

'Anyways, bro.' He coughed, and then closed his eyes again. I tried to imagine the place where he kept taking himself. Was it possible, I wondered, that even at a time like this, there could be a place where things were OK? If there was, Pete would have to give me directions to it. I'd needed to find it in the past, and no doubt I'd need to find it again in the future.

An odour rose up from Pete. It was bad. Very bad. Through the slight opening in his dressing gown, I could see the hairs on his chest, and the thought that they were attached to a body with only one leg made them more repulsive than they might otherwise have been. The same fascination that had led to my sexual relations with Ridge, desired a glance at the disfigured body that lay beneath the sheets.

'Pete,' I said.

'Yo, bro.'

Then 'Nothing,' I said. 'Nothing.' I changed my mind.

'OK, bro.'

I started thinking about the shoes. I'd given him thousands of rands' worth of shoes. I'd been happy to part with them be-cause they'd been serving no function in my cupboard. But now, again, they'd be useless. I considered asking for them back. But quickly silenced myself. I had to help Pete.

'What do you want?' I asked.

'Two things, bro. One I need you to do for me now. They won't let me smoke in here, but I really need to get stoned. I really need it, bro.'

'All right.'

'So I need you to make me some weed cookies, and bring them. They'll help me sleep, bro. I want to sleep.'

'I understand.'

'Second, bro. They haven't given me my shoes. But they say they got them.' He ran out of breath, and stopped speaking for a time. 'I'm on lank pain killers, I still can't sleep. I need some weed.'

'You'll have some.'

'I was wearing the boots when I crashed. You know, bro, the black ones. So anyways, I need you to take them home. The tin, bro, I hope, is still in there. I haven't checked, but I'm sure. Then you must plant the seeds. OK? We need this. I need this. Else I won't have any cash.'

'All right.'

We sat in silence for a few minutes. I could hear the rain falling against the roof, and there was a gentle yellow light that came through a window a few metres to the left of his head. Watching him lying there made me feel somehow better about myself. I knew it was the wrong way to feel, but I just couldn't help it. It wasn't that I felt a new and intense appreciation for my legs, or some such horseshit. It was just a simple case of comparison. I didn't have a job, and my house was being transformed into a museum. But that was fine. I'd been charged with a mission. I'd been summoned by a cripple. I was not completely useless. Or at least, I didn't have to be for much longer.

I wondered then, how many people in the world had the condition that, until recently, had united Pete and me. Did the surgeon notice the deformity? And when the nurses threw it in the incinerator, did they realise that they were destroying a unique – or at least highly unusual – specimen? And as the foot transformed into smoke and drifted off into the rainy sky, did God shed a tear over the destruction of his botched, and therefore – I'd like to think – prized creation?

'So I was thinking,' Pete said, drawing my mind back from the smoky foot drifting through the stratosphere. 'It won't be so bad. I can get one of those peg legs. You know the ones. Made of wood. Maybe an eye patch. Maybe a parrot.'

'Sounds all right, Pete.'

'Call a nurse. They have my shoes. They might be a bit messed, bro. Sorry.'

* * *

The left boot was virtually unrecognisable. It'd been squashed and tattered, and looked more like a leather jock-strap. When she gave it to me, the nurse said – and this she'd heard from the doctor, who'd heard from the paramedics – that as they retrieved his broken body from the side of the road, red lights flashing, drip in arm, paramedics speaking their nonsense-heightened lingo, Pete had still had the presence of mind to ask them to save his boots. Apparently the story had become something of a legend amongst the Groote Schuur medical staff.

As I stuck my hand down the inside of the boot, I put out of my mind the possibility that pieces of his flesh had remained behind as the paramedics had ripped it off his foot. If this had been the case, then by the time the foot had reached the incinerator, in fact by the time the doctor had cut it off, it would no longer have been bigger than the right. Perhaps the two feet, for the first time in his life – moments before they were forever parted – had been of equal sizes. And perhaps then, God's tears – assuming they were shed – came not as the foot was transformed into smoke, but as it was smashed by the bakkie.

There were bloodstains on the inside and the outside of the boot, the zipped compartment had been ripped from top to bottom. But somehow, the little ladies' pill box with the floral decoration on the lid had remained virtually undamaged. The top had been dented, some of the paint had been chipped off, and when I tried to prise it open I could feel that the hinges had been damaged. But as I sat at my desk, on a rainy afternoon, my door closed against the ever-increasing Susan Ridge posse, I felt a thrill of orgasmic proportions as I saw the six little seeds rolling about on the golden surface of the box.

* * *

My garden had been cordoned off. A large, colourful tarpaulin had been extended from the eaves to a tree in my back garden to two poles that had been fastened to the perimeter wall. The purpose of this, I was told, was to prevent a flood of the kind that had caused the bones to surface in the first place.

Ridge spent most of her time at my house. Working under her was Damien the Muppet man, and five or six others. Damien, as I'd recently learnt, was in charge of designing the launch party poster and advertising in general. The others had each been designated a room. In one they had placed a number of life-sized statues of Khoi warriors and women. In another there were boards filled with information regarding the lifestyle and history of the Khoi people. One was a memorabilia shop. I was uncertain as to the function of the others. Ridge had placed a number of hotplates and gas stoves along the counters in my kitchen. She'd also imported two deepfreezes, stocked with food supplies, which had been placed in the pantry. The lounge had been transformed into what she dubbed a VIP area. There were new couches, tables, a soft-drink machine, a small pool table. She'd even placed a number of single beds in the corner of the dark room, which she'd attempted to illuminate with designer light fittings – one an Elvis bust, the other Bart Simpson. Was I allowed to use this room? Of course, she said, of course. Why ask such stupid questions? Of course. This is going to be like staying in a hotel, she promised again, I would be waited on hand and foot, and get paid for it.

I noticed a number of interesting changes in Ridge. We had not discussed our sexual encounter: there had been no mention of taking a step forward, or a step back. There wasn't even the awkwardness that one would expect. But the event seemed to have brought about something of a sexual awakening in her. She had not been a virgin when I penetrated her, I knew this not from her lack of skill, but rather from the pure physics of the situation. I concluded that she was currently living in a delusional bubble. Victoria was beautiful, and when I slept with Ridge, Victoria had been my steady lover. Therefore, the foolish Ridge must have concluded that she had something going for her. Something seriously special. Something worth risking a steady sexual relationship with a beautiful woman for.

She'd taken the filthy mop of tangled hair, and had it straightened. She'd bought herself a pair of hoop ear rings, and yes, she had even taken to wearing skirts that ended above her knees. But the greatest change was in her mannerisms. She'd become more fluid – it was the way she spoke to men: her arm flopping forward like a dead fish, her fingers resting on their shoulders. She'd taken to smoking, without inhaling. The way she held her cigarette had evidently been copied from posters of fifties movie stars. Once, I even caught her trying to teach herself to blow rings in my pantry. I wanted to tell her that this was cool if you were going for the Puerto Rican gangster look; not the seductive fifties broad.

After Pete's accident I considered telling her that the drive that'd led me to undress her, had almost compelled me to look at the stump of a recently amputated leg. A dark desire, one which I had yet to understand myself. Wanting to see Ridge naked was like slowing down as you pass an accident on the highway. Perhaps if I'd told her this, her hair would've curled back up, her short skirt would have grown legs and the warm top would have returned from vacation to cover her buttocks.

But I didn't tell her. For although it occasionally annoyed me to watch her acting out these sexual predator delusions of hers, it also gave me a sense of pride. For I knew that it was me: me and my penis, that had brought about this metamorphosis in the strange woman.

* * *

I walked down my passage now and into the kitchen. Ridge was smoking a cigarette and having a conversation with a minion of hers known as Tara. She was a young woman, fragile, pale, ashy grey hair. She closed her eyes when she spoke, and looked as if she were reciting things from a list.

'Ridge,' I said.

She was wearing one of her knee-length skirts, and warm stockings to protect her from the cold.

'Yes, Byron,' she said. 'Can you not see we're having a conversation?'

I stood in the doorway and listened to the two of them speaking. Little Tara fiddled with her fingers and kept looking down at her feet.

'I also think it's important,' said Ridge. 'We have to give a voice to these forgotten peoples. Let us not forget that our ancestors played a role in their demise.'

'I know,' said little Tara. 'I feel, well you know how I feel. It's that I think it's a kind of calling for me.'

'As for us all,' said Ridge.

'I mean they were the original people in this country. Oh, I just, ah. I just feel so awful when I think of what happened.'

'And so you should. But you're following your heart!' Ridge said. 'It's more than most people do in their lives. And you must always affirm why you're doing it!'

'I do. I do.'

'I'm so glad you feel so strongly about this, Tara. I'm glad to have people with such honest hearts working on the project.'

'Thank you, Susan. I always feel better when I talk to you.'

Ridge smiled and the little ashy creature scampered out of the kitchen. Ridge came walking toward me.

'Yes, Byron. What is it that you want?' She held her cigarette as seductively as she knew how. In her mind, she was oozing sex appeal. Simply *oozing* it!

I wanted to lean against the counter, but was unable to do so, as my usual spot had been taken by a hotplate. The old wobbly table in the centre of the kitchen had been replaced with a sturdier one. In the corner of the kitchen there was a dishwasher, and Ridge had recently invested in boxes filled with paper plates and plastic knives and plastic forks.

'What was that all about?' I asked her.

'All about? You're so suspicious. Tara was just reaffirming her reason for being involved in this whole project. It's a calling for her. As for me. It's important to reaffirm one's reasons for doing things. In all aspects of life. Some people renew their marriage vows.'

'All right.'

'I suppose you could even do it if you were in a relationship.'

I felt my face go slightly red for a moment. Ridge blew a long line of smoke toward the ceiling.

'Well, Ridge,' I said, finding it hard to keep my composure with nowhere to rest my bum. 'I need to go into my back garden. But you've put in a security gate. When did you do that?'

'It was this morning while you were away. We need to be safety conscious. Your girlfriend agrees with me, Byron. She really does.'

'But where's the key?'

'Well, they only gave us three. I have one. Damien has one.'

'Can I have mine?'

'I need to keep it for Geoff. You haven't met him yet. He's a delightful young man. He's in charge of the excavation.'

'So how am I going to get into my garden?'

'If you absolutely have to, I guess you'll have to speak to one of us.'

'Ridge!'

'Byron, we agreed that you wouldn't be going into the garden anyway. I have to divide the place into zones otherwise there'll be *absolute* chaos!'

'You said I'd be like a guest in a hotel.'

'You are. But there are always places in hotels where guests can't go. That's sacred ground out there, Byron. Perhaps you have no respect for these people, but some of us do. That's just not your space.'

'It's still my house.'

'I don't think they'd agree with you on that.'

'Well, they're not here.'

'There you go again, Byron. It's because they're not white, hey?'

'No.'

'If these were white people's bones you'd be bending over backwards to accommodate us with the excavation.'

'Ridge!'

'What, Byron! They're worse than dogs to you.'

'No!'

'You just want to traipse all over their graves. You wouldn't do that in a church cemetery, would you?'

'That's different!'

'How? Because white people get buried in churches?'

'No. Because. Because, Ridge, this is my garden!'

'We're going around in circles here!' She walked past me and stood in the passage, took a drag from her cigarette, held the smoke in her mouth and puffed it into the air. 'Is there anything else?'

'No,' I said.

'Good.' She plodded off down the corridor.

I watched her from the kitchen doorway. She called to a man on the street, waiting by the gate. He waved back. She let him in. Up close I saw that he was a dirty white man with scraggly hair, stained yellow wrinkled skin, a tattoo on the forearm, a checked shirt, a pencil in the top pocket: just the way you'd expect that guy to look. She gave him instructions, pointed at the door handle in the lounge.

I made my way past them.

I needed to get to the grow-it-yourself shop. I would have to ask for credit. They knew Pete. I'd explain the situation.

I felt a strong sense of duty towards Pete. I felt guilty for feeling glad that I had the mission. But it gave me new meaning. I could be one of those people who said: I've got a friend who lost his leg and I support him. That's right, buddy, me. I support my friend with one leg. So don't come asking for any favours. Don't expect a handout from me, my friend. I support my one-legged friend through my own sweat and labour. And what do I ask for in return? Nothing. That's what. Nothing. So don't come asking for favours.

Yes indeed. That's the kind of guy I would become. I walked up the street with my hands in my pockets, a smile on my face.

I walked into the grow-it-yourself shop. Bradley, one of the owners – the friend of Pete's who'd sold me the growing equipment – came walking across the shop to greet me.

'How you doing?' he asked me.

'I'm OK,' I said.

'How your tomatoes coming along?'

'Ja. All right.'

'Excuse me!' A woman's voice came from behind me. 'You're the one who knocked into me the other day. You kicked all my books.' It was the Gothic girl from the street.

'I'll leave you two for a moment' said Bradley as he walked away to help another customer.

'I don't remember,' I said.

'Don't lie. I recognise you perfectly well. It was just across the road here too.'

'All right. It was me.'

'There's something wrong with you, isn't there?'

I moved my right foot back.

'What are you doing?' she asked me.

'Nothing. I came here to buy things.'

'There is something wrong with you. You're creepy.'

'You're dressed for a funeral.'

'This is personal expression. OK. Not creepiness.'

'Fine. So what you want me to do?'

'Nothing. I don't mean creepy in a bad way. When I say creepy, I mean it's the way you must appear to other people.' I could smell that same soapy sweat scent rising off her body.

'I came here to buy things.'

'I find people who seem creepy to others interesting. It's because I know the way I come across. People are very judgmental,' she said.

Jesus Christ, I thought. She's one of those people who think they're deep. I've met her type before. They have short cuts for dragging you into deep conversation; they speak in metaphors and think in metaphors and are so caught up in being deep that they've lost touch with everything.

'Can I just ask you a favour, please?' she asked.

'What!'

'I have this little book here.' She started shuffling through the handbag that hung over her dainty shoulder. She was an incredibly fragile creature. Her dyed black hair had clearly undergone so many treatments that it was beginning to thin. In patches her pale scalp was visible. Her ears were pierced all the way up the side; her nose was pierced; her lip was pierced; her eyebrow was pierced. She finally found what she was looking for in her bag. It was a tiny blue book, with faded gold letters on the cover.

'Would you write something in here please?' she asked, as she held the book up to me.

'What?'

'Well that's the point. Anything. I want you to write anything. It's just something I've been doing for a little while now. I ask strangers to write down a thought. Or a poem or anything.'

'About what? I don't know what to write,' I said, and started walking toward Bradley. But she followed me and put her wiry little hand on my shoulder, and tried to squeeze it.

'Please,' she said again. 'Just whatever happens to spring to mind. It's for my own interest. A project. A personal project.'

'I'm sorry I knocked into you the other day. But that's over.'

'That's why I want you to do this for me. I want to understand people.' She stuck it out toward me, her hand deliberately shaking.

I took the book from her.

'Pen?' I said.

'Oh, sorry.' She took one out of her bag.

I stared at the blank page for a few seconds then wrote: Don't expect any favours from me.

I handed it back to her. She read the words, her face remained expressionless.

'Thank you,' she said and looked up at me. 'And what's your name?'

'Byron.'

'Byron?'

'Winterleaf.'

She scribbled my name down.

'Thank you, Byron,' she said, gave me a half-curtsey, and went over to look at something on the shelf.

'Bradley!' I cornered the owner. 'Can I have a word with you quickly?'

'Sure thing, man. You're Pete's friend, right?'

'That's right.'

'So what's up?'

'Can we step outside?'

I astounded myself. I couldn't believe the ease with which I asked him to: *Please step outside.* I felt like a cop on a TV show: *Come with me please, Sir. Let's not make this any harder than it has to be.* Furthermore, I was astounded at his obedience. I had a mission, and it was fuelling me from within. Who could judge me for selling weed? I needed to support a guy with one leg. So now, not only was I a don't-expect-any-favours-from-me sort of guy; I was also a don't-judge-me guy; a you-never-know-what-you-would-have-done-if-you-were-in-my-place sort of guy.

I gave Bradley the *low down.* Yes, I fancied the phrase now had a place in my vocabulary: low down.

'Amputated?' he cried.

'Yes.' I shook my head. 'Tragic, isn't it?' I was loving it. Every second of it. I felt bad for enjoying myself so much. But then, I was actually doing something good. I was doing this to help a one-legged man.

'So you need credit?' he asked.

'That's right.' I shook my head again in mournful sorrow. 'But not for long. We'll pay you back.'

'No, man, please. It's like the least I could do.'

'Thank you. Thank you so very much.'

I told him what I wanted.

He gave me some special growing soil, and a variety of hormones and chemicals. I walked back home. My house was full of people. They were all going about their business. They were redecorating the walls of my passage, and installing speakers on large metal stands. For the launch party, I guessed.

But they were all lost souls. I was the one with purpose. I went and emptied the old soil and cheap seeds in the front garden.

'What are you doing?' Ridge asked me.

'Never you mind,' I said, and went back to my room.

I locked the door behind me. I cleared a few items of clothing off my table and then lined the pots up, one next to the other. I opened the growing soil, and was about to start emptying the contents into the pots when I realised I'd better close my curtains. I did so, then returned to the task at hand.

I filled each pot to what I imagined to be the three-quarter mark. I stared at them for a few minutes. I licked my fingers. For the first time in a very long while I felt pleased with myself. I was aiding in the act of procreation. I was furthering God's plans. But also, I was helping to support a cripple. I was doing good. I was a fucking saint. People should make statues of me and place them above their fireplaces. There should be a school named St Byron's, where rich people send their children.

I was filled with the holy self-righteous spirit as I gently stuck my finger into the soil and moved it in circles until the hole was open and asking for seed. I picked up the ladies' pill box, and heard the seeds knocking against the sides. I struggled to pull open the lid. And when it did come up, I made sure the movement was smooth. I didn't want to spill anything. I stared at the opening for several seconds, then dropped the little seed inside it. I lovingly closed it over, and kissed the side of the pot. I repeated the process six times.

I kissed each pot then placed them in the top section of the cupboard. I ensured that they were the right distance away from the ultraviolet light, then closed the door and dusted off my hands, dropping soil all over the floor.

There was a sharp knock on the door.

'Byron!' It was Ridge.

'What?'

'What are you doing in there? Why are your curtains closed?

'Nothing. I'm coming out now.'

'Open up now. Let me in.'

I hopped off my chair, kicked the soil under the table, and walked over to the door. I ripped it open.

'Listen here, Ridge. We'd better get something straight. We'd better get something very . . . ' I couldn't remember if the correct phrasing was something, or one thing. 'We better get it straight.'

'Yes, Byron!'

'That's right,' I said. I felt a little stupid, but I was still in control. I could see that Ridge was taken aback. She'd never seen this coming from me. I'd never seen this coming from me. 'I'm putting up with a lot,' I said. 'You know that. But this room is mine. You can't just come knocking. I can do in here whatever I want to.'

'Byron,' she spoke calmly. 'I don't want to fight with you. I'm not an unfair person. I never have been. You can keep your room –'

'You're right I can!' I was loving it!

'But Byron, you do still have to obey the rules. We're drawing up a constitution for the place. And everyone must agree to it.'

'Not in my room.'

'Yes, in your room, Byron. We'll respect your privacy, but you have to respect our rules.'

'No.'

'Yes, Byron. Next thing I know you're storing bodies in there or something.'

'I'm not storing bodies.'

'Then let me look around.'

'No, Ridge.'

'But you have nothing to hide.'

I removed the key from the inside of the door and pushed past her. Blocking her with the full force of my body, I closed the door and locked it from the outside.

'Byron. This is unacceptable.'

'You can't come into my room.'

'So you do have something to hide?'

'No, but it's my room.'

'Yes, and?'

'I'm *entitled* to it. Privacy.'

'Entitled!' she said sarcastically. 'And where are you getting these big words from? I'm entitled to know what's happening in a venue which I'm in charge of.'

'This is my room!'

She took a step toward me so that her body was just touching mine, cornering me against my door. I could smell her body. There was still that aura of something hidden. It was in her smell. The feeling one gets when you enter a bathroom after someone's taken a shit and sprayed air freshener. She looked up at me. There was an involuntary static in our groins. How disgusting, I thought. Not just me, but her too. All of humanity. The fact that unions such as mine and Ridge's could take place was a dark indictment on our species. The simple fact that she wore breasts on her chest, and hid a fanny twixt her legs, should not have been sufficient to bring me down.

She pushed herself against me. Closer. She was using whatever it was that she had to prod me. And I was being prodded. I stepped back against the door and raised my chin in self-defence.

'We know certain things, don't we, Byron?'

'What?'

'We know certain things. So don't tread on thin ice. It's bound to break.' She spoke the words through clenched teeth, then turned from me and walked away.

I went and had a look at the electricity meter. There were ninety days of electricity at the current rate of usage. Provided that I watered the little seeds before I left, I could safely leave them for several days. I needed to get out of the house.

It was heading to late afternoon. I phoned Victoria, she said she was home, I was welcome to come around. I watered the plants, making sure that on each entrance and exit from my room, I locked the door. When I had finished, I packed a bag with some clothes and toiletries, climbed into my car and left without saying goodbye.

* * *

Victoria greeted me in her dressing gown. She would frantically dry the hair on one side of her head, then move the towel and do the same to the other. I walked past her, she grabbed my arm and turned me around. She pulled me against her. I could feel the heat rising up from inside her gown. I felt my clothes getting damp from her body, but didn't care. I dropped my bag.

'Sorry,' she said, and held my face in her hands. 'About last night. I meant nothing. You know. I'm sorry.'

'Fine,' I said.

We kissed.

She pulled me toward her room, and fell onto her bed, opening her dressing gown. I took off my clothes and climbed under the cover with her. Our hands went frantically over each other's bodies. We fucked, then lay naked and still.

In the morning she had nowhere to go and brought me breakfast in bed. She made me lunch, she cooked me supper. She fussed over me like a mother over her infant child.

There were two competing theories that tried to explain her behaviour. The one was my own, and proposed that somehow she felt threatened by another woman. My once-off, meaningless, filthy, union with Ridge, had made an impression on her, she sensed competition. Perhaps she could smell it, like dogs smell other dogs on their owners. Her mind did not consciously register it, but some deep-seated cavewoman instinct told her she had better keep me, or I'd move to another cave and start killing mammoths for another cavewoman.

The other theory was that of her mother. She had explained to me that Victoria would alternately obsess over work and people. Now that her project was complete she had replaced the pictures of me with the real me.

But that one had to go, purely for my own sanity. If my theory were true, then there was some good which had come from the dark act of the night.

That was that. And I let it be.

On top of that, since I'd stopped smoking weed she'd stopped talking to me like a child. Or perhaps I'd actually stopped acting like one. Whatever the reason, at that point I felt happy in our relationship. I didn't have to hide the fact that I was smoking weed. She knew that I'd lost my job. I could be Byron.

'I sold them all,' she said to me on the third evening while we were watching TV. She'd adopted her offhand, not caring tone of voice.

'Sold what?'

'The pictures, of course, Byron. You know. The pictures.'

'All of them? Did you make lots of money?'

'Yes.'

'How much?'

'A hundred thousand.'

'No!'

'Come on, Byron. It's hard enough, you know that, already.'

'Hard enough!'

'Byron. You know. It's not me. I've told you already. I feel like it's not me.'

'But it is you.'

'So many, Byron. So many people want to have photo displays. When they get them, they sell maybe one picture. Maybe two, Byron, I mean this. It's hard being an artist. But not for me. My dad just made me, like that.'

'No one else thinks that.'

'Yes they do. Everyone, Byron, else, everyone, thinks that. Everyone.'

'So why did they buy them then?'

'Because. He told them to. Or, rather – but his way is just about the same as telling – asked them to. Nicely.' She made little bunnies' ear quotation marks.

'You should be happy.'

'I am.'

'So stop complaining.'

'I'm not' she shrieked. 'Byron. You're not listening.'

'I am listening. You're complaining about the fact that you're lucky.'

'No, Byron. No. You're not listening. Fine. It doesn't matter.'

'I don't know what to say.'

'It doesn't matter. You're right. I'm going to make some popcorn.' She left the room.

The next morning before I left – I needed to water my plants – Victoria stopped me in the passageway.

'Byron.'

'Yes.'

'I'm going to give you this.'

'What?'

She produced an envelope from behind her back. I'd had no idea she'd even been holding anything.

'It's a thousand. Just for now. You'll get more later.'

'A thousand?'

'Rand, Byron. A thousand rand.'

'Why?'

'I made all that money from the pictures. And it is in part because of you. You were the model. It's standard to pay. It's fair. Only fair.'

'Umm . . . '

'Don't argue with me.'

I wasn't. But I wanted to look like I was.

'I don't know if I can accept this.'

I knew that I could.

'Just take it,' she said.

'Are you sure?' I asked, but wouldn't have if I'd thought there was even a one in a million chance she wasn't.

'Of course, Byron.'

'Sure, sure?' I wouldn't ask again.
'Yes!'
'OK. Thank you.'
I kissed her, and left.

* * *

I was stopped outside my gate by Tara, the little ashy creature. She handed me a flyer saying 'We're having a launch party on –'

'Yes, Tara. Thank you,' I said and made my way inside.

I unlocked my door, threw the bag down on my bed before reading the flyer.

Khoi House
The launch
48 Trill Road Observatory
July 25
12h00 till late
Tickets R50, available at Computicket and the door
"You know you should be there"

The first question that popped into my mind was: who is she quoting? I got the distinct feeling it was herself.

The twisted Ridge.

I decided that I would be present. I couldn't wait to see who'd show up. It seemed that she had her target market pinned. She knew her marketing angle. The word *should* shimmered before me.

* * *

I threw the pamphlet on the bed, climbed onto my desk and opened the top cupboard. The shoots had yet to surface, and the soil was still slightly moist. I sprinkled a little water on the surface of each, locked my door and left the house. My mind was working wonderfully from not smoking weed. Perhaps it was true what everyone had been telling me. It was the weed that turned me into a moron. Without it I was able to function as a normal human being. Nevertheless I wanted cold beer. I felt I deserved it.

I walked into Scrumpy Jack's and ordered a pint. I was brought a bowl of popcorn, and sat quietly in the corner crunching through seeds and sipping ale. I noticed that on the wall, along-side a number of other posters, was one advertising the launch of the museum. Again, the phrase "You know you should be there."

After drinking ten pints and making my way through as many bowls of popcorn, I settled my account and stumbled onto the street. It was late afternoon and I was seeing double. The beauty of the situation was that I still had well over 800 rand in my wal-let. I put my hands in my pockets and looked at my feet. A home-less man asked me for money.

'I'm a fucking model, my friend,' I said.

'Eh?'

'I support my crippled friend. Don't ask me for any favours. All right?'

I pushed past him and turned into Trill Road, unlocked my gate. Little Tara was standing in the front garden. I placed my hands on either side of her head, and raised her face to mine. I could see the terror in her grey eyes. She had light spots all over her skin, miniature raised dimples. I leant forward and kissed her forehead. She closed her eyes.

'Care to go to bed with a model?' I asked her.

'He-he,' she giggled, before pulling herself away from me.

'Byron!' Ridge had appeared in the doorway. 'Are you drunk?'

'Fucked!'

'You can't show up drunk and expect a civil welcome.'

'Fuck off!'

I made my way into the house.

'Byron!' she grabbed hold of my shirt, but I spun around and forced her hand off me. 'What's wrong with you?'

'Nothing,' I said, whilst tapping my hands up and down my body in search of the key. Eventually I found it, and unlocked my bedroom door. She tried to follow me in, but I closed the door in her face, and even in my drunken state had the presence of mind to lock it again before passing out fully clothed on my bed.

The next few days passed in much the same manner. By Thursday I'd spent more than half my money and had nothing to show for it except red eyes and messy hair. Pete phoned me that day, the day before the opening. I visited him in hospital again. He said that he wouldn't be coming out for a week or more. They had to monitor his situation. He asked if I'd planted the seeds. I told him I had, but neglected to mention the other happenings in my house.

After our brief exchange of words he fell silent, and, as on my first visit, I was taken by the feeling that the silence was his to break. He stared silently across the room, occasionally closing his eyes for a few seconds, occasionally licking his lips. I spent most of the time wondering about his personal hygiene. I recognised the dressing gown, and a certain gravy stain on the white striped lapel, which had been there on my last visit. His body had an acrid smell. I was relieved when, after maybe twenty minutes, he said he wanted to go to sleep. Then he pulled himself up again and said in a barely audible voice 'Bro. Did you get a chance to make the cookies? The weed cookies.'

'There's some shit going on at my house, Pete. Can't really explain. But it's simply impossible.'

'Impossible?'

'Impossible, Pete.'

'OK, bro. Never mind then.' He pulled the duvet up to his neck, releasing the gases which had been collecting beneath it.

I left.

* * *

Friday arrived.

The usual noises of the house started in the earliest hours of the morning. It was still completely dark when I heard my gate rattling, opening and closing, objects being dragged down the corridor. Ridge – who'd taken to sleeping in my lounge – was barking orders at her minions. I closed my eyes and tried to doze some more, but, just on the cusp of sleep, was woken by a sharp knocking on the door.

'What?' I cried from beneath my duvet.

'Byron. It's me. Open up.'

'What do you want!' I pulled my duvet over my head.

'I need to speak to you. Now.'

Without putting anything over my boxers I opened the door and stared at Ridge. She was dressed in casual jeans, a casual blue top; she'd taken to wearing a large golden bracelet around her wrist. In the overhead passage light, I noticed her once perfectly straight hair was curling again towards the tips, her whiskers and barbel-like jawline were brought out by the careless application of her make-up. As I stood in my doorway, watching her watching me, I wondered how it was that such a controlling creature could consistently make this sloppy mistake with her own appearance.

'We've decided you shouldn't be here for the launch.'

'Rubbish!' I said, and tried to close the door in her face.

'Byron! Be careful!'

'I want to sleep, Ridge!' I sounded like a whining child.

'You will create a bad impression. We never know what you might go telling the guests.'

'I won't go *telling* them anything,' I mocked her tone of voice and then farted. She pretended not to have heard.

'Everyone has voted against it.'

'I wasn't invited to the vote.'

'We realise this, Byron. And for that we are sorry. But it simply won't work. Go stay with your lovely lady.'

'No. I'll be here. I'll wear a suit. If you want. I'll say nothing. But I'll be here. OK.'

'Byron, I don't believe I came for an argument.'

'Well, go away then.'

'If I go back and tell the others that you're going to be here, they'll see it as a sign of weakness. On my part.'

'Not my problem.'

'Our problems are connected. You know that.'

'What?'

'I don't like to look the fool.'

'Me neither.'

'I *really* don't!'

'Tell them you changed your mind. It was your choice. I need to sleep.' I shoved the door with all my weight into her plump body and locked it. She beat her fatty fists against the door.

I ignored her. No one must mess with my sleep.

When eleven o'clock came I climbed out of bed and went to the shower. I kept a piece of string around my neck onto which I'd tied my bedroom key, so that I could keep it with me when washing. The string did unfortunately retain a good deal of water, and so chafed my neck. But it was a small price to pay for my privacy.

I changed into my suit, and retrieved the smart black shoes given me by Pete. I laid them out on the floor and stared at them for several moments. I contemplated their partners, sitting somewhere in Pete's flat, the left shoe forever unemployed.

By twelve o'clock I was fully dressed, standing in the doorway with my right foot slightly back, my tie straightened, a forced smile on my face.

I noticed, for the first time, a table that Ridge had set up on the verandah. It was covered with nametags. Standing behind the desk was another of her minions, an attractive, but evidently naïve, young woman, with shoulder-length wispy blond hair and light freckles. Her name was Katie. The first time I'd seen her she'd been sitting cross-legged in the corner of my lounge, strumming a guitar to some Counting Crows number. She wore a long black dress, and smiled.

The first guests started arriving moments after midday. A tall man in a suit came walking up the front path. He smiled and mouthed his name: 'Denis' he said. Again he said, 'Denis.' He kept saying it over and over to everyone standing in the entrance. 'Denis.' Then he'd nod his head and smile, 'Denis.' He must have been in his late forties early fifties. He was going bald. He

wore a comb-over. The pale white skin on his neck was covered
with shaving nicks, and his chest hair sprouted out the top of his
shirt like pubic hair from panties. He was handed a nametag and
made an act out of struggling to get it on. He was advertising the
fact that he was the kind of guy who could have a good laugh at
himself, and when he finally got it on he said 'There we go.'

He made his way down the corridor and into the kitchen,
where, I was led to believe, he would be offered a glass of champagne.

'Who the nametags for?' I asked Katie.

'For the journos.'

'The who!'

'The journalists. Susie invited a bunch of journos from various
magazines and papers. It's kind of a press release, you know. Just
to get our name out there.'

'Katie,' I said.

'Yes.'

She turned and smiled at me. Her hair was thin and recently
washed. It looked so soft, I wanted to reach out and stroke it. She
had big brown eyes, thin lips. I was broken to think that such a
person could have voted for me not to be there.

I fetched myself a glass of champagne from the kitchen, and
was almost cornered into a conversation with Denis, Denis,
Denis, but got away just in time. I watched him move silently
through the house, long neck lowering his head around corners
like a curious giraffe.

I drank several glasses of champagne as the corridor of my
house slowly filled up with journos and other nametagless people. The RDFM people had done a fairly impressive job of redecorating my passage. Lights had been placed all along the walls
to combat the heavy darkness which had always hung over my

house. The bare walls had been covered with images of Khoi people, and patterned clothes.

The journos stood in small groups making polite chit chat. I drifted through them like a ghost, unnoticed. I leant against my bedroom door, to which I'd fastened the stop sign that had once been used for my coffee table. I hoped it'd get the message across. A young black journo of about thirty leant on the wall opposite my door, about a metre and half away from me. He caught my eye, and nodded his head. I nodded back.

Until half a moment after our mutual recognition, he'd been the only black person in the room. But then a large woman in a brightly coloured, one-piece outfit entered. As the stares of every individual in the room shifted toward her, I could feel the energy washing over me like a strong backwash rushing out to sea. The woman stood in the doorway, still, acknowledging her moment of arrival and making a show out of wiping her boots on the front doormat.

One of the female journos, a forty-something woman with clipped blond hair, wearing a white blouse came scampering down the corridor to meet her.

'Ooh, hellooo,' she cried. 'I'm so very glad you came. We've all been just waiting for you!'

She put her arm around the newly arrived woman. In the light I could see her face was soft and rounded, except for her cheekbones which were slightly pronounced, giving her an altogether pleasant air. I felt bad in fact, for having judged her grin as one of arrogance, for I saw now as she smiled to the perky blond journo whose tag identified her as Lynn, it was in fact one of slight fear.

She was led down the corridor with promises of champagne. Everyone crowded around her: their little mascot, to carry above their heads, like cheerleaders at a sports match. I watched her smile and shake hands. She was clearly used to this.

I went outside again, slightly drunk, and flirted with the innocent Katie; I had no intention of taking it any further, and even if I had, I would surely have been disappointed. Since my encounter with Ridge, I had no desire to be with any other female. I believed that I'd been driven to commit the heinous crime so that I might know for certain it was a mistake. The thought would often rise in my mind, I'd try to repress it, but it would, almost certainly, rise again.

'Where's Ridge?' I asked Katie.

'She should be arriving now-now, I think. She's giving the opening speech.'

I sat alone in the corner of my garden. Lynn, the blond journo came walking out onto the verandah. She scrambled through her bag for a box of cigarettes, which she frantically opened, removed one, put it in her mouth, had a few fast pulls, flicked it onto the floor and squashed it. For some reason I was able to visualise our friend Lynn changing her tampon with the same grace. I kept quiet, feeling that simply thinking such a thought was punishment enough for her littering in my garden. The mental image, of course, was punishment for me too; and so I lit a cigarette of my own.

'She's starting!' Katie called to me from her table.

'What?'

'Susie's giving her opening speech. Come. You must come.'

I went inside to find journos and non-journos alike standing silently, facing the stage at the end of my corridor. A podium had been placed at the front of it. Susan now made her way through the crowd, and I learnt that she'd been secretly preening herself in my lounge.

The sneaky Ridge.

She climbed onto the stage, behind which a large banner, with a drawing of two Khoi people standing in front of a stylised version of my house, was hung. The words *Khoi House* were written at the top, and below them the words, *You know you should.*

Ridge was greeted with a round of applause. I took a few steps through the crowd who filled my passage length and breadth. She tapped the microphone, there was silence. Her hair had been perfectly straightened, from this distance – five metres – I couldn't tell how effectively the make-up had been applied. She was wearing a long black dress with shining emerald pieces down the sides. My distance from her plus the six glasses of champagne made her look slightly appealing. I was sickened by myself again. She stood perfectly erect, raising a single cue card to her face.

'Friends, South Africans, countrymen. Lend me your ears.'

The clichéd Ridge.

And yet she received laughter: lots of laughter. Even a single, but swiftly aborted clap.

'I am so glad to see you all here today. You are doing the right thing by being here, and honouring this occasion.'

The manipulative Ridge.

She knew her audience. She knew her target market. I could almost feel the white guilt dripping off the walls and the ceiling like water droplets in a sauna.

'I would like to start by telling you all a little bit more about the organisation I work for: RDees as we affectionately call it. RDFM is its official name. Restoring Dignity to Forgotten Minorities.'

Oh the righteous Ridge! Who are we to condemn thee? You have only noble desires!

I could hear shuffling of feet. Perhaps there were some good ones amongst us. Some whose stomachs churned at the use of the phrase: *RDees, as we affectionately call it.*

I stepped outside. Hearing her speak made me need to spit. I lit up a cigarette and was surprised when Lynn snuck out the back and joined me. She had smoking lines creeping out from beneath her face. Death, slowly forcing its way through.

'What a load of crap,' she said, and lit a cigarette.

'Excuse?'

'I hate these things.' Her voice was husky, but I could see how – in the right situation, with the right words – it could be sexy. 'You have to be nice to everyone. It's not my scene.' She lit a cigarette and blew the smoke out in a big explosive cloud.

'Mine neither.'

'So what are you doing here?'

'It's my house.'

'What! Oh, I'm sorry.'

'No, it's fine. I agree.'

'So why did you offer your house?'

'I didn't. It just happened.'

'What do you mean?'

'Hard to explain.'

'Would you care to try.'

'Long story.'

'When we've got time.'

'What do you mean?

'This sounds interesting. We'll talk later. Come.'

We finished our cigarettes and went back inside. Ridge was finishing off her speech.

'I'd like to thank everyone who has helped me along the way. You all know who you are. This has been a dream of mine. A dream of ours, for such a long time. And once again to all of you. Thank you for being here. Enjoy the snacks and the champagne.'

She climbed off the stage. The journos and the non-journos went back to sipping their champagne and idling about. A few of them were taking notes, but, for the most, they seemed rather uninterested. I watched Ridge making her thunderous way through the crowd. She received pats here and there, smiled at all she met.

'Byron!' she looked surprised to see me. 'What are you doing?'

'Standing.'

'Yes, I can see that. Come make yourself useful.'

I followed her.

With a notepad in her hand, and a professional mask on her face, she'd managed to integrate her newly acquired sexiness with a businesswoman- of-the-new-millennium look. If she'd chosen herself from a catalogue, I imagine the description would have read: *sexy but smart; chic but sophisticated.*

A cold wind was blowing down the street. The grey air made all the buildings – the white house opposite mine, the Peninsula School Feeding Association – look hostile. There was a sudden gust of wind that picked up an empty plastic bottle, dragging it along the pavement, and finally lifting it off the ground and smashing it into my fence. The sky was grey and the buildings looked like morbid war hospitals.

Ridge walked past me and knocked on the window of a large white van parked on my pavement. The driver climbed out holding a clipboard in his hand.

'I was hoping for all this stuff to arrive *earlier*. Anyway, Byron, now it's here. Won't you help this man bring it in? Where must I sign?' she asked the driver.

Another man climbed out of the passenger side of the van.

'Cold, hey?' he said to me as he opened the back door.

'Now hurry up please,' said Ridge. 'I want all the journos to get a pamphlet and a Khoi House T-shirt before they leave. Do you understand? Byron! Do you understand?'

'Yes, Ridge,' I said. The delivery man gave me an I-sympathise-with-you-my-friend sort of smile. I helped the two men carry the boxes filled with T-shirts and pamphlets up to the house. We dumped them in front of Katie, who sorted them into piles, handing some to the first group of journos to leave.

When all the boxes were out of the van I made my way past the remaining journos in my corridor, pulled the string out from around my neck and unlocked my bedroom door.

I closed the curtains before climbing onto my desk to have a look at the plants. I opened the cupboard, and to my delight – I felt tingles of joy run up my chest – I could see tiny green sprouts popping out of the soil. Yesterday there had been nothing, and now, today, all six were a full inch out of the mud. They were bright green, young green. I understood as I looked at my little sprouts why the word green could be used to describe naivety. They were so small, so harmless. This was their first experience of life, and I was here to see it. I was their father. I felt so proud I almost fell off my desk. I bent down and picked up the small watering jug next to my feet, gave each sapling a tiny sprinkle, a final loving look; then closed the door and hopped off the desk.

I went back into the passage, no longer feeling so hopeless about the situation unfolding around me. I felt like a mad scientist with a laboratory in my basement. These fools tramped about in the light, while I hid in the dark and created life. And the life I created was used to help a cripple.

I walked outside and sat down on a plastic chair that had somehow made its way into my driveway. For the past week Ridge had instructed me not to park my car on the inside; and so the driveway stood empty. She assured me there were plans for it in the near future.

The journos, one by one, were making their way out of the house.

I lit up a cigarette.

Lynn came walking out the front door, paused, saw me and came walking over to where I was sitting.

'Hi there,' she said.

'Hi.'

She let her bag fall in front of her again, and started rummaging through her belongings. She was wearing black stockings and a skirt that came down to below her knees and a white blouse. She had short blond hair and showed a hint of almost wrinkled cleavage. The way she stood, spoke, searched through her bag, gave her the aura of a woman who liked to have herself on display. I could picture her shitting, shaving her armpits, spitting her toothpaste into the basin. And this, I sensed, she wanted. She was unashamedly human. The clothes she wore, the way she looked up and said 'Sorry' before continuing to look through her bag, yelled out: we both know we shit and fart and fuck, but we have to wear clothes and be polite. You know it and I know it. I think I liked Lynn. I stood up. She found her cigarette.

After a long drag she spoke, the smoke puffing out her mouth with each word, like steam from an old engine: 'We must speak, all right?'

'Yeah,' I said.

'I'm interested to hear how this all came about. Cause we

certainly weren't told about it. Here.' She started rummaging through her bag again. 'Take my card. Give me a call. Please. This could make a great piece. All right?'

'Sure thing.'

'OK. Cheers. What's your name again?'

'Byron.'

'Hi, Byron. I'm,' she paused, and pointed mockingly at her nametag, 'Lynn.' She smiled and walked away.

I milled around the front garden for an hour or more. Smoking cigarettes and watching Ridge talk to the journos as they collected their free T-shirts and pamphlets, and made their way onto the street.

Then, at about five o'clock a group of younger people showed up. There were five, six of them. I'd seen their type before around Obs. Two had dreadlocks. They were all dressed in expensive clothes that were meant to look cheap. One of the girls was wearing a trucker cap. They had the whole white trash thing going, a fad that has always puzzled me: rich kids spending their parents' money to make themselves look like they come from trailer parks. Ashamed of their wealth and taking full advantage of it. One of the boys had an African drum, still in its case, slung over his shoulder.

'Yo! Yo! Yo!' he shouted.

I saw Ridge hurriedly talking to Katie. The two of them carried the table, earlier used for nametags, down to the front gate. They'd placed a metal money tin on top of it. Katie was holding a stamp in her hand.

The gate was buzzed open, and one by one the six gave their money to Ridge and received a stamp on the wrist.

Four journos had stayed behind. They were taking full advantage of the free champagne.

'Looks like the younger generation are taking over,' said one.

'Yes.' It was Denis speaking 'They have come to inherit what is theirs!' He put on a mock ghostly voice, and they all laughed.

'Glad we're leaving behind a legacy,' said one of the others.

'We'd better get going,' said another.

'Leave them to it,' said the fourth. 'No one told them they had to be here.'

They all laughed.

A while later when the older crowd had fully vacated the premises, a man in his twenties, with a British accent, arrived with a steel briefcase in his right hand. It reminded me of the case Ridge had brought with her on her first visit. The one in which she'd carried the bones. Apparently this guy was the DJ. He got in for free.

The microphone had been removed from the stage, and re-placed with DJ equipment. A large desk had been placed in the entrance to the kitchen, a list with drink prices stuck to the wall. No one but RDFM members, who were now wearing bright orange access permits around their necks, was allowed into the kitchen.

'Can I help you?' a young woman standing behind the bar asked me.

I was silent.

The minions were busy cutting up onions and rolls. The hotplates were going, they were starting to precook boerewors rolls.

'Sorry, is there anything?' the young woman asked again.

I turned around and walked away.

It was almost dark now and a long queue had formed outside my gate. People were chatting and laughing. Although they had not closed off the road, it seemed that cars were avoiding it.

Katie sat by the gate collecting entrance fees and placing stamps on wrists. Evidently the majority had not gone through Computicket.

'Byron!' Ridge was standing next to me on the veranda. She was holding a cigarette in her hand, she gently touched my right shoulder. It appeared that her makeup had been professionally applied, her whiskers were well hidden. Unfortunately not even make-up and dim lighting could hide her masculine jawline.

'What's going on here?' I asked her.

'It's the launch party, Byron. You've known about this all along.'

'It's getting enormous.'

'No one said you had to be here.'

'Well, I am.'

'Are you going to complain?'

'Maybe.'

'I'm running around like a mad woman, Byron. Barely touching base.' She walked away from me.

I pulled the key out from around my neck, went into my room, packed a bag.

Victoria said she was at her house, and yes, of course, Byron, I'd love you to, of course, come around.

*   *   *

I returned to Victoria's flat each evening for the next week. Once I considered telling her about Ridge, but immediately decided it was a terrible idea; was shocked at myself for even thinking of it. That night I broke out in a fever, and when I woke in the morning alongside her, was covered in sweat, shivering. The whole day I felt slightly woozy.

Each day I would go to my house and check on the plants: they were growing fast, and toward the end of the second week their leaves had taken on the appearance of the world's best loved weed.

Every afternoon – loyal as a nun – I'd make my way to Groote Schuur hospital and report to Pete on the state of the plants. He'd always elbow his way up the bed, give me a little smile, a bro, maybe scratch the front of his head. Every time I entered the hospital I was struck by its sheer size, the passageways were wide and stank of disinfectant. It was hardly a place of love and joy. Even fucking would be a sterile activity in this place; the smell of genitals and hospital food: *amore!* Although, if I were pursuing a relationship with Ridge, the medical waste room would be the ideal place to propose. I'd slip a catheter ring around her finger and watch her saddlebag hips wiggle with glee.

The hospital brought on the dark thoughts.

One afternoon, midway through the second week of the plants' lives I noticed a card next to Pete's bed. On the cover was a picture of a cartoon smiling motorbike, and beneath it the words: *Get better soon.* Although I was certain that the artist intended the motorbike's smile to be honest, knowing the circumstances of the victim in the bed made it look sneaky and evil. I held it in my hand – not opening it – my look clearly asking for an explanation. He was silent.

'From your parents?' I suggested.

'Long dead.'

'I'm sorry.'

'Ag.'

We sat silently for a while.

'The plants are doing really well.'

'That's lank good news, bro. Lank good.'

Each time I informed him of the plants' progress some colour would come to his face and the brown freckles on his forehead would become less noticeable. But within fifteen minutes
– almost to the second – he would fade away again and become
silent. My powers of distraction would wane: I could almost see
the pain coming back into his eyes as he remembered his situation. I would try and draw him out again: make a joke, ask him
when he was getting out of hospital, but nothing would work.
He'd simply shrug his shoulders and stare blankly across the
room.

As I sat there now, I realised that I was still within my designated time frame, and so asked him 'Who sent you this card
then?'

'Strangest thing, bro. Strangest fucking thing. Old chick of
mine from back in Thabazimbi. Haven't seen her in years.'

'How did she find out?'

'One of the nurses here is from Thabazimbi. They were family
friends or something. The nurse reckons she remembers me. I
don't remember her.'

'And the bike?'

'What?'

'The picture?'

'Private joke, bro. Hard to explain. We used to ride on my
bike together. Joke about how we were going to die. We thought
it was lank cool that we didn't fear death.' He paused for a long
while, then said, 'But in the end I got it worse.'

'Worse?'

'Than death, bro.'

'No, Pete. That's not true. There's so much to still live for.' I
felt the heaviness of the cliché on my tongue. It tasted like rotten liquorice. I wanted to spit. Why, I wondered, when I should

have spoken honestly, was I talking the kind of shit people talk on American TV shows.

'No, bro. Don't need to lie' he said. He was right. I knew he was. I said nothing.

His pleasant interval had come to its inevitable and abrupt end. He lay silent now. I must admit, I was getting kind of bored with the whole game: waiting for him to roll over and pull the sheets up to his face, releasing the day's smell into the air. I just wanted to walk out. The excitement of visiting a man in hospital had long since passed. But I pushed on. He'd given me purpose in life! And I still did feel a little better about myself after watching him lying there like an upturned beetle.

When the nasty smells came wafting up to my nose, I knew it was my cue to leave. I got up, gave him a half-bow and made my way out of the hospital.

While still sitting in the parking lot I got a telephone call from a number I didn't know. As always, in such situations, I considered not answering it. But then, because I was in good spirits, I did.

'Hello,' I said.

'Byron' I recognised the voice immediately, the harsh vowels and the croaky consonants.

'Lynn?'

'Yeah. You remember me?'

'How did you get my number?'

'I'm a journalist.'

'Oh.'

'Listen, Byron. I really want to meet with you. OK. The story about your house, it could be a killer. What you up to today?'

'Not much.'

'You want to meet?'

'Where?'

'How about Obs Café? In an hour?'

'OK.'

When I arrived at Obs Café, Lynn was sitting in the smoking section on a leather couch next to the large glass window. I spotted her from the road, and was reminded of my first meeting with Pete.

I quickly walked down the alleyway that runs in between the two sections of the café. It's dark and looks like a back road of an inner city slum. In reality it's perfectly safe. I slipped into the men's bathroom at the far end of the alleyway. I wanted to check that I looked all right. I hadn't washed my hair in a few days and it was starting to get a little thick. But I pulled it off my face, and tried the best I could to mould it into a decent shape. In recent months my eyes had started taking on a yellow hue. But now that I'd quit the marijuana smoking, the whites had begun to re-emerge. My face was all right. I looked down at my feet. She wouldn't notice.

I went through to the smoking section. She was scribbling some notes on a piece of paper. I stood about a metre away from her, hovering between sitting down and backing off. She hadn't noticed me and I wasn't sure what to do. I raised my hand and softly said her name.

'Oh, Byron' she said, 'thank you so much for coming.' She pointed at the leather couch opposite her. I sat down, and tucked my feet up against the couch. She was dressed again in a knee-length skirt, black stockings and a white blouse. She wore an open winter coat over the other clothes. But on seeing me dressed in only a shirt, took the coat right off – perhaps in sympathy, perhaps realising it was actually warm inside – and folded it up next to her. Her milky skin looked beautiful in the afternoon light, even her wrinkles seemed to tell stories, as they do in cheesy adverts for menopause medicine.

'I ate before I came,' she said 'But you must eat something if you want. On me.'

'It's fine,' I said.

'But really.'

'Fine.'

'OK, get a coffee.'

I did.

'Listen, Byron. The reason I want to chat to you is because, well, as you know, your house. That Susan Ridge lady contacted a number of us journalists.' I wanted to go down on her for not using the word 'journo'. 'As she framed it to us, the house had been bought up by her foundation. Or donated, I wasn't sure. But you're saying that it belongs to you.'

'That's right.'

'I mean that's a really strange story. I write for the *Cape Times* and sometimes have longer pieces in the *Dispatches*. The *Sunday Independent*. You know it?'

'I've seen it.'

'I've chatted to the editor and he's keen. So it will probably appear two weeks Sunday. If you want this, that is.'

'I do. Yeah. It will help.'

'We want to get pictures of the house too.'

'My girlfriend's a good photographer.'

'OK, well, I mean, we've got our own. But we can see, I'm sure. There's an excellent artist called Francois Smit. He does stylised artwork for the cover of the *Dispatches*. So I'm sure with a photo of your house, and whatnot, he could make an excellent design. It'll be the cover story.'

'Great.'

'I was thinking of the whole white guilt angle. The way a white woman is exploiting a real historical tragedy to make – from what I can tell – personal profit. She's preying on a collective consciousness. It's fascinating. It speaks volumes for our current situation.'

'OK.'

'And then of course you. Caught in the middle. I'm sure she exploited your own guilty conscience, or am I wrong?'

'Well, I kind of got caught up in it.'

'Against your will.'

'Yeah.'

'I mean, did she offer you anything in return?'

'Well, she did sort of offer me money.'

'Oh. And that's why you accepted?'

'Not really. She hasn't given me any. I don't think she will.'

'So, what happened?'

'It all happened really fast. She was so persistent. Kept showing up. Told me I had a place in the whole thing.'

'And so you let her take over?'

'I suppose.'

'And so she used this idea of your having a place. As if you were in some way responsible for the bones being there.'

'I suppose,' I said.

And that seemed good enough for her.

She had a way of making me feel comfortable in her presence. Normally I felt like a bit of a twit around people I didn't know. But she was great: a despiser of industry lingo – the word journo had no place in her vocabulary; a hater of people such as Ridge; a smoker, a drinker, a fucker, a farter, competent but fucked up, and proud of all of it.

Before leaving, we shook hands: she said she'd see me soon. I agreed. I considered asking her again how she'd tracked down my number, but in the end decided her original answer had been good enough.

The walk home was short, no more than forty metres. But since the clearing of the brain I was able to process facts at a greater speed, and so was able to cram in a few kilometres' worth of thinking.

Although I hadn't discussed it with Lynn, I knew I would be able to use the threat of this article as leverage over Ridge. I wasn't sure if I wanted her out altogether. She could stay, but she had to pay me. If she refused, she had to go, and finally I had the power to tell her this.

I had become not only a don't-ask-me-for-any-favours sort of guy, and a you- can't-judge-me-guy, but now also an I've-got-leverage-over-you kind of guy. It made me feel powerful. I was going to walk straight up to Ridge and demand some money and a couple of changes. Then, I'd say something like: *If you work with me, I can help save you from imminent destruction.* I might even accompany it with a sideways glance. I'd make sure to be smoking a cigarette.

When it came to my infidelity, I believed I was partially cured. After the heavy night's sweating, some of the guilt had been soaked up by the sheets. I knew that I must have stunk that morning. I only hoped Victoria hadn't somehow smelt Ridge's aroma in my sweat. I didn't think she had. I didn't feel a confession was necessary. In fact, I saw it as immoral. A dramatic woe-is-me, woe–is-me, I-confess-please-forgive-me scene, would do no one but myself any good. It would cause unnecessary pain. There was a part of me that still felt bad for what I'd done. But the fact that I felt bad made me feel good. It meant I had a conscience. And if I had a conscience, then I couldn't be such a bad guy after all.

* * *

I walked down my road past the parked cars and the sleeping
hobos. A few people were sitting at tables outside the coffee
shops sipping drinks, smoking cigarettes. But the otherwise
calm scene was destroyed by the long loud line of young people
formed outside my gate. I made my way to the front of the cue,
and was stopped by an unknown frizzy-haired woman who was
watching the entrance.

'Sorry, sir,' she said, 'but there's a queue. You must go to the
back.'

'It's my house.'

'Do you have a pass then, sir?'

'No. I live here. I don't need anything.'

'We all have passes. Those of us who work here. Do you work
here?'

'I live here. Where is Susan Ridge?'

'She's inside, sir. But I'm afraid she's busy.'

'Fuck off!' I said and pushed past her.

'Hey!' Her voice suddenly rose a hundred decibel points. She
sounded like a shrieking hyena. I could not help turning around
in fright. 'Come back here! Either you need one of these orange
passes,' she held one up from around her neck, 'Or you need
to pay!'

Ridge came out onto the balcony. Behind her I could see the
long corridor, filled with people. They were making their way
in and out of the display rooms. Some were leaning against the
walls and making chatter. A group of three girls made their way
past Ridge with full plates of food in their hands. They went and
joined a small group that was sitting in the front garden enjoying a meal.

'Ridge,' I said to her 'Tell her that I'm allowed into my house.'

Ridge raised her hand in apology to the woman at the entrance.

'This is my fault, Byron. Sorry. I will explain. Come to my office.'

She was dressed functionally: a pair of blue jeans, a belt around which she'd hung a thick set of keys. She wore a dark blue hoodie with the RDFM logo on the back. Just past the entranceway I paused and looked inside the large room to my immediate left. It's the largest bedroom in my house, but I've always found it too cold to live in. It has a fireplace in the corner – the chimney's blocked – large wooden floors, a high patterned ceiling, rounded bay windows which look out onto the mulberry tree in the front garden. It had been cleared, except for two large piles of mattresses in the far corner.

'What's going on there?' I asked Ridge.

'Come, Byron.' She was busy unlocking the lounge door.

We went inside, and she locked it behind us.

Despite her promise that I should be able to use this room whenever I liked, I hadn't set foot in it since her arrival. There were several beds in the far corner of the room, below the small window. There was a soft-drink machine, a pool table. Despite the installation of two designer lamps, the room was still covered in the thick molasses-like darkness, which has always filled every corner of my house. In the other corner, nearer to the entrance, in between the fireplace and the cupboards, she'd placed her desk.

'Take a seat, Byron.' She made her way round to the back of the desk.

'I will.'

'I really must apologise.' She leant forward on her desk. Had she been wearing a low-cut blouse, her boobs would have been showing. Her hair was starting to frizz again, and she'd tied it back in a ponytail. 'It completely skipped my mind to give you an access pass. Do you have an ID photo on hand?'

'Ridge. This is my house!'

'We're doing this for you. It's for safety reasons. We don't want just anyone traipsing in off the street.'

'But you recognise me.'

'There are new people working under me now. I can't tell them all. It just makes it so much easier.'

'I don't have an ID photo. This is mad!'

'Don't worry. I have a Polaroid in my cupboard. I'm having to make so many at the moment. Oh, you won't believe how difficult it's been. Running this place is a nightmare.' She started laughing as she got up and unlocked one of the cupboards. She brought out a camera. 'Would you just stand up for a second, By. It would help a lot.'

'Ridge. I don't – .'

'Come, By. Let's just get this over and done with.'

I stood up and took a few steps back. She held the camera up, said 'Smile,' and the light flashed.

'There we go. I bought this camera especially for taking these pass photos. It's unbelievable. So expensive.'

She sat behind her desk, and started putting my access card together.

'We've had to spend so much money on this whole thing. It's really beginning to cost way more than I thought. I don't even know if we're going to make a profit. Not important. But. Here you go.' She'd finished laminating my access pass and handed it to me. 'Just hang it around your neck and you can come and go as you please. No one will hassle you now.'

I looked down at the card. My hair was messed in the picture.

The card was orange, and said that I was an employee of RDFM. Then there was a section that said, VIP, yes, no. She'd ticked the no block.

'What's this here?' I asked her pointing at the block.

'That's nothing. It's just to get into *this* room. It's because we're sleeping in here now. And we store all our things in the cupboard.'

'And the garden?'

'That's still out of bounds. We have to be careful who we let where.'

'Has the excavation started?'

'Not yet. We're waiting for all sorts of things to clear.'

'Have you sent the other bones to the lab?'

'We don't want to have people traipsing mud through your house. We want to keep it clean for you.'

'Do you know yet?'

'What?'

'About the bones. The one I found. Others. Are they Khoi bones?'

'There's all sorts of paperwork. But yes. We can be pretty sure. I think that's all for now.'

'What's happening with those mattresses in the lounge?'

'Oh those. Yes. Hang on a second.' She leant down and brought out a flyer from a box on the floor.

'Khoi Lodge!' I said.

'Yes. There's been an interest in a backpacker's.'

'By who?'

'Guests. Foreigners passing through. Some suggested that we turn it into a backpacker's. So we're using that front room over there. It's the one that I think is best suited to it. What do you think?'

'Why didn't you ask me about this before?'

'An executive board was elected. It has the power to make these sorts of decisions. It's not that we want to exclude anyone. It's just to make decision-making more efficient.'

'Who's on it? Why not me?'

'It consists of myself. I'm the chairman. Then it's Katie. And then Alison. The girl at the front gate.'

'Why didn't I get an invite?'

'You haven't shown much interest in the project. We thought you wouldn't care.'

'When am I going to start making some money from this? You haven't paid me!'

'Just as soon as we cover our costs. The start-up costs have been large. Larger than expected.'

'When will I start getting money?'

'Soon, By. Very soon.'

'You must pay me.'

'I will. Just bear with me, OK? We have to cover our costs. I can't give out more than I bring in! It doesn't make economic sense. But I must get to work now. Is there anything else?'

I considered playing my trump card, but decided to keep it up my sleeve for a little while longer.

'Nothing,' I said and left the room.

In Ridge's mind she was a step ahead of me. But she didn't know that I'd gone nuclear. I could blow her out of my house as quickly as she'd come upon it. The slimy little bitch. If she didn't start paying me soon, I'd let Lynn go ahead with the article. I'd be a hero then, and Ridge would be finished.

* * *

I slept over at Victoria's house that night and was woken the next morning by a phone call from Lynn. She wanted to come back to the house and take some photographs, maybe speak to some of the people from RDFM. Was Ridge going to be there?

I asked to meet her around the corner so none of Ridge's people would see us. I parked three blocks away and walked along the dirty streets. I stopped at the vendors and bought myself a packet of chips for one rand fifty. When you walk along the pavements in Obs there are always concrete coverings above your head. They're the underside of balconies that hang over the street, but you feel like you're walking along a corridor. The vendors always have fires going on which they cook the boerewors rolls and chicken pieces, and the smoke has stained the overhangs black, like the pavements and the walls on which the dirty people lean. There are only three vendors but about fifteen other people who hang around them. Some are their friends, others hobos looking for change. One of the hobos tried to make small talk with me. But I knew it was foreplay for begging and walked away.

I kept munching on my chips and looking down at my feet. I was feeling nervous. Another hobo sitting in a doorway called out for some coins, I pretended not to hear him. When I rounded the corner of Station onto Lower Main, I dropped the empty chip packet into the dustbin. I could see Lynn standing outside Obs Café: she was extinguishing a cigarette with her foot. I kept walking toward her and when I got near said, 'Hey!'

'Hey, Byron. How you doing? Where were you?'

'Girlfriend's house.'

I reached her. We were past the phase of shaking hands,

and not yet intimate enough to hug or kiss. There was an awkward stammering, a step forward, a step back. A should we, or shouldn't we. In the end we didn't embrace, and both sort of laughed. I picked up my right foot and ran it down the back of my leg.

'So,' she said 'Should we go down to the house?'

'Yeah.' She had a camera case slung over her shoulder. 'Are you?' I said, pointing at it.

'Digital. Yeah, I take photos too. Why didn't you want to meet there?'

'Because. Well, how are you planning to get inside?'

'With you!' She was visibly shocked by my question.

'I don't know if I can. Get you in.'

'What! Byron. It's your house' she said.

'I know. But.'

'But?'

'It's hard to explain. *I* even need a pass to get in.'

'Oh, Byron.' She gave me a look of motherly affection. 'You poor thing. You've really let them walk all over you.'

'Come,' I said.

There was no queue and so we went straight to the front of the line, where Alison, the bushy black-haired wonder, gave me an exaggerated benign smile. I in turn made a show out of shoving the pass in her face.

'Are you a student, ma'am?' she asked Lynn, with no trace of irony in her voice.

'I'm a journalist.'

'Oh,' she said. 'Well. Do you have your nametag from the first day?'

'No.'

'Umm . . . ' Alison looked up to the front door, expecting

some sort of help. But none came. 'Susan said we could let in journos.'

'Let me in then.'

'All right. You'll only say good things, I hope.' Alison giggled.

We walked up the front path, the garden was filled with people eating curry and rice off paper plates, drinking beers. They were laughing loudly, some smoking cigarettes. Ridge had indeed found a use for the carport which I had been forbidden to use. A number of her cronies had set up tables selling T-shirts and small booklets. There were pamphlets being handed out for free, and confectionaries on sale.

The corridor inside had continuous traffic, people making their way in and out of the various display areas. While I'd been away the first room to the immediate left had been filled with steel bunk beds and the mattresses had been placed on top of them. On some there were sleeping bags and rucksacks.

The entrance to the kitchen was still blocked, by a now more permanent feature. On the wall, below the drinks list, was a daily menu. On Wednesday, for instance, you would get curry and rice. On Sunday there was a roast. On Monday macaroni cheese. Three of Ridge's minions were in the kitchen and Katie was serving. Lynn kept taking photographs, and was even ambitious enough to climb onto the stage so that she could get a better view of the garden, as the DJ-ing equipment and microphone made it completely invisible from the passageway.

'Do you think Ridge is here?' she asked me.

'I don't know. Could be in her office.'

'Which is . . .'

'Here.' I took her to the lounge. 'Do you want me to come with you?'

She shook her head, then knocked on the door. Ridge opened.

Lynn introduced herself, then disappeared inside. The door was closed.

I went out the front door. My swing seat was gone. I looked across my front garden at the groups of people in their late teens and early twenties, sitting in groups, eating food and chatting. I saw Alison scribbling down notes in a small book. Multiple branches had been stripped from my mulberry tree, and some hippie in a tie-dyed T-shirt had used them to make dream catchers. He'd set up a stall in my driveway.

My swing seat had been replaced by a row of plastic chairs decorated in cheesy African designs. As I sat there and looked at the fake beads wrapped around the legs I really wanted to cry. I felt so upset that my swing seat had been taken. It was my one true joy. I'd spent so many hours sitting on the cushions watching the world pass me by and hoping for nothing, wanting nothing. But now, I could no longer do that. That simple joy had been stolen from me.

And then, as if God had decided to grant me a small mercy, a picture appeared before my eyes. The skies were grey, and there was a single patch in the centre of my vision where the sun was creating a golden split. The white houses had a yellowish tinge, the rooftops suddenly appeared self-conscious, ashamed of how normal they were when compared to the two creatures strutting down the road. One was a tall man with messy hair, a thick beard, khaki clothes. Beneath his arms were two large wooden crutches, the type I would have sworn had gone out of use in the Middle Ages. The top part of his leg – the only part left – was covered in a bandage. The end of the bandage was tied in a knot. It made me think of Ridge: the way in which I'd imagined the back of her head to be tied up like the end of a sausage; the dark craving in the soul to see things unbeautiful.

The other was a short man, with a long grey ponytail, a barrel chest, an innocent smile the size of a watermelon plastered across his face.

'Hey there, Byron!' Roddy called out.

I jumped to my feet and was unable to stop myself from smiling. The two men were stopped at the front gate by Alison.

'No, Alison!' I shouted. 'These are my friends.'

'It's a forty rand cover charge if they're students!' she shouted back.

'Yes. But these are my friends.' I was standing right next to her now, half a metre from Pete and Roddy.

'Either you have an access pass, or it's fifty rand. Forty rand with a student card.'

'What's going on here, bro?' The only thing keeping Pete from falling over were the two oar-shaped crutches that rested within his armpits.

'This is a museum,' said Alison, punctuating her words with a twitch of the head. 'And there is an entrance fee!'

'These are my friends. OK, just wait. I'm going to Ridge.'

I ran inside and knocked on the lounge door. 'Ridge!' I cried. 'I have some friends who want to come and visit me. You must tell Alison to let them in.'

'What?' she shouted.

I repeated myself.

'I'll be out just now, Byron. Wait. I'm in a meeting.'

'Please, Ridge. This can't wait.'

I heard her get up and walk across the room, the door opened.

'How many are there?'

'Just two.'

'Humphhh!' She let out a long sigh, then pushed her way past me. 'Alison. Let them in, it's fine.' Then to me 'But you'd better stay in your room.'

Pete came crutching up the front path, Roddy walking behind him. They stopped at the front door.

'Bro. What in God?'

'Come to my room.'

I pulled the string out from around my neck and unlocked the door to my bedroom. Pete had a bag on his back and was struggling to use his crutches. They propped his body up too high, he looked uncomfortable. He gave me a smile as he made his way into the room and sat down on the chair next to my desk. His sausage leg didn't quite make it to the end of the chair, and I found myself looking away too fast. I looked back again. Then away.

He seemed to have incorporated the half-leg fairly well into his personality. He slunk his weight back on the chair and displayed the stump the way a vulgar man might display his cock.

'Couldn't of spent another day there, bro.'

'How'd you two arrive at the same time?'

'Met on the street. Know each other from around Obs,' said Pete.

'We know each other, Byron,' said Roddy. 'I've been busy, man. I've been doing all sorts of things that are the crazy things, man. I must tell you about them.'

'And the crutches?'

'This is what bums like me get from the hospital.'

'How you get around?'

'Catch a ride to my house now-now. I want to check out the plants, bro. For myself. They going to have to see me through. Isaiah reckons, bro, that his people are fizzing at the poes to get their hands on this shit. We'll make a killing.'

'I can help you guys out,' said Roddy 'I know all the right people to sell it to.'

'It's fine, Roddy,' said Pete.

'I'll show you,' I said. 'Stay seated.'

'What else am I going to do, bro.'

I made my way around Pete and climbed onto the table. I unlocked the top cupboard and found the plant that I believed looked the healthiest. I handed it to him.

He stared at it for several minutes in absolute silence, then placed it on my table, turned his head away from me and raised the inside of his arm against his eyes. He covered them for several seconds. I could see his chest gently heaving. I felt terribly awkward. I'd seen Victoria's body contort with sorrow when she had her serious crying sessions. But she was a girl. And no matter what anyone said, it was all right for girls to cry, and a little strange for boys. Especially when they were big hairy boys with one leg. I didn't know what to do. I walked over to the corner of my room and pretended to inspect the quality of my curtains.

Roddy came over and joined me. Like a moron he tried to open them. I grabbed hold of him and forced him across the room away from me. He made little squealing sounds. Our tussle helped break the awkwardness of the situation.

Pete brought his arm away from his face and started laughing as he wiped his tears. I walked toward him and tried to rest my hand on his shoulder. But I just couldn't bring myself to do it. I did feel sorry for Pete. But my sorrow was outweighed by my disgust. Now that I could see his body in its full mutilated horror, his presence made me feel uncomfortable.

'Are you all right?' I asked him, trying to sound as polite as possible.

'It's from my mom, bro. I haven't cried since I was a little fucking kid. I'm fucking sorry.'

I saw some toilet paper sitting on my bookshelf, and handed him a strip.

'Thanks, bro,' he said.

'Did you know, Byron,' Roddy started speaking, 'when they went to the moon, Neil Armstrong and Buzz Aldrin, they were arguing about who was going to walk first. So I pushed my way past them both. I was on the moon first. I planted a weed seed on the moon. It's still there man. But NASA had to cover the whole thing up. So I lost my place in history.' He threw the pamphlet he'd been reading onto the floor and fell back onto the bed in despair. This old injustice coming back to haunt him. Pete giggled through his tears. He evidently enjoyed Roddy's nonsense. At that point anything that distracted me from the blubbering one-legged man was welcome, and so I smiled.

'Well done, Roddy,' I said.

'Yeah, well done,' said Pete.

He wiped his eyes again with the back of his sleeve. It was the same top he always wore – like the standard GI Joe kid's toy: outfit and man in one.

'I'm sorry, bro. But I never knew until now if you were telling the truth or not. About the plants. No offence. I wasn't sure.'

'It's all right' I said.

As the tears cleared away from his face I stopped feeling disgusted by him. My chest began to tingle a little, and then started bubbling. I knew what it was: a feeling I'd almost forgotten existed – pride. I was proud of myself. The don't-ask-me-for-any-favours guy! The I-support-my-one-legged-friend-and-ask-for-nothing-in-return guy! The don't-judge-me guy! That guy was reaping his rewards.

'It's my mom, bro.'

'What?'

'She was flattened by a truck, bro. Long ago. Nothing left. But some ou at the hospital gave me some shit which hadn't been totally fucked. In her handbag, bro. The little pillbox. That's how come it's got flowers and shit on it. It was filled with anti-depressants. But I kept it with me all the time, bro. And again. It's saved me. Cause of my mom, bro. She must have cared. Do you still have the box?'

'Of course.'

I fetched it from my top drawer and handed it to him. He held it to his face then placed it in one of his many pockets. He dropped his head back, closed his eyes.

'We must move them to the lower section, bro. Right now.'

'What?'

'The plants. To the lower section.'

'Already?'

'I told you, bro. These things grow lank fast. They're ready. Is the HP light still set up?'

'Ja.'

'Let's do it.'

'OK.'

'Wait,' Pete said. He opened up one of the many pockets on his khaki jacket and took out a bankie of weed. 'Got it on the way down here,' he said. 'Let's smoke.'

He started mulling it in the palm of his hand. I watched the weed heads break up into little pieces and could smell the fresh green scent filling my room. I must admit, I really wanted some at that moment. But when Pete had finished rolling, and had a few drags, he handed it to me, and I just said, 'No.'

That's right, the way they tell you to say no in posters. A new guy was emerging from within. An I-can-say-no kind of guy. Add that guy to the I-support-my-one-legged-friend guy, and you had a real somebody.

When the joint was finished and the room filled with smoke, Roddy and I started unpacking the small plants from the top shelf and moving them onto my desk. Pete had leant his crutches on the bookshelf and moved himself onto my bed where he sat scratching what was left of his left leg. The stump was still wrapped in a bandage, but toward the top you could see his dark skin and black hair. I wondered if Pete would ever have sex again.

He gave us instructions, and both Roddy and I obeyed. Somehow his injury had lent him an other-worldly quality. I guess this was because he knew, in part, what it was like to die. He was, literally, one foot in the grave.

When we'd raised the plants to the right level, and the high-powered sodium lamp had warmed right up, we all sat on my bed and admired the scene. The light gave off an extraterrestrial glow, like one might expect from a UFO. In the light, the plants looked like seaweed at the bottom of the ocean. And the light seemed to turn us yellow, giving each of us the look of a wax statue. Our brief moment of fame.

'What's going on in your house, Byron?' Roddy asked me.

'Ja, bro, what the hell?'

I jumped off the bed. 'It's hard to explain. It's a museum. Long story.'

There was a knock at the door.

'Byron!' It was Ridge.

'What?'

'I need to come in there.'

'No.'

I quickly shut the cupboard door, and locked the outside latch.

'What's wrong, bro?' Pete asked me.

'I must speak to you!' Ridge shouted.

'Five minutes. Please!'

She let out a loud and deliberate sigh.

'Sorry guys, I, umm . . . ' I felt terribly stupid. It must have looked to them like I'd become a prisoner in my own home, and there was no way I could spin it. If only I could explain that I was really in control. That I was really calling the shots. That I had a nuclear trump card up my sleeve. But it didn't matter. They'd know soon enough. I'd start making money from the house and the weed at the same time. I'd also be able to say no to drugs. I'd be the ultimate man. I'd be featured in men's magazines. But for now, they had to go.

'You gotta go, guys,' I said.

'What the fuck is going on here?' Pete asked again.

'I'll tell you soon.'

'All right,' said Pete. 'Fucking weird, bro! Anyways, I'll be here each day to check. Must go home now anyway. My electricity's probably finished. Fridge fucked.' He hobbled across the room and paused at the door. He tried to unlock it himself and lost his balance for a second. I stepped forward trying to help him.

'Fuck off, bro!' he said.

'Shit. I'm sorry.'

'I'm sorry,' he said. He stared at the floor for a few seconds. 'Just let me out.'

I moved toward the door, and rubbed up against his jacket. I could feel the weight of the dirt that had collected in the material. I saw a small red mark on the edge of the bandage. I didn't like being near him. He shuffled into the corridor. Everyone stepped aside, not even bothering to hide the fact that they were staring. They must have thought he was a hobo. A few of them glanced in my direction, as if asking what sort of a man I was to associate with a guy like Pete. He kept on hobbling very slowly along the corridor. He was a rather tragic sight. The crutches pushed his body out of line, the bandage was a little bit dirty. Just by looking at him, you could see that he stank. Unable to take any more, I looked down at my feet and pretended that nothing was happening.

When I looked up again the two men were gone and Ridge was staring at the electricity meter.

'Just this morning it said I had ninety days' electricity at current usage' she said to no one in particular. 'And now it says there're only thirty days. That doesn't make any sense.' She spun around. 'Oh, Byron. Come with me.'

'Where?'

'My office.'

She pulled out the thick set of keys that jangled on her belt, and unlocked the lounge door.

'Come inside, sit down. Where's your pass?'

'I don't have it on me.'

'You have to wear it at all times.'

'It's in my room.'

'I'm going to start fining people for not wearing their passes around their necks. You people are making it impossible for me to run this place.'

'Where's Lynn gone?'

'She left twenty minutes ago. That's what I want to speak to you about.'

'What?'

'She tells me she's doing a piece on the house.'

'Yes.'

'I got the feeling, Byron, that it's not going to be particularly flattering.'

'Maybe not.'

'You know this lady.'

'I do.'

'It wasn't a question. I don't want any bad publicity. Do you hear me?'

'Well then,' I felt power surge through me like electricity. 'Perhaps we need to talk.' I shifted my shoulders.

'Perhaps we do.'

'I can get her to pull the article.'

'Good.'

'Yes. But, if you want me to help you. You have to help me.' I couldn't believe I was talking like this. I was the star in a thriller. The good guy.

'OK.'

'I want my money. Firstly.'

'I've explained it to you, Byron. I can't give you money until I've brought it in. There can be no pay without profit.'

'That's not what we agreed.'

'It is. What else?'

'Well, if you can't pay. Then. You have to. You must leave. I've decided. It's final. You must leave right away. Else she'll print an article that will ruin your name.'

'Please. And how are you planning to make me go?'

'I'll get her to print it! I swear. I have the power.'

'Remember, Byron, how I told you our problems were related?'

'Yes.'

'I don't think you want to get yourself in a tangle, do you?'

'What?'

She sat silently for a few moments. I could hear the commotion in the corridor outside. People chatting and laughing, making their way in and out of the display rooms.

'I want to show you something,' she said, and leant down to unlock one of the drawers at the bottom of her desk. When she sat up straight again she was holding a wooden box covered with golden designs. She placed it on the desk in front of her and stroked the top of it with her hand.

'This was my mother's,' she said, and gave me a smile.

'That's nice.'

'She died.'

'Oh.'

'My father's a drunken lout. My brother's an electrician. Did you know that?'

'OK.'

'I've worked for everything I have, Byron. I wasn't given anything. And I don't have sympathy for lazy people.' She unclipped the box. 'I also don't have much time for stupid people.'

Out of the box she took a small purple bean bag and placed it on her desk. Then she took something else out. A bank bag. She held it up against the light at the end of her desk.

'What the fuck is that!' I made to grab it from her, but she retreated.

'What the fuck is it?' I asked again. But I knew. Of course, I knew what it was.

'You weren't the best I've ever had,' she said while admiring the packet. Inside was a used condom filled with semen. Next to it the silver red packet in which it had once been kept.

'That's mine,' I said.

'Mine,' she corrected me. 'It's really a very simple rule. During sexual intercourse, the man willingly gives his seed to the woman. That's the whole idea behind it. It was yours. You gave it to me.'

'You're fucked! In the head!'

'Not at all! If you hadn't been wearing this it would've landed up in my uterus. It's the same thing in the end. The ancient and sacred exchange between man and woman. I thank you for it. But don't forget whose it is.'

I sat lifeless and still on the chair. I could feel cold tingles in my feet.

She put it back in the box.

'This,' She indicated the purple bag 'This is for keeping it warm. To prevent it from coagulating. We wouldn't want that.' She placed the purple bag on top of the bank bag, closed the box and put it back in her bottom drawer.

'What the fuck are you going to do with that?'

'Nothing. Probably. Unless you give me no choice. I've told you before, Byron. I really don't like looking the fool. So you make sure that article doesn't appear in the paper. You say you have the power.'

'What if I don't?'

'Then I'll take your lovely lady out for tea and give her a similar demonstration.'

'She'll never believe you.'

'I'm sure she won't mind waiting for a DNA test.'

'You would never. She'll think you're mad.'

'It doesn't matter what she thinks of me. The point is she'll know you're a cheater. An unfaithful lout. And that will be that. I know that you do love her. Despite what you may have done.'

'Fuck you, Ridge!' I stood up. 'I will not let this happen!'

'Get out of my office.'

'Ridge! This is not fair!'

'Get out!' she stood up. 'It's up to you. You can save your relationship. You know what you have to do. Now swim along!'

*   *   *

I ran into the corridor and unlocked my bedroom door. I kicked
through a pile of clothes on my floor, and threw another off
my bed. I picked up my phone. I needed to get onto the street
where no one would be able to hear my conversation.

'Byron!' Alison shouted as I made my way past her. 'Where is
your access pass?'

'In my room.'

'You must have it on at all times! Susan is going to start fining
us! You should set the example.'

Ignoring her, I made my way up Trill Road against a heavy flow
of young traffic. Tens of people were making their way toward
my house. Some had bags on their backs, sleeping bags in their
hands, a few had drums around their necks. I made my way past
them, bumping into a very fat guy with a red face and dirty black
hair. He shoved me out of the way with his fatty man-breasts. I
could smell his armpits.

I turned onto Lower Main Road and nearly bumped into the
old-style red postbox on the corner. My phone was struggling to
get reception and so I continued along the road, past the bottle
store and stopped alongside a restaurant dumping-alley. I had
signal. I scrolled through the names in the phonebook, and dialled Lynn. It rang for thirty seconds and went to voice message.
I dialled again, and this time she answered immediately.

'Byron,' she said.

'Yes, it's me.'

'Yes, Byron. Sorry I left without saying goodbye. I couldn't find you.'

'I need you to pull the article.'

'What! I thought you wanted it.'

'I did but –.'

A group of people with dreadlocks and pierced lips came walking past me. One of them shouted 'Hurry up, bru!' to a lagging friend.

'Byron, are you there?'

They passed.

'Yes. I need you to pull it. I've changed my mind.'

'That's impossible, Byron. It doesn't work like that.'

'Why?'

'An article that was meant to appear this Sunday has been pulled. They need my article this Sunday.'

'What! No, please. Please try get rid of it.'

Music started playing in a venue upstairs.

'I can't hear you, Byron.'

'I said, please try and pull it!'

'I can't. That's ridiculous! The editor's already approved it. It has to be in tomorrow. Printed Sunday.'

'Lynn!'

'Bye, Byron.'

I ran down my road. The people I'd passed on the way up were now queuing outside my front gate. I pushed to the front of the line.

'I must get back in.'

'Access pass?'

'In my room.'

'Byron!'

'Alison!' I placed my hands on her desk. 'Please, Alison. Please. Please. Please!'

'It's not fair to put me in this situation,' she said, and looked down at her money box. I took this to be a turning of the blind eye. I scampered up the path and was blocked by a large group of people loitering outside the front door. I pushed through them.

'Chill, bru,' one of them said to me.

All the beds in the large room had been taken: they were covered with sleeping bags, rucksacks. On one of the lower bunks a young couple was making out. People were standing around, laughing, smoking.

Ridge came storming down the corridor past me. I felt a rush of nerves run up my sides as I got a whiff of her acrid perfume.

'What is causing this!' She frantically tapped on the electricity meter. 'This can't be the DJ equipment! Where is Ben? Somebody!'

'I think he's just arrived,' someone muttered.

'Bring him here. I must speak to him.'

Ridge looked at me, but her eyes carried no hint of our earlier conversation. It was as if I had disappeared from her world: I served no function right then, and so being the solipsist cunt she was she'd made me disappear. It gave me a measure of comfort. I flattened myself against my doorway, and as her eyes moved past me, I made to walk toward the lounge door. Ben, the DJ, came in through the front door, and Ridge started tapping her finger against the electricity meter. He shrugged his shoulders.

I rapped my fist against the lounge door, hoping that somehow I would be let in by one of her lesser minions. There was no answer. I knocked again. And again: silence.

'What are you doing, Byron?' Suddenly she was standing in front of me.

'I was just checking. If you were. In there?'

'Oh, please. You just saw me!' She looked away. 'Ben! You're sure it isn't your equipment causing the drainage?'

'Yes,' said Ben. 'It's not even plugged in now.'

'OK,' she said 'Go and set up. I want to get the music started. Byron! Can I help you?'

'Ridge. Please. Just give me the thing.'

'What thing?'

'Please, Ridge. This will ruin my life.'

'Move, Byron!' She pushed me aside.

'Ridge!' I dug my fingers into her shoulders. 'You have to give it to me! You have to!'

She didn't even bother responding, but simply shook her body free of mine: a shake without sex. Her features now defined her differently: where once they had weakened her sexuality, they now enhanced her power. Her masculine jawline gave her an air of authority; even the frizzy tips of her hair looked like steel wool, touching them would rip open my fingertips. Her shoulders were wide like an ox's. Her green eyes shook like those of a psychopath. What the fuck was I up against? I lowered my eyes and walked away, and in that instant we both knew that she was the bigger man.

I walked into my room, kicked a pile of clothes along the floor. Sat on my bed. Stood up. Tried to call Lynn, she didn't answer. My head was spinning, I could taste acid in my throat. I couldn't sit still; but then, I couldn't move.

Recently I'd been enjoying a clear head. I'd even managed to say no to a joint. But now my thoughts were all shaken up again. My mind felt like the liquid in a spirit level: the contraption being played with by a lunatic child. I felt like the old Byron. The stupid stoned Byron. All the improvements I'd thought I was making would count for nothing now. I paced. I took a cigarette out of my pocket and lit it up. In order to calm myself, I imagined the path the nicotine would take through my body. I visualised the smoke entering my lungs, being absorbed by microvilli, nicotine sent to my heart, pumped through my body. Whether it was the drug or the exercise, I could not be sure, I began to feel a sense of wellbeing pass over me. A sense of resignation: I accepted my powerlessness and it made me feel powerful.

But it was only an illusion, and seconds later I was panicking again. But within the panic there was now a sense of order. This was a time to be rational. There was no chance that Ridge would hand me the condom voluntarily. There was no chance that the article would be pulled. But I had a greater chance of stealing the condom than I did of convincing the editor of a Sunday newspaper to drop an article. I needed to find a way of getting into my lounge and stealing the box.

I walked over to my window and made a tiny gap in the curtain. The two stands directly outside my window were selling T-shirts, small books, and giving away pamphlets. Angling the curtain slightly I was able to see the hippie at the end of the driveway selling dream catchers that he'd made from my mulberry tree. He'd managed to make about thirty of them and I'd earlier seen that they were selling for between one and four hundred rand. Surely I was entitled to some of the revenue. But that was not for now. It was getting dark. The garden was full. The music had started playing in my corridor and the crowd was starting to dance.

I hadn't seen my house at night since the museum, slash, whatever the fuck it was, had opened. I opened my bedroom

door now. I did not like what I saw. The passage was completely packed, and people were dancing hard. I could feel the old
wooden floors shake under their weight. There were lights flashing off the stage, and the music, the bass, each note was intense.
The DJ held the crowd like Hitler at one of his rallies. People
held their hands in the air and responded with tiny adjustments
of the body to every whirl that came from the speakers. The
DJ was loving it. The genre's called trance. And once you've listened to it, it's easy to understand why. It would take a team of
crack scientists to tell where one song ends and the next begins.
It blurs into one hypnotic drawl and drives the crowd wild.

Outside there was a similar lunacy, and the moon, almost full,
was looking down on all of it.

People were sitting in circles drinking beer, smoking joints
and cigarettes. In the corner of the driveway was a man I recognised from the street. I'd seen him a few days earlier collecting
a rat from a trap he'd set by the railway lines. I'd thought it was
a little strange at the time, but hadn't thought of it since. And
now, here he was, roasting rats over an open flame. I looked
around and saw, beneath the bare mulberry tree, a young man
eating a roasted rat off a skewer. I walked over to him and asked,
'What are you eating?'

'Hey, bru!' He was dressed quite normally, this one: a T-shirt,
long pants. 'I bought it from that dude over there. It's called
ixyong, it's an ancient Khoi delicacy.'

'All right!' I said.

'You should try it, bru. It's lank good.'

I walked away from him. The beat of the trance music reached
into every corner. All the people looked hypnotised. I noticed
large pupils in some, red eyes in others. There was evidently no
shortage of drugs.

Some of the groups of stoners were reading pamphlets handed out by Ridge. I overheard one young man explaining what
he'd read to the rest of his group. It was clear that he was high
and drunk.

The T-shirt stand was doing good business. I noticed one with
the RDFM slogan on the back. Another said: *Look what we have
done.* A third read: *You know you should.*

Out of the corner of my eye I saw a young woman I recognised
standing in the line to buy a roasted rat, or ixyong, as it'd be
marketed to her. It was the Gothic girl from the street, the one
whose notebook I'd written a message in. I stood still for a while
watching her as she paid for her roasted rat, took a big bite and
walked away from the fire. She stood silently in the corner of
the garden eating it, and when she'd finished wiping her hands
and face and disposed of the empty skewer, she started walking
through the crowd. She'd walk up to a person, tear a page out
of her book and hand it to them. They'd have a small chat, fold
the page up and place it in their pocket.

I stood under the mulberry tree and lit up a cigarette, then
leant my head against the trunk and looked backwards at the
moon through the bare branches. The hippie had really done
a number on my tree. It was mutilated. There were no leaves,
no mulberries, and the branches left behind were short and
stumpy.

'Hey!' a voice called out to me.

I brought my head forward and saw the Gothic girl standing
two metres away from me. She was holding a book in her hand.

'You remember me?' she asked.

'Ja.'

She started walking toward me. I hadn't noticed before but
she had a definite sexiness to her swagger. Her voice was still

rough. She was the inversion of Ridge, with her manly body and feminine voice. She came right up to me, took a cigarette out of her bag and lit it up.

'This is the next stage of my project,' she said. 'Remember I was getting people to write down whatever they wanted? Well now I'm giving these things away to different people. Randomly you know. You know what I mean?'

'No.'

'Well, here.' She tore a page out of her book and handed it to me. 'Here's a thought for you. Someone else wrote this down off the top of their head. Now you can be inspired by it.'

'What happened to mine?'

'Byron, right?'

'Ja.'

'Byron, Byron, Byron,' she said as she flipped through her book. 'I must have given it away already, Byron. To someone else. No idea who, I'm afraid.'

'What am I supposed to do with this?' I asked, holding the piece of paper toward her.

'I want you to muse on what's written there. Then later, I'll come around again. Maybe only tomorrow or something. And then get you to write whatever this phrase inspires in you.'

'Ah, fuck.'

'What?'

'Nothing. I must go.'

'I never knew you hung out at Khoi House. It's fantastic, hey?'

'Ja,' I said, and walked away from her.

'Don't forget to read your message!' she shouted after me.

I scrunched it up and placed it in my back pocket.

I walked up to the front door, and at the entrance was accosted by Ridge.

'There you are,' she said.

'What's wrong?'

'There's only one option left!' She took me by the arm and dragged me toward the electricity meter. 'You see this meter here,' she screamed over the noise.

'Yes. I can't hear you. Too loud!'

She brought her mouth toward me and let her tongue touch my ear as she spoke.

'This meter tells you how many days' power you have left. It estimates from current usage. This morning it told me I had ninety days left. Then suddenly this afternoon it tells me I have thirty days left. I've looked through the rest of the house. Yours is the only room I haven't checked.

'So?'

'What are you doing in there, Byron? What's suddenly taking up all the power?'

'It's none of your business.'

'You know it is!'

'Nothing. Leave me alone.'

'I've had a key cut for your room, Byron. I've been hugely respectful, and not broken our agreement. I haven't set foot in your room. But clearly you have no respect for me.'

'Piss off, Ridge!' I tried to walk away, but she gently grabbed hold of my shirt, and I froze like a man turned to stone by a witch.

'Come with me. Show me around your room.'

'No, Ridge. Fuck off. It's my room.'

'Then I'll look by myself.'

'No, Ridge!'

She marched away from me through the crowd toward my bedroom door. I watched her pull out her heavy set of keys and shuffle through them until she found the one for my room. I forced my way through the crowd, until I was standing right next to her. I tried to block her with my body, but she got the door unlocked and pushed it open.

'What's going on in here, Byron?' She shut the door behind us, and the hypnotic rhythms of the passageway faded slightly. She walked straight over to my cupboard and started tapping on the door.

'Why is this locked?'

'I keep my clothes in there. You lock yours too.'

'What is going on in there?'

She placed her ear to the cupboard door and listened to the loud hum created by the HP bulb.

'Please, Ridge.'

'Unlock it!'

'No.'

'Now.'

'It's my clothes.'

'Byron.' She looked at me the way a grade-school teacher looks at a naughty, but pathetic boy.

'You have to leave this alone. Please trust me, Susan. This is important. I'm supporting that guy with one leg. His whole life depends on this. Please!'

'Just open it.'

I felt like a hypnotised moron listening to the hypnotist. Every part of me wanted to refuse her, but somehow I found myself obeying. I pulled the string out from around my neck. My hand was shaking. I undid the lock, and stepped back. She opened the cupboard door, and as she did so the light crept across the room. There they were, standing in front of her. All six plants, beautiful and healthy, basking in the bright light of the high-power sodium lamp. The culprit in the power-sucking scandal had been found.

She stood silently for several seconds staring at them. I could feel her thoughts. She'd always considered me a useless sack of shit, and this was confirming it for her. What sort of a man spends all his time nurturing a plant that makes people stupid, she was thinking. Oh, how she was loving having it all confirmed.

Then there was a pause. I could feel her thoughts shifting. The rhythm, or something I could not describe about her, had changed.

'I'm calling the police. I'll let them deal with this,' she said without looking at me.

'No!' I screamed after her. But she ignored me.

I felt something rise in me. It was a primal drive that reminded me that no matter what Ridge might have over me, I was still stronger than her. I was a fucking man! In the next moment I felt like I was watching myself from the corner of the room, as I lunged at Ridge, grabbed her by her shirt and pulled her body close to mine. I felt her chest inflate as she gasped with shock. I pushed her against the table and brought my eyes close to hers. She was trying to look tough, but I could see she was afraid. The little whore was shitting herself. There was still a child somewhere in Ridge.

'Listen here, you fucking bitch!' I said.

Her psycho green eyes were shaking. 'You will not tell the police anything. This is all I have left.'

I could smell her breath, and feel the hot air on my face. Then suddenly, she shifted gear again. Something in her switched and she screamed: 'Don't you dare!' She hissed like a neurotic cat. I jumped back, I suddenly felt vulgar and hairy. The power surged across the room. I'd given myself away.

'I'm giving you a choice. And you should be very grateful,' she said, pushing her curly hair back behind her ears. 'Either you throw these things away. Cut them up. Or I call the police.'

'Ridge. This is my room. We said I could do what I wanted in here.' I sounded like a little boy in trouble with his mommy.

'This room is still subject to the rules of the house. You can do as you please, so long as you do not violate any of the greater codes. Now make up your mind. I'm giving you twenty minutes.'

She turned around and walked out the room. I stood still, my heart racing, the palms of my hands heavy with sweat. I ran the sweat through my hair. There must be rationality in the mind of Ridge, surely. I could plead my case before her. I'd swallow my pride. I'd grovel. I'd beg for forgiveness. I'd beg for understanding.

I knocked on the lounge door. It opened immediately. She must have been standing by it, waiting for me.

'You've made up your mind?'

'Please, can I come in, Susan?'

She let me in, locked the door. Except for the two of us, the room was empty. She'd turned off the designer lights, and the only glow came from the laptop computer sitting on her desk.

I was silent for a few moments and could hear my thoughts mumbling about in my head. I needed to sound perfectly rational.

'What!' she snapped at me.

'Susan.'

'Byron.'

'I really need to ask you to be understanding. It's so important to me. I need to support that guy with one leg.'

'Do you know that Gothic-looking girl?'

'Yes. Why? Please, Ridge, it's serious. Please just show some mercy.'

'It's funny how our old selves can come back to bite us. Isn't it?' she said, and took a piece of paper out of her jacket pocket.

'What's that?'

'She said it was the second phase of her project. I didn't participate in the first. But anyway. Read it.'

I unfolded the piece of paper and was greeted by the distinct scrawls of Byron's hand: Don't ask me for any favours.

Byron Winterleaf.

Below it the Gothic girl had recorded the date, and the fact that I'd written it down in the grow-it-yourself shop.

'I didn't mean it like that,' I said. 'It was meant only as a joke.'

'You should have thought about it.'

'You would let me off it weren't for this?'

'You leave things all over the place. Not a care. If it isn't your seed, it's some half-baked thought. A recurring theme in your life.'

I'd let her lecture me. If it would help my case, I'd let her do it.

'Yes,' I said.

'Oh! Some agreement. I think you need some consequences. That's what you're missing in your life. A bit of concrete.'

'I know. Please just let me go on this.'

'My offer stays the same. You have ten minutes to decide.'

I fought my way through the hypnotised crowd, and back into my room. The only option available to me was to take the plants somewhere else. I didn't want to involve Victoria. Pete had told me at the beginning that his place was out, which meant that the

only person left was Roddy. I took all six plants out of my cupboard and placed them on the desk. I had to ensure that none
of the guests saw what I was transporting. I had to find a way to
disguise them.

I took some clothes out of my cupboard and wrapped them
around the plants and the pots. The little bits of green that stuck
out were then covered with socks or the tight pairs of underwear
I used at Bhakhuba. I had no idea what anybody would think
they were. But right then I didn't really care. I just had to get
them out of there.

*   *   *

I had to make three trips to my car, which I'd parked in the lot
alongside the park that borders the community centre. Neither
on the street nor in my house did many people take notice of
me. It was a quiet night in the rest of Obs. The hobos had gone
to sleep against the walls, even the vendors on the corner were
doing slow business. They stood around chatting loudly.

On each trip to my car the guard would come running up to
me clapping his hands and I'd look away pretending not to see
him. When all the plants were in the car and I started reversing
out of the parking spot he stood behind me guiding me with his
hands. I was feeling so worked up from the situation and from
running back and forth that I put my foot on the accelerator,
and he had to jump out of the way. He was still stupid enough to
put his hands by my window and ask for coins.

I drove up Station Road and turned into Arnold. There was
no one about, only cars parked along either side of the street,
lit up by the old streetlamps. I drove past a small park and a cat
came running across the road. I slowed down and let it cross. In

my rear-view mirror I watched it scamper up a concrete wall into someone's garden.

At the end of the road I turned right, out of the white quarter. A couple of Muslim guys were hanging around on the street. But otherwise it was all quiet. The houses are connected all the way down the road, and the sunflowers growing in the front gardens were drooping their heads like drunk women.

I finally got onto the main road that runs to Salt River where Roddy lives. The road is wide and the buildings that rise up from the sides look like saloons in old Western movies. His building is opposite an enormous traffic circle, but at this time of night there was no one about. On the far side of the circle a few men strolled in and out of the shadows. All the shops along the road are gated up with iron, and like Obs, the pavements are roofed in by overhead balconies. But unlike my side, people live in the overhangs. From the street you can see cheap television sets and broken pot plants.

I hopped out the car and walked over to Roddy's building. Like the shops, it's closed in by a metal gate, and you have to stick your hand far in to reach the doorbell. Without saying a word, Roddy buzzed me in.

I made my way up three flights of stairs. I can't imagine that Roddy's building ever looked good. But now it's disgusting. The concrete stair railings are cracking. The paint on the underside of the stairwell is peeling off in fat flakes. It smells like cat piss. I knocked on his door.

He opened up, and stood silently staring into my eyes, like a woman offering herself up. His ponytail was hanging proudly down his back.

'Can I come in?' I said, and pushed my way past him.

The room smelt of weed, incense and unwashed feet. For the

most part the room looked as it always did. The small wooden floor tiles were loose. His single bed sat in the corner, unmade. His chest of drawers was open, and the ceiling light was hanging out of its fitting. But in the far corner, just short of the Indian blind that partitions his kitchen, Roddy had placed four boxes, one on top of the next. Resting on the top of the pile was his tiny black-and-white television, and on top of that his aerial. Thick rope had been tied through the hoops of the grey antenna, and attached to an unplugged toaster that he'd fastened to his ceiling. There was no other light source, and as the black-and-white flashes darted across the room, I felt like I'd just walked into a scene from a fifties horror movie.

Without saying a word to him I walked over to the Indian partition and pulled it aside. My body cast a thick shadow across the room, and the light that made its way around me was sketchy and dim. But I could see that the dishes were piling up; on top of the large pile was a bar of bath soap. I spun around and looked at him. He was sitting on a cushion on the floor staring up at the television. I had never seen him this way before. His madness had always been playful. I had in fact often wondered if he were not perfectly sane, a straight-faced shit talker who'd latched onto me because I went along with his nonsense. But this was something else. I watched him silently with my hand in my back pocket as he sat staring at the flickering screen at the top of the room.

'I need your help, Roddy,' I said, and walked toward him, placing myself between him and the screen.

He raised his finger to his lips but said nothing.

'I mean it, Roddy. I need your help.'

Again: the finger to the lip. Then he flicked his right hand, indicating that I should move out of his way.

'Please, Roddy!' But I realised my requests were in vain. I found his house keys and let myself out. I took the first two plants out of the car, and carried them up the stairs underneath my arms. He didn't look away from the television for a second. I opened the door that led into his spare room, turned on the light – it didn't work. I took my cellphone out of my pocket and used the light from the screen to find my way through piles of magazines, statues, other junk. I eventually made a clearing large enough for six plants. I brought them all up, and placed them side by side.

'Roddy. I need to go to my house to fetch something. I'll be here in fifteen minutes. I'm taking your keys.'

'He said that no one else should know.' These were the first words Roddy had spoken.

'What?'

'I must wait for the message to come through the screen. He told me how to see it.' He didn't make eye contact as he spoke. His voice seemed to be a few octaves lower than usual. Had I been a religious man, I might well have believed him possessed.

I ensured that the door to his spare room was locked, then set out, back into the night. I managed to get the light out of my room and back to his house with relative ease. Finding a place to fasten it, on the other hand, was anything but easy.

The spare room was the ideal place for the plants. It was small and the blind covering the window was completely black, so no natural light could fuck with the plants' cycle. I realised that a few months ago I wouldn't have even known that that was impor-tant. I felt good about myself for a few seconds. I was a practical, I-can-do-things-with-my-hands kind of guy.

I found the rope that Roddy must have used to fasten the toaster to his ceiling. I took it through to the spare room, and all the while had only the light of the television in the next room to

work by. I used the rope to hoist the lamp up. I created an elabo-
rate scaffolding by running it between the old mock chandelier,
and then through the curtain railing at the far side of the room.
I tested its strength with rapid pull movements, and it seemed
surprisingly strong. I cut some separate strands of rope and fastened the light to the newly constructed system. I used some of
Roddy's old *National Geographic* magazines to raise the plants to
the optimum height. On my way out I again locked the spare
room door.

I was then taken by an idea that could work for both Roddy
and me.

I went into his kitchen and opened his ancient fridge. There
was nothing in it except a shrivelled rotten tomato, and a half-
eaten can of pilchards that stank like hell's fish market. I picked
them both up, gagging as I walked across the room to throw
them away. There was no black bag in the dustbin. I placed them
both down next to his sink, and made my way to his bathroom.
The light was broken, but using my cellphone screen, I could
see that there was no toilet paper.

'All right, Roddy!' I spoke loudly, but still got no response.
'I'm heading out now. I'll be back just now.'

I locked the door behind me and made my way to the car. I
drove to the Shell Garage on Main Road, and parked outside
the 24-hour shop. I sat in my car for a few moments counting
the money in my wallet. I had 230 rand. I needed to speak to
Victoria soon. I needed my royalties.

I walked through the brightly lit shop seeking out the best
and cheapest supplies for the old man. I would probably only be
gone for a day, but considering the unpredictable chaos my life
was in, I decided to get him enough food to last a week. I bought
two loaves of bread, a packet of smoked ham, some cheese, some

cans of tuna, some fruit, some milk, a box of Pronutro, several light bulbs, some black bags, some toilet paper, some juice, and – although I was pretty certain he wouldn't cook them – a box of fish fingers. It cost me nearly everything I had. But fuck, there was no other option.

I got back to his house, and started off by replacing the bulbs. It felt bizarre, I'd never even been this efficient about fixing things in my own house. I did everything at quite a pace, and all the while felt good about myself. I made a lot of noise, but still he took no notice of me. When the kitchen was again in light, I set to work on his dishes.

Mainly because I had no choice, and partially as a means of honouring his ways, I decided to use the bath soap to clean the dishes. When I was done, I dried them and placed them back in his cupboards. I lined his bin with a black bag, and threw out the dirty food. I put the food in his fridge, the toilet paper in his bathroom.

'All right, Roddy,' I spoke to him from the corner of the room. 'I need you to listen.' But I realised anything I'd say to him would be a complete waste of time, so I just told him that I'd left him some food and that I'd be back soon.

He nodded his head.

I knew that there was no other option. It was lucky that he'd been here now, but he could easily disappear and the plants would die.

'Right then, Roddy,' I said. 'I'm on my way. I'll see you soon.'

I checked that the spare room door was locked, then locked the front door behind me, and checked it several times. I made my way down to the car. I'd taken care of one problem, and was hugely pleased with these hidden resources of mine that had made themselves known. I was convinced that several months before I would not have been able to do what I'd just done. All the chaos. All the havoc. It was making me stronger.

I had the strength to overcome the final challenge. The one thing that stood between me and prosperity. On Sunday morning Ridge's reputation would be ruined. If she was in possession of the condom, so would mine. But if I had it, then I would win. I would be free. I drove slowly, my hands twisting on the steering wheel, my eyes focused on the darkness before me, my mind on the next move.

*   *   *

One thought kept rolling through my head: Regereman; Regereman and his guns. There was more chance of a Sunday paper pulling a lead story because some unknown powerless fool asked them to, than Regereman giving me a gun. I had accepted a long time ago that he didn't think much of me. And I was fine with that. I didn't think much of him. But his guns. I wanted to get my hands on one of those. The more I thought about it, the more the idea appealed to me. Even if there was some other way to get the condom from Ridge, I'd prefer to do it with a gun.

The only way I could get into Regereman's house was with Victoria's set of keys. I knew that she carried them with her at all times. It would simply be a matter of getting her drunk and making love to her. Then, as she dozed sweetly in her post-coital slumber, I'd silently ransack the house, until I found the keys. She'd look for them, of course, but keys go missing all the time. When I'd done what needed doing, I'd place the keys back in her apartment, perhaps between the cushions in her couch. Eventually she'd find them and think: I'm sure I looked there before; strange.

I wanted to go straight to Victoria's flat now, but there was something awful eating away at me. As much as I longed to deny it, I felt that I had to check in with Ridge. Even though she'd made it quite clear that she was able to enter my room at will and see for herself, I felt I had to tell her that I'd thrown the plants away. And what was worse – sickening to the very core – was that I wanted her approval. I wanted to see her pleased.

But no! She was the villain! I owed her nothing. I would not check in with her. As with each decisive move – the making of a rope scaffolding, the buying of sandwiches for Roddy, planting the seeds to begin with – this decision increased my power, my faith in myself. Making a decision, a firm choice, was as strong as tying a knot. I tightened the grip on my steering wheel and drove on through the darkness.

Fifteen minutes later I was outside Victoria's flat, pounding my fist against her knocker, buzzing her bell. I hadn't phoned before I came; I was taking a risk, I knew. But when she answered the door, dressed in her gown, toothbrush in hand, hair wrapped up in a white towel, her smile told me she was glad I'd come.

'Oh, Byron. You didn't say. But come please. You must come in.'

'Do you have any wine?'

'I've just, um, cleaned up. Was going to sleep. No wine.'

'I'll go get some from the Seven Eleven. Let's chill a bit.'

'Um, OK. I've got, I suppose, nothing on tomorrow. Have you got any money left?'

'Umm . . .'

She gave me two hundred bucks.

Twenty minutes later and I was back outside her gate, four bottles of red wine in a blue packet.

'Wow!' she said.

She'd changed into her pyjamas.

We made our way through the first bottle and my mind started playing games with me. I ran over what I had done and what I was about to do. I'd locked a madman up in his flat. I was going to get my girlfriend drunk so I could steal the keys to her parents' house, then steal her father's gun. I stopped there. Were there any moral problems with this? Over the past while I'd noticed myself becoming increasingly pragmatic in my approach to life. My plans were more logical, and seemed to have only the outcome in mind. I was pleased with myself. Yes, I was a pragmatist. I went to take a piss and looked at myself in the mirror. I ran water through my hair and said: 'Byron the pragmatist!' It made me feel good.

Morality was simply a trick. I opened the second bottle of wine and knocked back a full glass as if it were water, or I were a bandit. Yes. Victoria was talking to me, but I wasn't listening. I was thinking. In life we're constantly faced with problems. We need to make choices. There is nearly always an obvious choice, or if there isn't, careful consideration will reveal to us the right option. The right option will bring the best consequences. Morality is simply thrown in to fuck with the heads of fools. Fuck morality, I thought as I slammed down my glass and filled it up with red wine. I took a long slug. I'm Byron the fucking pragmatist!

I leant over and kissed Victoria on the cheek 'Mweoh!' I made as much noise as I could. She giggled and tucked her feet up against her body, she stuck her hands out toward me. I could see she was starting to think naughty thoughts.

Two bottles of wine later and I was nearly too fucked to perform. Thankfully youth and necessity were on my side. I came, and immediately felt myself falling asleep. In my last waking moments I realised that I'd forgotten the age-old rule of human sexuality: women like to cuddle; men fall asleep. Perhaps I was still too stupid to be a pragmatist.

Thankfully I woke up in the middle of the night. I checked my cellphone. It was four o'clock. Desperate to pee, I stumbled out of bed and made my way to the bathroom. After urinating I turned on the tap and drank from it without looking up for a full minute. I looked at myself in the mirror. My hair was standing up in tufts, there were crease marks on my face. I could smell my sweat and Victoria's groin. I splashed my face.

I made my way back into the room. I was still very drunk, and there was a burning sensation in my gullet. I turned on the bedside light and whispered Victoria's name in her ear. She moaned, rolled over and pulled the duvet up to her face. I found her handbag and searched through it. There was no sign of the keys. Probably because I was drunk, and thinking like a moron, I decided to look for them in the couch. Even as I was doing it, I knew I was being a fool. I went back to the room, picked up her pants and shook them, but the pockets were empty. I went to her cupboard and started shuffling through all her coats. Finally I heard a jangle. I stuck my hand in the outside pocket and felt a set of keys. I took it out. I'd struck gold.

I set my alarm and woke up early. I went through to the bathroom and took a piss, dribbling all over the floor. I took some toilet paper off the roll and bent down to wipe the piss up, and happened to look under her bath. I'd completely forgotten that I still had a bankie of weed lying there. I picked it up and put it in my pocket. When all this was over, I'd reward myself with a fat joint.

I brought her breakfast in bed and kissed her on the head. I'd hidden the keys in my cubby hole before waking her. I made idle chatter, but slowly turned the conversation toward her parents, their whereabouts, and plans for the immediate future. Her mother, it transpired, was away at a spa. Regereman had sent her there to recuperate. From what? It was unclear. And – from a pragmatic point of view – unimportant.

This was excellent news, it could well mean that Regereman would be living it up, drinking with his friends, hunting maybe.

'Is your dad in town?' I asked.

'I think so. Why do you ask?'

'No reason. Haven't seen him since the gallery.'

'That's true I suppose. We'll see him soon, I'm sure.'

She'd become so chilled these days. She could spend hours just sitting and talking. I thought back to the way she was during the last weeks of her photo project. She barely had time to speak to me, I'd felt like a constant annoyance. And now that I was sober she always spoke to me like an adult. Perhaps I was just more comfortable pretending to be one. I wished she'd never treated me like a fool and ignored me, then perhaps I'd never have had my affair with Ridge. Perhaps it was her fault as much as mine, and what I was doing was necessary to save us both from a mistake we had jointly made.

Late morning I kissed her goodbye, and said I'd see her soon.

That afternoon I got a phone call from Vusi.

'Byron, bra.'

'Hey, Vus.'

'We need you here tonight, man.'

'What? No, not tonight.'

'We really do. There's a big party going on here, my man. You've been asked for by name.'

'Me?'

'Ja. Look, bra. I swear I'll make it worth your while. You know what I mean!'

'Vus. This is bad timing.'

'Byron, man. I'm *telling* you, my friend. You're still employed here. We said you'd come in from time to time. Come, my man. I'll make it worth your while.'

'What time?'

'The guests are coming round eight, half past. You be here seven. Half seven latest.'

'Shit, Vus. OK, fine.'

*   *   *

It was a spanner in the middle of my works. Performing the robbery before nightfall would be suicide, and it was getting dark around six o'clock each evening. If I was waiting outside his house at dusk and broke in as the sun went down, I'd still have an hour and a half in which to get the condom from Ridge and make my way to Bhakhuba. I'd be cutting it fine, but there was no other way.

I went to the second-hand clothes store behind the Spar. There was a large wire basket with an assortment of items in it: socks, large woollen jerseys with buttons missing, and yes, just what I needed, a black balaclava. I pulled it over my face. It fitted snugly, and I paid for it with the last ten rand note in my wallet. I stuffed it into my pocket and walked home.

As I sat in my room waiting for darkness, I wondered if there wasn't perhaps an easier way to get the condom back from Ridge. There probably was. But I didn't only want it back. That wasn't enough. I wanted Ridge to squirm a little. I wanted to see urine dripping from the bottom of her pants. I wanted to smell something brown.

So as the birds made their way home and the shadows grew in

length, Byron strolled unnoticed through the streets of Observatory and climbed into his car. I packed my balaclava and the key to Regereman's front door in my cubbyhole. All I could do now was hope he wasn't home. I climbed onto the M5 to Muizenberg. In the distance the mountains looked like scrunched up toilet paper and the clouds loomed overhead like big black bottoms. I took the Constantia off-ramp and drove through the leafy streets of the pretentious suburb as the last light of the day faded. I was stopped at a security check. The guard handed me a logbook into which I had to sign my name and vehicle registration number. I called myself Clive in honour of the cunt I was about to rob.

I drove past his house. The large stone driveway was empty, and a gentle rain was coming down. I drove on for a few seconds, then spun around and drove back again. I did this for about fifteen minutes as I waited for darkness to fall. I didn't want to be noticed. Eventually I pulled up outside his front gate and searched about for the remote control I'd stashed in the cubbyhole. I pointed it at the gate and pushed the top button. A small part of me hoped it wouldn't work; hoped that I could just go home and tell Ridge I'd done my best, that it wasn't possible. But then I realised there was no one to excuse myself to, and anyway the gate was starting to open.

It was dark now, and in the strip of light cast by my headlights I saw the stone cherub holding his stone cock in his stone hand. And yes, the elegant green fungus that clung to Regereman's roof: I could just make it out. I sat still for a few moments and considered abandoning the entire operation. But no, it had to be done. I opened up the cubbyhole and took out the ridiculous black balaclava I'd bought from the second-hand charity clothes store. I pulled it on and looked at myself in the rear-view mirror.

It was starting to rain and the drops made cracking sounds as they hit the roof of my car.

'Dear God,' I mumbled, 'please don't let Regereman be in his house. Please. I'll start going to church on Sundays if he isn't. Please. Please.'

I wasn't even religious. But this was a serious situation, surely God could give me an itsy-bitsy olive branch.

I opened my door and walked across the courtyard, past the cherub and up to the front door. Standing on his doorstep I activated a sensor light and saw my face reflected in the brass knocker that hung against his door. I raised it up a little to see how it distorted the image. It bent the front part of my face, causing me to look like a donkey. I was getting wet and the balaclava was giving off an unpleasant smell. I wondered who'd worn it before me and how many times it'd been used to commit a crime. If indeed it had been used in a crime, the charity shop was acting as a launderer. I fiddled with the key in the lock and as I pushed the door inwards a sound most awful exploded through the entire residence. I'd set off the fucking alarm! Regereman! Of course a cunt like him would have an alarm!

In a state of panic I pulled the door shut, then realised how suspicious I must look, unlocked it again and shut it behind me. I fumbled around for a light switch and as it came on I saw the large table covered with pictures of Victoria. I noticed for the first time how – in her late teens – she'd had the appearance of a troglodyte. Her features were all too big for the face: her chin, her ears. Thank God she'd grown into them. And the alarm was howling and I could see the box into which the code had to be typed. I decided to try my luck and typed in C-L-I-V-E. But instead of turning it off I simply caused it to start howling a dif-

ferent tune. The armed response mother fuckers would be here
any second and I still had a task to complete.

I ran up the stairs and was forced to pause at the top to catch
my breath. I took the fact that the alarm was armed as a sign of
Regereman's absence. And so I slunk along the corridor, over
the soft fluffy rug up to his bedroom door. I pushed it open and
was overwhelmed by the scent of his aftershave; and yes, there
was still a light fog from his shower. Sniff sniff. Indeed I could
even smell a shit and some bathroom spray. I think it was straw-
berry and cream flavour. He must have left moments before I
arrived; perhaps he even saw me driving up and down his road.
Besides the smell of Regereman's ablutions the room was un-
changed from my first visit. His bed was made, his exercise bike
stood silently in the corner.

I made my way into his walk-in cupboard where his greedy
scent hung heavier than before. I flicked on the light and immediately noticed a glass of whisky resting on the upper shelf,
where he stacked his shoes. I couldn't remember in which suit
pocket he'd kept his key, and wasn't certain if he always kept it in
the same place. But as I walked through Regereman's nest I noticed that the moron had left his safe door lying open. Through
his glass of whisky I could see the set of keys, bent and distorted
like my face in the knocker. I reconstructed the scene in my head
and watched in my mind's eye as the cunt sipped his booze and
stroked his guns. He must have been so pissed when he left.

I bent down and peered into the safe. It was higher and went
back further than I'd remembered. I was struck by the smell of
steel and gunpowder, and the alarm was still howling and my
palms were sweating. I stuck my hand in and touched the side of
the gun. I could hear the fucker's words: *the most legendary pistol.*
It was heavy and felt so good in my hands. And just to complete

the moment I picked up the glass of whisky and took a nice long sip, then took the sleeve of Regereman's nearest jacket, stuck it down my pants, and wiped my ass.

But as with all good things in life the moment passed too soon. I ran out the cupboard, through his room and down the stairs. I had no idea how long I'd been in his house, but there was still no sign of the armed response. As I reached the bottom of the steps I realised that I hadn't switched off Regereman's lights. I swung around, gun in hand, and for an instant considered running back up the stairs to switch them off. But as I stood there I noticed that I'd left behind a clue more telltale than if I'd signed my name on his glass. All the way up the stairs, and all the way back down were nice fat muddy prints. And each time the right was noticeably larger than the left. Oh, Jesus Christ, I thought. There was no time to fix the mess. If it ever came up I'd deny everything. *Deny everything!*

I tucked the gun under my shirt and ran out through the rain toward my car. I put the gun inside a packet in the cubbyhole, opened the gate and reversed onto the street. I knew that driving past the same security checkpoint would be the end, and so I wound my way through the dark streets, water mixed up with leaves crashing onto my windscreen like big bird shits. I found the on-ramp and headed for home.

As I entered my house I was hit by the immense heatwave created by the mass of hypnotised sweating bodies. But as I walked through the crowd, I felt like a man swimming silently through underwater reeds. There was no resistance, only a gentle sway aside. All the eyes looked like eyes in paintings. And like the eyes of painted people they followed me mechanically.

Then I was standing outside her door, holding the packet by the handles. It swayed from side to side. And then I was knocking. Rat-tat-tat. And the door was opening and she was standing there before me, a look of confusion on her face, and I was asking her if I could please come inside. She looked down at the packet in my hand, and must have wondered what it was, but never, never, in all her years of stupid experience could she have guessed. I bumped her, and found myself pointing at the chair behind her desk. Without resistance she made her way toward it and sat down. Our eyes locked on one another like animals. The moment was still. I felt primal. I could feel the sweat in my asshole and on my balls. I could taste the spit in my mouth. I could feel my heart beating. I could feel my lungs.

The whole world felt silent.

'Ridge! Give me the fucking box!' I yelled as I quickly untied the handles of the packet and pointed the gun at her face. The silence was gone and the primal feeling with it. I felt uncomfortable now. Like a human. My right foot was large. My hand was shaking.

'Give me the fucking box!' I screamed again.

She slowly raised her hands. Was this an instinct, I wondered, or had she learnt it from watching TV?

'Byron, you don't want to do this,' she said to me.

'I've thought this through,' I said.

'I don't have it here.'

'Then where is it!' I screamed, and turned to make sure the door was locked. The room was dark, the only light was coming from Ridge's desk. She'd been reading in here, silent and scheming.

'It's at my flat. In Rondebosch.'

'We must go fetch it then!' I said.

'Byron. Are you sure you want to do this?'

'Ridge. I'll kill you. You've pushed me to the end!'

'You can't kill me, Byron. Everyone will know it was you. You come in here. There's a large explosion. You walk out. I'm dead. Don't be ridiculous.'

In the light from her desk I could see that she was awfully composed. Her hands were on the desk, and yes, how hadn't I noticed? She was wearing a pair of glasses: reading glasses, which she now took off.

'It doesn't matter. I'll bury you. You'll be dead. Why would you care!'

'If you want me to get it. I'll get it for you. Just calm down, Byron.'

She was scared of me. And seeing her scared brought back the primal feeling. I could smell it, like dogs smell it.

'I'll get my coat. We can go and fetch it. Just stay calm.'

I backed away into the corner of the room.

'And when you've given it to me,' I said 'You have to leave! Or pay me lots of money! Lots of money!'

'We can discuss that, Byron.' She was calming down. 'Now how do you think you're going to march me through the crowd, without getting caught. Hmm?'

I walked right up to her and put my arm underneath her jacket. I could feel her bra strap and the heat of her body. She hadn't put on perfume for a while, and was smelling of sweat. I stuck the barrel of the gun into her armpit.

'Now we must walk. Like lovers. Come!'

She opened the door. In order to keep the barrel of the gun inside her armpit, I had to maintain a rather unnatural position. I didn't know if the gun was loaded. If I tripped I could well blow a hole right through her arm and separate it from her body. I pictured the bloody stump as I walked right behind her. It made me want to laugh, but I didn't want to do it. I was bent like a spastic cripple, holding onto an able-bodied friend. We got surprisingly few stares, and made our way off my street onto the dark side road, where I let go of her.

'Keep moving,' I said.

'Where are we going?'

'To my car. Then to your house.'

We got to my car. I unlocked the door for her and she climbed onto the passenger seat. She sat silently. None of the car guards bothered me. It seemed I was giving off the aura of a psycho.

'How do we get to your flat?'

'Get onto the M3. Then take the turn-off by UCT. It's probably the easiest.'

Ridge was remarkably calm. The original adrenalin surge that had marked the start of the encounter had faded, and everything seemed completely normal. It was as if we were going to the shops, taking a stroll. Only now I had a gun, and Ridge was my captive. I was almost disappointed by how mundane the whole thing was.

We got on the highway, I could see Devil's Peak. The sky was beginning to clear. I kept the gun on the far side of my seat, I could feel the steel against my pants. And then suddenly, as if someone had injected adrenalin into my heart, I was overcome with panic and fear. What am I doing? I thought. This is terrible. I wanted to park the car and throw the gun away. I wanted to tell Ridge to forget everything. I wanted to apologise to her. I wanted to abandon my car and run off into the mountains and join a forgotten tribe, that at that instant, I was certain, must live somewhere nearby. I patted my pants and found a box of cigarettes. I lit one, and felt myself calming down.

Then in my rear-view mirror I saw a police car. They were driving at exactly my speed. I looked over at Ridge. She was staring at the road in front of her. Had she called them? Were they coming for me? It was only a few hundred metres to the UCT off-ramp, but if I took it would they think I was trying to run away from them? Perhaps they were just patrolling and that would seem like suspicious behaviour. Or perhaps if I kept driving they would assume I'd panicked, and therefore had something to hide.

Before I could make up my mind, I took the off-ramp and got stuck at the red traffic light opposite the law campus. The cop car was still behind me. I could see the policeman's face. He had dark hair. His skin was yellow; his black eyes knew the truth.

The light turned green. I turned left. He was still following. When we reached Main Road, I asked Ridge which way we must turn, and as she started answering the cop car pulled up alongside her in the left hand lane. She looked at him.

'I'll kill you,' I muttered under my breath. 'I'll do it,' I said. At that moment I meant it. And she could hear that I meant it.

'Right,' she said.

The robot turned green. The cop car went left.

I felt alive. I felt in control. I was powerful. This was my situation and I was at the helm, no one would dare question my authority. She directed me along Main Road up to the traffic lights in the centre of Rondebosch. The pavements were lit up by various coloured lights attached to the fast-food joints and the video store. There were lots of people walking about. The music coming from the car behind me was so loud that the windows were shaking. An Indian guy wearing a red cap was slumped down in the driver's seat of the car. He reckoned he was pretty cool. But I was cooler. At that moment, I was the fucking king!

When the robots went green we drove on until we got to Stardust, a cheesy looking restaurant, lit up in white and purple. We turned left and pulled up outside her block of flats.

'I'll go in and get it,' she said.

'I'm coming with you.' I sounded like a dictator. My tone left no room for argument. I remembered how, in my room, I had dealt with Ridge using my physical strength. Afterwards I'd been ashamed of my manliness. But with a gun in my hand, I felt no such shame. I'd handed all my brutal qualities over to a small steel instrument, so I could remain civilised.

'Will your flatmates be home?' I asked her.

'Sarah's away,' she said. 'No. No one will be here.'

We walked across the road beneath the lamplight. The air was crisp, the classic Cape Town post-rain freshness. She unlocked the gate and we made our way into her complex. I slipped the gun inside my jeans pocket, and started worrying again that it might be cocked. I could end up castrating myself. I took it out, and tried to hide it behind my back. I knew that I looked suspicious, but I didn't care.

We went into her complex, then her flat. It had a long wooden passage, with two large rooms on the sides, and a kitchen at the end. We went into her room. It was painted red. She opened up a wooden chest of drawers and there lying on top of her underwear was the box. She picked it up and without any resistance or comment, handed it over to me.

'Good!' I said.

I put the gun in my pocket and opened the box. The purple covering was still there, and underneath it the bank bag with the used condom inside it.

'I'll leave you here,' I said.

'No, Byron. You must take me back to Khoi House.'

'No!' I said.

'Byron!' She stepped toward me. I pulled the gun out of my pocket and held it into her stomach. She backed away.

She was looking bookish this evening. Her hair was neatly clipped up around her head. In patches the frizz stuck out from beneath the clips. Although she was no longer wearing her glasses, they'd left behind their academic shadow. She had her hands in the pockets of her red RDFM hoodie.

'You could have asked me,' she said.

'I did ask you.'

'I didn't realise how important this was to you.'

'Don't lie, Ridge!'

She looked down at the ground. Again, a stillness descended upon us. I had the box in my hand. I'd won the game. I put it down for a moment as I surveyed the scene.

The light in her room was dim. There were shades over the light in the ceiling and next to her bed. Her duvet cover was white and dotted with small red flowers. Her bed was a replica of an antique, the metal deliberately tarnished. She had a printer's tray stacked with a mix of different items. Along her railing she'd hung ribbons which she'd won in gymkhanas. I pictured the horse's face as it landed after a jump, Ridge on its back.

'Poor animal,' I said.

'What?'

'Never mind.'

On the top of her shelf was a bottle of cough mixture. There was fresh syrup running down the label.

'Were you sick, Ridge?' I picked up the bottle.

'Recently. I'm better.'

I looked at the gun in my hand, then at Ridge. She felt very human to me. For the first time I could see that she was a human.

'Come with me, Ridge,' I said.

'Byron. Please, can't we just go? I'm not enjoying this any more.'

'I said come. To the bathroom.'

'No, Byron, why?' She started walking out of her room.

'To the bathroom!' I yelled.

The bathroom was just short of the kitchen, and, like her room, was cluttered but ordered. There was a washing machine and tumble drier at the entrance, a bath, but no shower, and of course a toilet. I closed the door behind us. I locked it.

As in many bathrooms there was a large mirror that covered the entire wall behind the bath. I saw myself. My dark hair was still wet and sticking onto my forehead. I looked at the weapon in my hand. I suited a gun. I was a gun man, and I'd never even known it.

'OK, Ridge,' I said. 'It's time to pull down your pants.'

'No, Byron. No, please,' she said, and started shaking her head frantically. I could feel her fear filling the room. Nervously twitching she backed away into the corner of the room, against the toilet.

'I'm telling you, Ridge. It's time to pull them down. Do you think I'm a clown!'

'Byron, please don't do this to me!' She was on the verge of tears. I knew what she was thinking, and seeing her so scared gave me a sense of delight. She was afraid of me. In awe of me. I was holding Regereman's gun.

I was Regereman!

'Off!' I screamed. 'I ask once more, then the room gets gooey!'

'Please!' She started crying, and at the same time slowly undoing her belt. 'Stop it, Byron. I'm sorry I ever did anything. Please stop it!'

I leant right over her and pointed the gun at her head.

'Hurry the fuck up,' I whispered into her ear. She finished

undoing her belt and dropped her pants to the floor. She hadn't taken off her underwear. They were white, with frills on the edges, different to the ones she was wearing when I fucked her.

'Considering your current state,' I said 'I think my next request will be easy enough. Take off your fucking underwear and sit on the toilet.'

'What do you want me to do?' She was really sobbing now, to the point where her chest was heaving. The tears were running down her face. Crying didn't suit her.

'I told you what to do. Take them off. Sit down.'

She sat down on the toilet, and bent her chest over her legs. I took a step toward her and placed the gun against the top of her head. My finger wasn't on the trigger, but she didn't know this.

'Come on!' I shouted.

She raised the back of her butt cheeks and dragged her underwear down her legs until they reached her knees. She looked up at me.

'Why are you doing this?'

'Are you shit-scared, Ridge? You know the phrase?'

'Yes.'

I stepped away from her and leant against the door. I looked at myself in the mirror and had a good smile.

'I want you to do a shit for me, Ridge.'

'What?' She sat up straight. Between her legs I could see the edges of her pubic mound, the outer reaches of her hair. The texture of her pubes, I remembered from the night I'd fucked her, was similar to the hair on her head. Or rather the hair on her head felt like pubes. But they were darker than her hair, and looked as if they'd been covered in motor oil.

'I want you to take a dump for me. Have a shit. Press a coil. Do it for me!' I screamed.

'No!' She pulled the lower edges of her RDFM hoodie onto her legs. 'I won't shit for you!'

'What's your name?'

'Susan, Byron.'

'Sue.'

'No. Susan.'

'Sue Ridge. Suits you!'

'Stop it, Byron!'

'What's your organisation called?'

'What? You know, By-ron!' She dragged out my name as she cried.

'Say it for me!'

'RDFM.'

'Which is.'

'Restoring. Byron, why are you insulting me like this?'

'Restoring . . . '

'Dignity to Forgotten Minorities.'

'Restoring?'

'Yes. It's my life. Why are you doing this to me?'

'*Your life!*' I said with all the sarcasm I had in me. 'And you're wearing the top now, aren't you?'

'Yes. You can see. Please!' She kept weeping, and pulling the front of her top further forward.

'Not restoring any dignity to *you!* Is it?' I was laughing and screaming at the same time. Finally, I knew what it was like to be powerful. This is what power hungry men dreamed of. This is what they lusted after. And I had it. Right now I had it! I wanted the feeling to last for ever.

'Shit for me, Ridge!' I screamed.

'Byron, please. I'm so sorry I ever . . . '

'Ever what? Ever what, hey, Ridge?'

'I've given you the box, Byron. Please.' She was crying and squirming on the toilet, just like the little bitch she was. My God, I was *loving* it!

'If I'd wanted the box, Ridge, I could've gotten it from you. I want you to shit!'

'No, please, Byron!'

'Shit! I want to smell your crap, Ridge. You stole my cum. I want to steal your shit. I want to keep it in a box!'

'No!'

'Why not? I want to keep some in a printer's tray. Come on, Ridge!'

'Byron. Please stop it!'

The top part of her body was bent right over her naked legs, and tears from her stupid eyes were falling onto her feet. She kept shaking her head frantically like a child that doesn't want to go into the dentist's room. I was the dentist and Ridge was my patient. I was going to drill holes right through her smelly teeth into her gums and make her bleed.

I put the gun on the top of her head and pushed the barrel hard into her skull.

'You're hurting me,' she said.

'Come now, Ridge,' I said. 'I'm not letting you go until I hear something.'

'Please, Byron.'

'Push!' I screamed.

She kept looking down at the floor. The top of her head was moving up and down as her body shook. Then she took a deep breath and stopped sobbing for a few moments. I could see the muscles in her arms tensing as she tried to shit. But nothing

came. She relaxed again for a few seconds, and then started tensing again. This time she even made a groaning sound. Then, out
of her anus came a tiny little fart.

'Excellent!' I screamed. 'Now something solid!'

'Please. That's all I have. There's nothing more.' She broke
down.

There was nothing left to say. Silence was hurting her more
than all the words I could conjure up in a lifetime. She'd made
a noise, and I felt good.

Then she raised her head slightly. Not enough for me to see
her eyes. But it looked as if she was preparing for something.
Not a shit, but something else. It looked like she was regaining
her strength. I remembered the way she'd swung the situation
around when I'd had her against the desk in my room. I couldn't
let her do it again.

'Little bitch!' I said.

'What's wrong with you?' she asked me. Her tone had changed.
The energy was switching. She sounded curious, not afraid.

'Nothing!'

'What's going on with your feet?' she asked as she sat up
straight.

'Nothing!' I shifted my right foot back.

'Not nothing, Byron. Your right foot is twice the size of the
left.' Her voice had regained its musical quality and rose up
from her stinky body like a spirit leaving a corpse.

'How have I never noticed that before?' She pulled her pants
up and climbed off the toilet.

'Sit down, Ridge. I still have the gun!' I screamed as I jumped
back into the door.

'You're a little freak, aren't you?'

'I'll shoot you, Ridge.'

'No, you won't.' She turned around and flushed the toilet, then continued to button up her pants.

'Give me the gun, little boy.'

'No, Ridge! Fuck you!' I unlocked her bathroom door and ran into the passageway.

'Come here,' she said, following me toward her bedroom.

At that moment my pants started vibrating.

I took the phone out, all the while still waving the gun about like a madman. My arm was getting tired from holding the heavy weapon.

It was Vusi. I hung up.

'Why don't you answer?'

She was coming toward me. I tried desperately to change my tone as I pointed the gun straight at her and said 'I *will* fucking kill you.'

But she kept coming toward me and my phone started ringing again.

'Answer it.'

'Why?'

'Because I said so.'

I pushed the green button and held the phone to my ear. Ridge slipped into her room.

'Byron, bra. Where the hell are you? You meant to be here.'

'What, Vus? I'm coming now.'

'No, Byron. Get here right now! The guests are about to arrive.'

'OK!' I hung up.

'Who was that?' Ridge was standing right behind me.

'Shut up' I said, and walked into her room to fetch the box which I'd left on her shelf. I picked it up. It's fine, I told myself. You got what you came for. Now leave.

'I'm going, Ridge,' I said to her as I stood in the corridor.

'Take me back to Khoi House.'

'No,' I said, and walked out the front door.

'Byron! Come back here!' she screamed at me.

'I'm going,' I said, pressed the buzzer, opened the gate, and walked out to my car.

* * *

I sped along the N1 towards Bellville. The highway was dark and my car was rattling. Vusi phoned me twice as I was driving, but I didn't bother to answer. I'd told him I was coming.

I took the Stellenbosch turn-off and went left. I knew the route so well. Right, under the bridge, left at the stop street. The roads are dark, but there's an enormous sign to Bhakhuba ten kilometres from the restaurant, again at five kilometres, and again at one. All the signs are lit up by large footlights buried in the earth in front of them. I turned down the unlit, unposted maintenance road that only us workers know about. It's terribly kept. My car rattled like a man having an epileptic fit, and by the time I pulled into the parking lot I'd had almost all I could handle for one day.

Vusi's BMW was there, as was Charlie's bike. The chefs were there, the waitresses were there. It was just Byron who was late. But he was going to be a little bit later. Because in his cubbyhole was the bankie of weed he'd found under Victoria's bathtub.

I felt like I'd earned myself a joint. I wasn't pleased with the way Ridge had treated me toward the end of our encounter, but I'd humiliated her enough, and no one could take that away from me. Secondly, if I were going to be playing the part of praise poet tonight, I'd need to get into character. I'd never done it sober before, and I wasn't about to start now. I mulled the weed onto the box I'd confiscated from Ridge. It felt as good as pissing on her face. I'd won!

I lit the joint up and smoked it slowly. Every drag felt like a little orgasm, a tiny explosion of happiness. It had been too long. I hadn't even realised how much I'd been missing it. I felt the warmth pass through my chest into my head, through my veins, down to my toes. Things were going to be all right.

When I'd finished the joint I had a cigarette to get rid of the smell. The weed was beginning to really kick in. I felt like I was sinking underwater and things were blurring, but at the same time the outlines of shapes were becoming more defined. I'd almost forgotten what it was like to be stoned. My phone started ringing. It was Vusi. I stubbed my cigarette out, took my tog bag off the back seat and headed for the change room.

'Wena, Byron!' Charlie shouted at me as I came stumbling into the dirty room. 'Where have you been? Haai, man!' He clicked.

'Sorry, Charlie. I was held up. Big problems.'

'Yo yo. Byron. You are a strange one. Get changed quick-quick!'

I walked toward my locker. A large puddle of water had collected in the centre of the room. I stopped short of it and stared at my reflection for a few seconds, then realised that I was acting stoned, hopped over it and started changing out of my clothes.

'Ah, shit!' I said.

'What's wrong, Byron?'

'I forgot my tight briefs. No way to put my balls into the triple P.'

'Byron! Byron! Byron!' He slapped his hands on his knees. 'Are you smoking that shit again?'

'Uh, no,' I said. My mouth felt dry, my eyes red.

'You are smoking!' He came walking toward me.

'No,' I said, and turned away from him so he couldn't see my face.

'Eish! I have spare one. I can borrow for you. But I never want it back.'

'Thanks, Charlie. Shit, man. Thank you so much.'

I slipped into the tight briefs that Charlie fetched from his bag and pulled my balls into the triple P. I took the leather skirt out of my bag and shook it out. It had been in the bag for quite some time. Whenever it sits for too long it develops a distinctive smell, like rotten Bovril. I shook it out then pulled it on and tightened the various safety straps, sat down on the wooden bench and strapped the ankle ties around my lower legs.

'What time they coming, Charlie?'

'Byron. Come sit here, wena. We must speak.' I shifted along the bench until I was sitting next to him. 'The men who are coming tonight, they are the rich ones. OK. This man!' He pulled a newspaper clipping out of the pocket he'd sewn to the inside of his skins. 'This man she is called Shanghai Blowshark. This one, eish. Too much, too much.'

'Is he coming here?'

'Sure. She's coming. It is her birthday tonight, nè. She wants to have her praises sung nice-nice! OK!'

'Sure. OK. Which routines we doing tonight?'

'For Mr Blowshark we will be doing some original. We can go over it now now. For the other one, Byron, we have to use all the routine.'

'Even four?'

'Byron. Come, my friend. You mustn't forget number four tonight. You understand?'

'Let's run over them all quickly, please.'

'Very quick. OK. Number òne!' He held out one finger as he spoke. 'Number one is for? What do we say for number one?'

'Umm, money? He's got lots of money,' I said, trying to hide my red eyes from him by looking down at the floor. I'd remembered it without great effort.

'Good, Byron. OK. So, number two, what we say for that?'

'Two is for strength. Hey?'

'Eish!' He patted me on the knee. 'Not so stupid! Nè. OK, now. What we say for number three?'

'Um. Three. OK. What's that again? We say he's wise? Wisdom? Is that the one about wisdom?'

'For the wisdom. Sure. We say he is the wise one. OK?'

'Got it!'

'And now, my friend. Let us see if you can remember what is number four. Hey? The one you like to forget.'

'No. I know. It's just that I forget when I'm out there. In the moment.'

'What is it?'

'Power.'

'Say it again!'

'Power.'

'One more time!'

'Power.'

'That is correct. You are the praise poet. And you must tell the man how very much power he has. You understand me? If I say number four. You say power. You do not for-get!' He stuck his finger into my knee, tapping out each syllable.

'All right.'

'Why do you always forget that one?'

'I don't know.'

'No, you must tell me. You don't like to sing to a man how powerful?'

'It's not that.'

'Is because you like to smoke the weed?'

'No.'

'Why then. Me and Vusi, we both say, why he do like this.'

'I don't know. Not tonight.'

'Eish. It make no sense. But fine. Lastly we have number five!' He held his palm fully open and counted the tips of his fingers. 'One two three four five. How many, Byron?'

'Five.'

'And what is for number five? What is for?'

'Children.'

'Many children. We say this man, he have many children, he is wealthy in children. OK. Now we must go over quick what we say about the main one.'

He ran over what he'd planned for the main man. I memorised it as best I could. I considered taking a pen from my bag and making some crib notes on the inside of my hand. But when I thought about it again, I couldn't decide if it was a normal thing to do, or if Charlie would then know that I was stoned.

'What's the guy's name again?' I asked him.

'Shanghai Blowshark.'

'I'm sure I've heard of him.'

'You've seen him on the television. In the newspaper. You do know him for certain.'

'No. Shit. I'm sure I know him from somewhere.' I couldn't remember if I did know him, or if I'd just convinced myself in my stoned state that I did.

'Come now. Let's go. And Byron. This man. They speak Xho-

sa. They know English. But Xhosa is their home language. Nè.
You must not mix tonight. No mistake. They will catch you.'

'OK.'

'And Byron.'

'Ja.'

'OK. Good luck!'

We walked along the raised wooden boardwalk through the
centre of the inkundla, past the bonfires, the tables, the bars.
The bright Christmas lights had finally been taken down and replaced with decorative African bulbs. Since I'd been away they'd
brought in large clay pots with designs cut into them. Inside the
pots they'd placed candles and the light flickered through the
gaps casting strange patterns across the wooden boardwalk. I
started getting slightly paranoid. Perhaps I'd underestimated
the importance of the evening.

I looked upward trying to calm my stoned mind. The sky had
cleared and the temperature was just right. I didn't feel too
cold in my skins. We slipped through the entrance and stood
in the guest parking lot. Like the staff lot it's made of dirt, but
the dirt somehow looks stylish, and well kept. Next to the main
entrance, two large flames were burning. Above the reed entranceway, the word *Bhakhuba* was carved into a designer piece
of rust.

Charlie was standing next to me, jogging on the spot, mumbling under his breath, and gently hitting his legs. He does this,
he's told me, to get the blood flowing properly.

I in turn looked down at my feet and tried to imagine them
the same size. The image of Ridge sitting on the toilet was still
fresh in my memory. How I wish she'd made a proper solid shit.
The humiliation would have lasted for ever then. But that didn't
matter now. I looked back down at my feet. I imagined myself

in a far-off land where my people respect me. My name is Byronkhulu and I am mighty.

I looked up and noticed that two Mercedes Benzes, one green one maroon, had pulled into the parking lot, their headlights carving yellow columns through the dust. Charlie continued to mumble. Two bright lights were suddenly turned on from on top of the main building. The whole parking lot lit up.

I felt more exposed.

'Byronkhulu,' I said under my breath.

A tall, dark-skinned man climbed out of the green car, and straightened his jacket. A beautiful young woman climbed out from the other side. She was dressed in a green satin dress, with a V-shaped front, exposing smooth skin, slightly lighter than that of her man. She walked around the car, and slipped her arm through his. Neither made any attempt to move toward the entrance where we were standing. Suddenly, I felt a hand take hold of my naked arm. I turned to my right. It was Vusi. In all the time I'd been at Bhakhuba, I'd never known him to come out and greet the guests.

'Hi,' I said, looking away and hoping he hadn't noticed my red eyes.

Another couple climbed out of the maroon car. Again the man was dressed in a suit, his female partner in an evening dress.

'Byron,' Vusi spoke under his breath. 'Listen to me. I forgot to tell you, none of them are going to change out of their clothes. Don't even offer. When Blowshark's secretary booked it for him, she said he wasn't interested. Right?'

'Sure.'

The two men walked across the dirt parking lot and took hold of each other's hand. They were both well built, tall, and had the classic swagger of powerful men. They came toward us, and first the men, then the women, in turn, took Vusi's hand in theirs. The one man turned his gaze to me. He was very dark, clean-shaven; but his skin was coarse, as if perhaps he'd been plagued by acne vulgaris in his younger years. His hair was shaved short, his nose solid and definite, his eyebrows bushy and long.

'What have we here?' he said eyeing me, but clearly directing his question to Vusi. I was cold, I could feel my nipples were erect.

'His name is Byron,' Vusi said.

'Byron, hey?'

I nodded. Byronkhulu was slipping away, I could feel Byron returning. I slipped my right foot back, and gave a stupid grin.

At this moment – with the thunderous power of a god – Charlie raised his hand in the air. He held it first to the left, baring three fingers. Then moved it to the right, and held up two. To a layman, it would appear that he was counting us in. But I knew what this meant: the man to the left was wise; the man to the right strong.

He jumped up and raising his shield in the air began to scream in apoplectic fits:

'Uyindoda ehlakaniphileyo! Wonke umntu uyasihlonipha isiqqibo sakho!'

This was my cue and I jumped into action, throwing my big foot into the air, and bringing it down on the sand with a thunderous clap. As it slapped the ground I felt adrenalin surge through my veins, my pupils dilate. I was on fire. I was Byronkhulu!

'You – the man with the green tie,' I looked him in the eye, moving my feet as I spoke to imitate Charlie. 'You are the wisest of your people! All the people respect your decisions!'

Charlie moved onto the next man.

'Amandla akho agqithisile! Akekho umntu onokugqitha! Bazakubuya bangxengxeze kuwe!

'Your strength is legendary!' I started screaming at the other
man. 'No man should ever cross your path for they will come to
know of your might!'

The second man to receive our praise moved his lips in an in-
verted contemplative smile; then nodded his head, a smirk making its way across the face. Charlie and I stood still now, catching
our breath, the underside of my feet felt bruised and dirty. I'd
slammed my big foot on something sharp, and could feel a light
trickle of blood emerging from the sole.

Not willing to show any signs of pain, I stood still, my teeth
held tight together. Just then another car came off the dirt road,
and drove all the way through the parking lot stopping next to
the grove of eucalyptus trees. A middle-aged white man with a
ponytail climbed out of the car and took some equipment from
his boot. He was, it transpired, the official photographer for the
evening, and set his camera on a tripod, at the entrance. By the
time he'd set up, there was a small crowd gathered on the dirt
outside the restaurant's reed fence.

Vusi ordered one of the waitresses to take a tray around with
full champagne flutes to all the guests. Everyone stood and chatted, some smoked. All the men were dressed in suits, the women
in dresses that matched their partners' ties. The bright overhead
lights had been dimmed to suit the formal mood, and the large
flames had been cranked up a notch, so the shadows were dancing on the dirt.

We moved around the outside area singing the praises of the
guests. My big foot was sore, and I could feel dirt clinging to the
open wound. But I didn't allow myself to give in to the pain.
Anyway, it was too dark for anyone to notice.

It was a long while – perhaps forty minutes – until the hero of the evening arrived. By the time the two Bentleys entered the dirt parking lot I was tired, my body covered in sweat, my lungs sore. Vusi removed the orange beacons put down earlier to reserve the spots for the two cars.

Both Bentleys were black and the windows were tinted. They drove slowly, but somehow the presence of whoever was inside the vehicles was so intense that it showed through the steel and the black windows. I felt nervous.

The cars came to a standstill. No one budged. The general chatter that had accompanied the champagne and photographs subsided. Everyone was waiting for the doors of the cars to open.

Then, slowly and deliberately the back door of the first car began to move. Even after it was completely open there was no sign of the inhabitant. Then out come the legs, covered in black suit pants. And then came the body. It was a black man of medium build. His partner climbed out from the far side of the car and walked around to join him on his side. They stood next to one another, arms wrapped around each other's waists as the photographer took multiple snapshots and everyone clapped their hands. By the manner in which both the man and the woman conducted themselves, I could tell they were no strangers to attention. Charlie tapped me on the side, and we started moving toward Mr Blowshark. This was the man!

'Uyeyona ndoda emphambili kuwo onke amadoda. Ubutyebi bakho bulilitye elingena kususwa mntu. Amandla akho angonaphakade. Njenge ngonyama ilele bhu!' 'You are the greatest of all the men!' I screamed. I felt myself running out of breath, but focused on the image I'd created. The other me. The one who didn't tire. I went on: 'You are peaceful and do not bring harm to those who respect you. But woe to your enemies, for they shall know how mighty you are. They shall know what awaits them, when you come down on them with thunderous strength.'

He made his way past us toward his guests, and shook their hands and kissed the women's cheeks. There was much laughing and joking.

But I kept watching the other car. Neither of the doors had opened, and it had the look of a car that was about to explode. In my stoned mind I convinced myself that a group of terrorists had followed Mr Blowshark and were about to blow him up. But then suddenly, very suddenly, the door began to open. As with Blowshark, a leg came out first, and then the body. Somehow he managed to get himself out without showing his face. He stood with his back to the crowd and made a show of dusting down his arms and straightening his jacket. He was bald, white, and had no partner, and as he turned around – the flashing lights of the camera bringing out all the definite, arrogant features of his face – the image of Blowshark that I had seen before came back to me. He hung alongside Regereman on his bedroom wall.

And Regereman was here to enjoy the party.

Asked for by name, I thought. Asked for by fucking Name! How many times had I told the cunt that I was no longer a translator? I'd done all I could to hide myself from him, and he had done all he could to expose me. I pictured the mismatched footprints running up and down his stairs. Then I visualised his gun sitting snugly in my car and felt a warm feeling pass over me as I remembered using his jacket to wipe my asshole. I ran over the last words he'd spoken to me: *Big dogs bite harder than puppies.* What a wanker.

As he approached, Charlie raised his hand in the air, all five fingers exposed. I ran through all the praise routines in a matter of seconds. My mind was working fast, but unproductive-ly. It was tying itself up in knots. Three times I ran over what five meant, and each time I came up with a new way in which Regereman would interpret it. Five praised one's wealth in de-scendants. The first time I thought it over, I realised that he had only one child. He would simply think me dumb to be telling him how many children he had. The second time I thought it over, I believed that he'd consider my translation a mockery. He'd think I was ironically pointing out the failure of his loins to produce more than one child. Then the third time I thought he'd consider my translation a roundabout way of asking for his daughter's hand in marriage. Not that the idea was something unappealing to me. But to openly announce that I enjoyed fucking his daughter so much that I wanted to do it for the rest of my life, was not the way a sensible man would approach Regereman with a marriage proposal. Whichever way it went, routine five was out.

I tried to tap Charlie on the shoulder, but he was already lunging forward, the words already making their way out of his mouth: 'Hayi indoda enamandla yakwaXhosa. Waqhwanyaza nje! Intando yakho inyenzeka!'

Regereman was nearing the rest of the crowd, everyone was watching; people listening. I wanted to say the right words, but I couldn't, and suddenly I found myself reciting the words to praise routine number four. There I was, dressed in my skins, jumping about like a fool and screaming 'You are the most powerful of all the men! Your power is legendary! You are so great!'

I don't know what it was that ran through me. It could have been the nervous energy, or perhaps somehow I believed that if I praised hard enough I'd erase Charlie's words and my translation would be correct. Whatever it was, the praise that came from my mouth was greater than ever before. I was the master praise poet. All my blood and my soul and my heart went into screaming these words of praise up into Regereman's cold eyes. He looked at me through the flickering light, and as he leant his bald head to the side, he gave me a wink.

Charlie spun around, a look of anger, almost hatred in his eyes, and I feared for a second that he was going to lunge at me with his stick. But he simply stepped away from me, and looked down at his feet.

Regereman was embraced by his friend, Blowshark, and the crowd began to make its way into the inkundla. The dust settled. The sky was black. The moment lost. Charlie didn't look back at me. He slunk away through the crowd, off to the change room. I had to continue serving drinks for the evening; but he was finished. He didn't say goodbye. I heard his motorbike starting up. I wanted to run out and explain my behaviour. But as I tried to slip away Vusi caught me by the wrist, pulled me close and gave me an aggressive look.

I stayed on serving the guests drinks, until it came time for dinner. I spent the time in the change room smoking cigarette after cigarette, pacing up and down. I couldn't make sense of what had happened out there. For weeks I'd been forgetting praise routine number four. Although Charlie had said we'd be using it during the course of the evening, not once had he held up four fingers. It was as if the routine had been brewing inside me, waiting for the moment when it could explode upon the world. I'd never praised like that before. Had Regereman placed a spell on me, I wondered. Perhaps his friend Blowshark was into black magic, perhaps he still consulted sangomas. But no, I was just being stoned and stupid.

Maybe it was because of what had happened with Ridge. I'd
felt power for the first time, and so I was free, finally, to sing
about it. And I'd felt it because of Regereman's gun. Perhaps I
was thanking him. I wish I knew.

I walked up and down the dirty change room smoking cigarette after cigarette, these thoughts pounding away at the inside
of my head. I was relieved when Vusi finally came to call me. I
couldn't spend another second alone with myself.

I made my way back into the inkundla. The waitresses were
clearing up the plates and cutlery. Some fresh logs had just been
placed on the large fires in the centre of the area. There must
have been at least two hundred people, both black and white.
But not one of them had changed into the skins. Jazz music was
playing in the background.

My job was again to take drinks to the guests. Now, however, I
had to get orders. I went up to the first group, three men and two
women, and asked what they would like. None of them wanted
something simple. It was all, this mixed with that, a double this
and that, a that on ice, a this with soda. I nodded and pretended
to have remembered, but couldn't recall a single order. So I was
glad, for half a second, when I heard the distinct coarse voice calling me. Perhaps someone else would have to take their order.

'Hey!' It was Regereman. He was with a few other men. They
were near to the largest fire. He was on the sand, and next to
him was the main man. Slightly raised, on one of the wooden
boardwalks, was the man with the bushy eyebrows, the first to
arrive earlier in the evening. I made my way over to where they
were standing, and stood silently in front of them.

'Shanghai, meet Byron.'

Mr Blowshark stuck out his hand. He was an incredibly strik-
ing man, his features sharp and angular. He had an awesome

presence. He shook my hand for a long time and looked me up and down. I buried my large foot in the sand.

'We have met already' he said. 'You were the one who sung to me in English. I do speak Xhosa, you know. It's unusual – I am saddened to say this – but it is unusual to find a white boy your age who can speak the language. I am glad, of course.' He eventually let go of my hand. I bowed my head, thanking him for his compliment and made to walk away.

'Where you going, Byron? Have a drink,' Regereman called after me. He'd taken off his jacket and rolled up his sleeves. He had a cigar in one hand and a glass of whisky in the other.

'I. I can't drink when I'm on shift.'

'What nonsense!' said Blowshark 'It's my party. *I* paid for everything here!' He waved his arms around. 'And *I* say you can drink.'

'Sir, Vusi would –.'

He raised his hand toward me. 'What do you want?'

'Come, Byron. He's offering you a drink,' Regereman said.

'I would like a beer then.'

'I'm paying for it,' said Blowshark, 'get yourself what you want.'

I turned and looked at the bar. I saw Vusi watching quietly. Blowshark raised his hand in the air and called one of the waitresses over.

'Get this man what I've been drinking. Make it a double for him. Do you want ice, Byron?'

'Yes.'

She disappeared, and returned moments later with my drink. In the time she was gone, Blowshark and Regereman spoke as if I were no longer there. And then, once I had a drink in my hand, they began to speak to me again: as if it were some sort of passport into these powerful men's conversation.

'Byron,' Blowshark continued, 'My friend here tells me that you're dating his daughter. Is this true?'

'It is.'

'You must be a brave man, Byron. To date Regereman's daughter.'

He and Regereman had a good laugh.

'What do you say to that?' Regereman asked me. He was in a festive mood.

'I suppose,' I said.

'You suppose?' Blowshark asked me.

'Yeah.'

'Not the kind of girl whose heart you'd want to break now. Is it, Byron?'

I giggled nervously.

'What do you say to that, Byron?' Regereman asked me.

'For sure,' I said 'Would never want to break her heart.'

'And I hear you enjoy a bit of boxing. You have a nimble frame. So you welterweight, or what?'

'Welter. Yeah.'

'Where do you train?'

'I mainly just practise at home.'

'And compete?'

'I compete . . . ' I looked over my shoulder pretending I'd heard something from the bar. Vusi was still standing there in silence, leaning against the counter. A woman was trying to get his attention, but he was focused solely on my situation, and brushed her aside.

'I compete with friends and other people.'

'What organisation?'

'I used to belong to an organisation called . . . ' The words seemed to speak themselves. 'Boxing Federation Front.'

'Boxing Federation Front!' He hit each word hard, firing the consonants off like gunshots. 'That sounds like a political party. A conservative party. Maybe something Constand Viljoen would have started.'

The three men roared with laughter at this comment, I too decided to laugh, if only to divert the issue.

'And Byron,' Blowshark continued 'Are you planning to work at this place for ever?'

'I think I would rather do something else. Later on perhaps, I'll get another job.'

'What sort of job? We're all bosses here. What sort of job would you like?'

'Any job. I would prefer not to have to dress up.'

They liked that. They laughed.

'So, Byron,' Regereman started speaking, 'would you ever consider being a manager at this restaurant?'

'Maybe.'

'Maybe, he says. Maybe, hey, Byron. Maybe. Maybe seek a promotion. Within the business.'

'Perhaps some day.'

'Why you playing with your feet in the sand there?' Regereman asked me.

'I hurt it earlier.'

'Shanghai, you have to see this. Wilson, you too.' Regereman addressed the bushy eyebrow man. 'Show us your feet, Byron.'

I pulled the big foot out of the sand with great speed, as if I were not in the least embarrassed by it.

'Put them next to one another,' he said. 'Wilson move to the left a little, you're blocking the light. See that?' Regereman had a look of absolute pride on his face, as if he were a general showing off a newly conquered land to his king.

'Isn't that something?'

'I have never,' said Wilson. 'Not in all my years. What a thing. Does it cause you trouble?'

'No,' I said.

Blowshark simply nodded his head, as if taking in an everyday fact. Then he asked, 'How is your drink doing, Byron?'

'Good.'

'Let me ask you something. Can I ask you to do something for me? As a present. For my birthday.'

'OK.'

'I want you to show me how you box.'

'I don't have anything . . . '

'No, just shadow box. Show us how you move. Come, show us here in the inkundla. Let's move to the fire.'

He guided us with his hands, and we walked toward the main fire that was burning in the centre. It was enormous, the largest flames reaching higher than my head. It was evident to many of the guests that something was happening, and various groups started coming toward us. Vusi too, came closer.

'I take your drink,' said Blowshark.

I gave it to him.

'OK. Now move a little in the sand. Move your feet from side to side. Come on, you know how it's done.'

There were people standing all around the fire, some at my level, some on the raised areas that surrounded it. People were quiet, they listened as Shanghai spoke. As I moved, I could feel the skins slapping against my thighs, and my ankles.

'Hey, barman,' he shouted across the inkundla. 'Turn that music down.'

And the music went down.

'OK now, Byron, show us.'

The flames from the fire were towering up above me and casting long shadows across the crowd.

'Come on, move on your feet, fists up at your face.'

I did as he asked, and jumped around, fully conscious that I looked completely unskilled in this particular art.

'Move, Byron. Come. Now throw a punch with the left.'

I watched my shadow move across the sand as I gave an uncoordinated jab.

'Now with the right. Then a combo. Come on.'

I kept dancing around and throwing my hands about in spastic fits.

'I wouldn't want to be your enemy,' Blowshark shouted. His little quip was greeted with much laughter.

'Now, Byron,' Blowshark said, 'I want you to pretend this is not a boxing match. I want you to pretend that you are beating your sworn enemy. Come now, what do you say to him when he's down?'

I kept dancing from foot to foot, and sending out lashes into the night air.

'Um . . . ' I muttered, uncertain as to what I would say if indeed I had knocked my sworn enemy to the floor. Blowshark naturally assumed that my enemy would be a man. Of course, the truest enemy I had was Ridge. I pictured her lying on the floor, I'd punched her while she was taking the shit she was meant to take.

'What would you say to him?' Blowshark screamed.

I wanted to say 'Bitch!' But in a last ditch effort to save some pride, my brain-tongue filter kicked in and added a 'Son of a' before the bitch.

'Good!' yelled Blowshark. 'Let him know who's the boss. Let him know!'

'I'll kill you!'

'Yes!' Blowshark's voice rose up above the flickering light and the shadows.

'Now, Byron, imagine that this man has stolen your woman from you. He has taken your pride.'

How did he know this? Could he see who I was picturing? Did he know my secret? He was coming so close to spelling it out, but just slipping past the details. Had he told Regereman of my infidelity?

'You will pay!' I screamed.

'Good.'

I kept moving.

'And now, Byron. Imagine that this man, this man who has taken your woman from you; this man who has shamed you, disgraced you; this man who has robbed you of all your manhood. I want you to imagine Byron, that this man is a Xhosa! There's a Xhosa lying there in the sand, and you want to tell him who's boss. In his own language. So he knows! Tell him, Byron!'

I felt the blood coming from my foot. I was Byron and my foot was sticky. The sand was clinging to it. It felt enormous, as if the whole world would be sucked up inside it. He knew nothing of the woman lying on the floor. He knew another secret. He was an evil puppet master, and he'd come to choreograph my swan song. I lost my rhythm; my pace was thrown. I could no longer move as I had been. My feet were tripping over themselves. I was drunk. I was stoned. I was stupid.

'What would it be, Byron? Your worst enemy! Xhosa is a powerful language; we both know that. Now use it, to *punish* your enemy.'

'I –.' I stopped dancing and moved toward Blowshark. My surroundings were painfully there. All of it. There was no escaping. There was no music. No one spoke. Some of the guests – including Blowshark, Regereman and Wilson with the bushy eyebrows – were on my level. Others were on the raised areas around their tables. The flames reached up to where they stood silently, drinks in hands, their enormous shadows dancing around Byron.

'I am not so good at speaking. Only translating.'

'Just give something simple then. Tell him in a few words.'

I tried desperately to conjure up some of the phrases that Charlie used. But I could only get sounds, parts of words, or incomplete phrases. And anyway, they were all used for praising, not insulting. It would be useless to tell my enemy that he was a great man, a wise man. A bright light was shining in my eyes; but I could still see a mass of expressionless silent faces. All people. They were so very people-like. All their hair and their eyes, and their clothes. These were people. This is what they did. This is how they congregate to bring glory or shame upon a single person who must stand in the centre and receive their judgment. And there was no praise for Byron. He had always lived his life in the shadows. He was not meant to stand trial.

'I don't know,' I continued. I was feeling the heat of the fire against my bare skin. I could feel the sweat running down the valley of my spine.

'OK. I will tell you what I would say if I had my enemy down. Then because you are a translator, you can say it in English for him.'

'No, I would rather –.'

'Come on, look down at this man who's stolen your pride. Tell him, ndisisiphukuphuku senkwenkwe yomlungu! Nolwimi andilwazi naisisibhanxa! Andina ndawo apha!'

'You are my enemy,' I said.

'Come on, Byron. Say what I really said. I would never have said anything like that. Say what I really said.'

'I will make you pay.'

'What *I* said, Byron. Not what you imagine. I said ndisisiphuku-phuku . . . ' He went through all the words, pronouncing them slowly so there was no way I would be unable to hear them. I started looking around. My senses were patchy, and broken. Everything came to me as if through a television with bad reception. I'd see one mouth smiling. Then a head of hair; and another man's laughter. I saw glasses. Groups of people standing with no expression. The people were breaking up. There was no union, nothing was complete. I kept looking around from side to side.

'What *I* said. What *I* said, Byron. What *I* said. Not what you want. Come on.'

'I don't know,' I mumbled.

'What I said! What I said!' His words seemed to echo like ancient chants bouncing eternally through an eternal valley.

'I'm sorry,' I said.

'What's wrong, Byron?' It was Regereman's harsh voice. 'Has the cat got your tongue?'

'No,' I said, and kept looking down at my feet.

'Vusi!' Blowshark shouted across the inkundla. His call was obeyed.

'Yes, Mr Blowshark.'

'Get it out of here,' he said.

Vusi stuck his hand into my shoulder and led me away from the central fire. Still no one spoke, and as I moved everyone turned to watch. I could feel their eyes all over me.

Vusi unlocked the gate to his office and led me down into the dark room. I made my way around the clutter and sat down at his desk, folded the skins between my legs and stared at my hands. He was silent for a long time. From the tops of my eyes I could see he was twirling his beard.

'*Proud* of yourself?' he asked me.

'No.'

'Proud of yourself?'

'No.'

'What's going on at your house at the moment?'

'Not much.'

'Got a phone call from Susan Ridge the other day. Used to know her quite well at one stage. Says she's thinking of starting a cultural franchise. Wants to know if Bhakhuba would be interested in buying shares in Khoi House.'

'No! They leaving soon. As soon as they get all the bones.'

'Oh yes. That's right, hey, Byron? The bones. How much money have you made so far?'

'Not yet. But soon.'

'That's right.'

'She hasn't made a profit yet.'

'Of course not.'

'No, she said she hadn't.'

'I used to know her quite well. She's got top lawyers working with her at the moment. She's trying to get the deeds to the house.'

'No. Impossible. It's mine.'

'You can't beat her.'

'I can.'

'I really do want to help you. But you make it very hard for me, Byron. You're not going to have a house for much longer. I can never bring you back here after tonight. What are you going to do?'

'I'm not sure right yet.'

'He's not sure. Where you going tonight?'

'I'm going now,' I said and got up off the chair. I started making my way up the chipped stairs toward the bright light coming down from the inkundla. The music was blasting again, people were talking and laughing. I pushed the gate open.

'Byron!' Vusi shouted after me. 'I do want to help you!'

I slunk silently along the raised boardwalk toward the change room. A group of young men passed me, one of them shouted 'The Xhosa boxer!' They all laughed.

In the change room I dropped my skins onto the floor. I'd never need them again. I pulled up my jeans. I still had the keys to Roddy's house. Oh well.

And then in the back pocket I felt a scrunched up piece of paper. It was the one given to me by the Gothic girl. I unfolded it. There were crease marks all over it and little pieces of burnt weed from half smoked joints I'd tried to hide.

In black ink the words: *Ikhaya lam likhaya lakho.* There was no name beneath it. How disappointing. Just another thing I'd never understand.

I threw it on the floor.

I looked at my phone and saw five missed calls and one text message. All the calls were from Victoria. The message was from Ridge. It read: *I suppose by now you've opened the box and realised what an idiot you are. You are an idiot, Byron! And you'll always be an idiot!*

Sitting in the driver's seat I opened the box up and sure enough the condom wasn't in it.

I called Victoria and through her tears the only thing she could say was 'Please tell me it's a lie. Please tell me it's a lie.'

'I'm afraid not' I said. 'I'm an idiot. And I'll always be an idiot.'

So I hung up the phone and drove along the bumpy dirt road out of Bhakhuba, onto the highway and off into the dark night. Somewhere.